# WHITETAIL DAWN

# Whitetail Dawn

by

**Duncan Dobie**

**Illustrated by**
**Allen Hansen**

SAFARI PRESS

Dobie, Duncan

First edition

Safari Press Inc.

2006, Long Beach, California

ISBN 1-57157-321-6

Library of Congress Catalog Card Number: 2004099491

10 9 8 7 6 5 4 3 2 1

Printed in the USA

Readers wishing to receive the Safari Press catalog, featuring many fine books on big-game hunting, wingshooting, and sporting firearms, should write to Safari Press Inc., P.O. Box 3095, Long Beach, CA 90803, USA. Tel: (714) 894-9080 or visit our Web site at www.safaripress.com.

For Jack Crockford, the best man I’ve ever known.

## Table of Contents

## Epigraph

I think the reason I have always loved the sport of deer hunting so much lies in its inherent challenge, for the whitetail is the smartest creature to walk this earth. It has eyes for anything that makes the slightest movement, it has a nose that can pick up just about any scent, and it has ears that act like radar, warning it of any sound that is out of place. To outwit a creature as well tuned to its environment as the whitetail takes some doing.

Fred Bear
*The Archer's Bible*
1968, New York

# Acknowledgments

Special thanks to *North American Whitetail* magazine for granting permission to reprint the stories in chapters 1, 6, 7, 8, 12, 17, and 18. Several of these stories originally appeared in "Trails and Tails," and several others originally appeared in the "Misadventures of Arnold and Waldo."

Also, a very special thanks to a gifted artist, Allen Hansen, for doing the superb illustrations in this book.

# A Game Warden's Folly

## Chapter 1

It was one of those unforgettable days in the woods that make a deer hunter glad to be alive. The temperature was just right. It was not unbearably cold, but cool enough to give a crisp feeling to the morning woods. Not a cloud could be seen in the deep blue sky.

A gentle breeze was blowing, and the mountains were alive with fall colors. The hickories and maples were aflame with brilliant shades of yellow, while the oaks and dogwoods boasted an almost blood-red hue. Underfoot, the soft, crunchy carpet of leaves—fresh-fallen and still damp from the morning dew—beckoned the cautious hunter to move along as quietly as possible, ever mindful of the fact that a fine autumn buck could materialize out of the maze of color at any moment.

"Man, what a great day to be deer hunting!" Mort Wilson sighed as he slowly made his way back down the winding trail toward his truck.

Mort owned a service station out near the interstate. It was late October, and he was taking one of his rare days off to enjoy the splendor of the fall woods. He was hunting alone. His longtime hunting partner, Billy Carruthers, had become sick the day before. Both men had been drawn for a special quota hunt at Beaver Lodge Refuge. A week earlier, they had driven up from the city to scout out a good place to hunt.

Now, Mort had returned by himself. He had hiked up the steep mountain in the predawn darkness to hunt near a fresh scrape. So far, he had not seen a deer all morning, but that had not dampened his spirits in the least. Just being in the woods on a day like this was more than enough. Anything else, such as seeing a gnarly old ridge-runner, would be icing on the cake.

Mort had parked his truck near a roadside camping area. On his way in he had forded a mountain stream a short distance from the road. Now, on his way back to the truck for lunch, he paused alongside the stream to take in the picturesque view in the daylight.

As he was standing there, a ripple in a small pool forty yards upstream caught his attention. It was definitely some type of fish feeding on the surface. Mort slipped closer for a better look. As he peered down into the twelve-inch-deep pool from his hidden position on the bank, he saw three fish fanning water near a submerged log.

*Trout!* he thought. *Rainbows!*

Mort just happened to have an ultralight rig in the truck, along with a good assortment of small spinners. Fresh trout for lunch, cooked over an open flame, certainly would be an added bonus to an already perfect day outdoors. He hurried back to the truck to get his fishing gear. During the next forty-five minutes, Mort caught seven feisty trout—all between eight and ten inches in length. Anxious to get back to his deer stand up on the mountain, he quickly cleaned the fish and headed back to the truck.

Mort had noticed a fire pit at one of the empty campsites. Since no one was around, he gathered up a supply of hardwood sticks and quickly built a small cooking fire. While he was waiting for the coals to burn down, he put the trout on a piece of aluminum foil and seasoned them with salt and pepper. He took out several slices of bread along with a stick of butter he had packed in his lunch kit. He planned to sauté the trout in a bed of butter while slowly grilling them on top of the foil.

"*Mmm-umm!*" he said out loud. "Ol' Billy doesn't know what he's missing today. This is gonna be a real feast!"

Mort had not seen a soul all morning long, but just as the coals of his fire were almost ready for the fish, a green pickup slowly pulled into the camping area. From the insignia on the door panel, Mort knew it was the game warden.

Suddenly, Mort's heart felt like it was in his throat. Now, for the first time, it dawned on him that he might be in serious trouble. He didn't even have a fishing license with him, much less a trout stamp. Furthermore, he didn't even know if trout season was still open!

"How ya' doin'?" the game warden asked as he stepped out of his truck.

"Howdy," Mort replied.

"Any luck this mornin'?"

"Naw, didn't see a thing," Mort answered. "Well actually I take that back. I did see a fox squirrel and two grouse. Isn't it a gorgeous day?"

"Beautiful!" the warden agreed. "Whatcha doin' there?"

"I'm just cookin' myself some lunch," Mort replied. "You're welcome to join me if you haven't eaten yet. I love trout cooked over an open flame better than anything else in the world. My wife thawed these out for me last night, so I could have 'em for lunch today. Caught 'em back during the summer, over at Bear Creek."

Mort hated to lie, especially to a game warden, and he knew he was not very good at it. He was surprised that he had sounded so good.

"Is that right?" the warden said, eyeing the fish closely. "They sure look fresh to me. You know, trout season's been closed two weeks."

"Oh, these fish have been in the freezer since August," Mort insisted. "My wife has a special way of freezin' fish that keeps the freshness in."

"Well, I tell ya' what," the warden said. "That sounds better than the peanut butter and jelly sandwich *my* wife fixed for me today. I love trout, too. Your offer sounds pretty doggone good. You sure you got enough?"

"Oh, more than enough," Mort said. "My wife always freezes them in packets of six or eight. I've got more here than I can say grace over. I was just gonna cook 'em all and save some for tonight when I come back out of the woods."

While the fish were cooking, Mort introduced himself. When the trout were done, he got out some paper plates, toasted some buttered bread over the fire and poured them each a cup of tea.

"Boy, these trout are delicious," the warden said, after he had eaten his fill. "I just can't get over how fresh they taste."

Mort proceeded to give the warden a detailed description of how his wife always prepared fish for the freezer so that the freshness could be retained. Every word was true!

"I'll sure try to remember that," the warden said. "Every time I keep something in the freezer longer than several months, it always seems to get freezer burn real bad."

The two men finished their lunch. They talked about deer hunting and several other topics of mutual interest.

"Well, I guess I'd better be gettin' on up the mountain," the warden said. "Couple of deer camps just over the other side I need to check on."

"I've really enjoyed talking to you," Mort told him. "I guess I need to be getting on up the mountain myself. Can't kill a buck sitting around camp chewing the fat."

"That's for sure," the warden said.

The warden got up and started to leave. "Thanks again for the lunch," he said. "Those trout were something else. I'm sure gonna try to remember your wife's formula. I swear, those fish tasted like they were just caught this mornin'!"

"It oughta be pretty easy to remember," Mort said.

Deep down inside, Mort was beginning to breathe a big sigh of relief.

As the warden got into his truck, he paused. "Oh, by the way," he said, scratching his head. "I almost forgot. Would you mind doin' me a small favor?"

"Sure, anything," Mort answered with a puzzled look. "Just name it. . . ."

"Well, it's like this," the warden said. "Next time you decide to lie to a game warden, how 'bout cleanin' the fish scales off your boots first."

He smiled and drove away.

# Strange Happenings at Chickamauga Creek

## Chapter 2

The lone hunter had been following a sparse blood trail for over two hours now, and it looked as though his greatest fear might be realized. The scant blood sign was beginning to peter out even more. John Forrest feared it might disappear altogether. Although he was sure he had made a lethal shot, serious doubt—the enemy of every competent bow hunter—was beginning to creep into his mind. As always, John had been hunting with a recurve bow, and as always, he had been shooting instinctively, with no sights. Despite the difficulty of hunting this way, he seldom had to travel more than one hundred yards to recover a deer he had arrowed.

It was mid-September in northwest Georgia. Archery season had just opened the day before. John had taken over a dozen deer with his fifty-four-pound Hoyt recurve. Being a purist at heart, he had even taken two mountain gobblers with the old recurve, aided by a handmade wing bone turkey call.

Ever since first light on this second day of the brand-new bow season, however, the woods had become increasingly strange. All morning long, John had heard an odd rumbling sound off in the distance, much like far-off thunder. Although the weather report had indicated patchy fog in the area just west of Chickamauga Creek where he was hunting, the skies were supposed to clear by late morning with little to no chance of rain.

*To heck with the weather report,* John had told himself shortly after first light. *That rumbling has to be a thunderstorm, and it sounds like it's headed my way.*

Now, as he painstakingly followed the blood trail across a series of rolling hardwood ridges, the curious thunder was getting louder. What's more, a peculiar mist began to roll in and fill the woods around him. It was like no other fog John had ever experienced, and it seemed to bring with it a strange odor.

*Could there be a fire in the woods somewhere off in the distance?* John wondered.

John rehashed the events of the morning over and over again in his mind. Having scouted these woods several weeks earlier, he had found a series of rubs and scrapes on a well-used trail that crossed a gap between two steep hardwood ridges. He had built a primitive brush blind on the downwind side of this natural saddle. He had hunted here the day before, opening day, with no luck.

The eerie noise had begun on this second day of archery season about an hour after daylight. It had continued all morning long, but the woods around John had remained quiet. Around 10:30 A.M., three does came over the saddle. An hour later, the buck appeared. It was a nice eight-pointer with fairly long tines and a good spread, and it was walking rapidly down the trail. It kept looking back, as if something were following it. Being well hidden, John waited until the buck was within twenty yards. Then, quietly coming to full draw and aiming carefully behind the buck's shoulder, he released his arrow.

The shot appeared to be right on target. The arrow passed through the buck's midsection just behind its shoulder. The buck turned inside out and quickly bounded back over the saddle in the direction from which it had come. John recovered his blood-soaked arrow. Then, after waiting about fifteen minutes, he began following a fairly good blood trail. Two hours later, the blood trail had all but disappeared.

*Better find him soon,* John thought. *That thunder's getting closer, and it's really starting to get hazy in these woods. If it rains, I'll lose the trail for sure.*

John decided to take a short break as he passed a large outcropping of rocks. He sat down on one of the high, flat rocks and carefully rested his bow across another.

*It can't be a forest fire,* he thought. *But it sure does have a strange smell to it.*

John pulled out a large chocolate brownie that his wife had made and started eating it. Just as he was finishing up, he heard another strange sound. This time it was very close. The noise appeared to be the distinct clanging of steel. Someone, or something, was coming through the woods toward him.

*Must be some greenhorn squirrel hunter,* he thought. *No one else would make that kind of racket walking through the woods.*

John was surprised to see three men with rifles emerge from the rolling mist forty yards away. They were walking three abreast, and they were coming straight toward him. One of the men was limping slightly. As they drew closer, John's mouth fell open. Two of the heavy rifles the men carried were topped with long bayonets, and all three men were wearing the soiled gray uniforms of Confederate soldiers.

*They must be reenacting a battle today over near the battlefield,* John thought. *Maybe that's where all the noise is coming from. But they sure do look real. . . .*

One of the men suddenly spotted John. Stopping dead in his tracks with a startled look on his face, he halted his two companions. All three men stared at the lone hunter sitting on the rock.

"Howdy," John yelled. "What brings you men out here in the middle of nowhere?"

"You from around here?" one of the men asked with a challenging tone.

"I don't live too far from here," John answered.

"What're you doin' out here," another asked.

"I've been following a wounded deer," John said, nodding toward his bow. "A buck. He's headed in the direction you boys just came from. You haven't seen anything, have you? I've been following him quite a while."

"Nope," one of the men said, staring at John's recurve bow. "A wounded buck's about the last thing we'd expect to see around these parts today."

"Are you huntin' with that bow and arrie?" one of the men asked.

"That's right," John said. "An old Hoyt recurve."

"It's a good thing you're deer huntin'," the oldest of the three men said. "We thought you might be a Yank."

"No, I'm not a Yankee," John said, smiling. "I'm a pure-blooded Georgia cracker through and through."

As the three Confederate soldier look-alikes stepped closer, they continued to size up the strange man with an even stranger weapon. John was wearing a dark green wool jacket that had belonged to his grandfather. It was ideal for bowhunting. He also had on an old pair of brown corduroy pants and Old Western-style leather work boots. On his head he wore his favorite weathered felt hat with a copperhead-skin hatband. To any stranger, he might easily have looked like a nineteenth century homesteader, except for the modern bow he was carrying. The recurve bow with its attached quiver of arrows seemed to baffle the three strangers.

"Are you an Indian?" the oldest of the three men asked.

"No," John smiled. "But I take that as a compliment. The Cherokees and Creeks that used to live around these parts were great hunters."

John noticed that two of the men were extremely young, practically boys. *Probably still in their late teens,* he thought.

The third man had a heavy beard and was probably in his thirties. The odd gray uniforms that each man wore were all strikingly different in appearance. All three men looked as if they had just walked through a burning forest. Their uniforms and faces were smeared black with dirt and grime. Only the oldest of the three wore a hat.

"It's been a long time since I've done any huntin'," one of the youngsters reflected. "I'm a sandlapper from Lower Carolina. We used to hunt the swamp country with buckshot and hounds when I was a boy. I've heard tell of people huntin' with a bow and arrie like that, but I've never seen it with my own eyes."

"Hell, you look like you still are a boy," John said in a friendly tone. "You don't look a day over eighteen."

"I'll be seventeen on December 20," the boy announced. "I been away from home a right long spell."

The second youngster spoke up. "You reckon you could spare a drink of water, Mister? We're plumb parched."

"I've got a little here," John answered. "You're welcome to it. I've also got a couple of apples if you're interested."

John held out his leather water bottle as the men stepped closer. Then, knowing that a good-size creek flowed into the much larger Chickamauga Creek somewhere just ahead, he added, "Didn't you boys just cross a big creek back there?"

"Oh, we crossed it, all right," the bearded man said. "That water ain't fit to drink if you know what I mean." He made a strange face.

John had no idea what the man's comment was supposed to mean.

"You boys really look convincing," John said. "I didn't know anything like this was going on today. Where's the battle taking place?"

"Just over the ridge, yonder," the bearded man answered with an incredulous look on his face. "Less'n a mile away. It was pretty rough out there today, but we give them bluecoats a run for their money. We got separated from our outfit early on, but we heard tell our boys sent 'em skedaddlin' all the way back up toward Chattanoogy. We done our part today, though. So we just been takin' it easy through these woods. We ain't in no hurry. I reckon we'll ketch up with our outfit 'fore the sun goes down."

"I haven't seen a soul in these woods all morning," John said. Then, as an afterthought, he added, "It's a good thing you're doing today. I had a lot of kinfolk who fought in the war."

"Which side?" the older man asked.

"The South, of course," John answered.

"They all dead?" one of the younger men asked.

"Why, yes," John answered. "They've been dead quite a while." Then, addressing the bearded man, John asked, "Where're you from?"

"I'm from east Tennessee," the man answered, putting the emphasis on the first syllable. "Ike, here, he's from Alabam."

The young man with the limp nodded. "We're with the 23rd Tennessee Volunteers," he added.

"Are those new Springfield rifles you boys are carrying?" John asked.

"Yep, we got 'em off a couple of Yanks," the man said. "They weren't needin' 'em any more."

"You men are bein' pretty hard on the Yankees, today, aren't you?" John asked kiddingly.

"Actually, they were pretty hard on us," the boy from Carolina answered, taking a swallow of water, "'til we got the best of 'em, that is."

"We better be gettin' along," the Alabamian said nervously.

"OK," the older man said. He looked at John. "Say, you mind partin' with one a' them-there apples?"

"Not at all," John said. "Here . . . ."

John reached into his jacket and pulled out two red apples. The men took the apples.

"We hope you find your buck," one of the boys said.

"Me, too," John said. "I hope you find your outfit."

"We'll ketch up with 'em somewheres hereabouts," the Tennessean repeated. "You better be careful your own self, though. They's lots of stragglers roamin' these woods today." He smiled oddly.

The three men clambered off noisily through the hazy woods and disappeared.

*What a strange encounter*, John thought. *They sure looked convincing. What a crazy day!*

Thirty minutes later John found his buck. It was stone dead, partially submerged in a shallow pool in the big creek. Oddly enough, the entire pool had turned a dark crimson color.

*My buck couldn't have had that much blood left in him,* John thought. Then he noticed that the stained water seemed to be coming from upstream.

John spent the next two hours dragging his buck out to the nearest dirt road. He then pulled his truck around and loaded the deer in the back. Just as he reached the paved highway on his way home, he noticed a historical marker near the intersection. Pausing at the stop sign, he read the inscription on the marker.

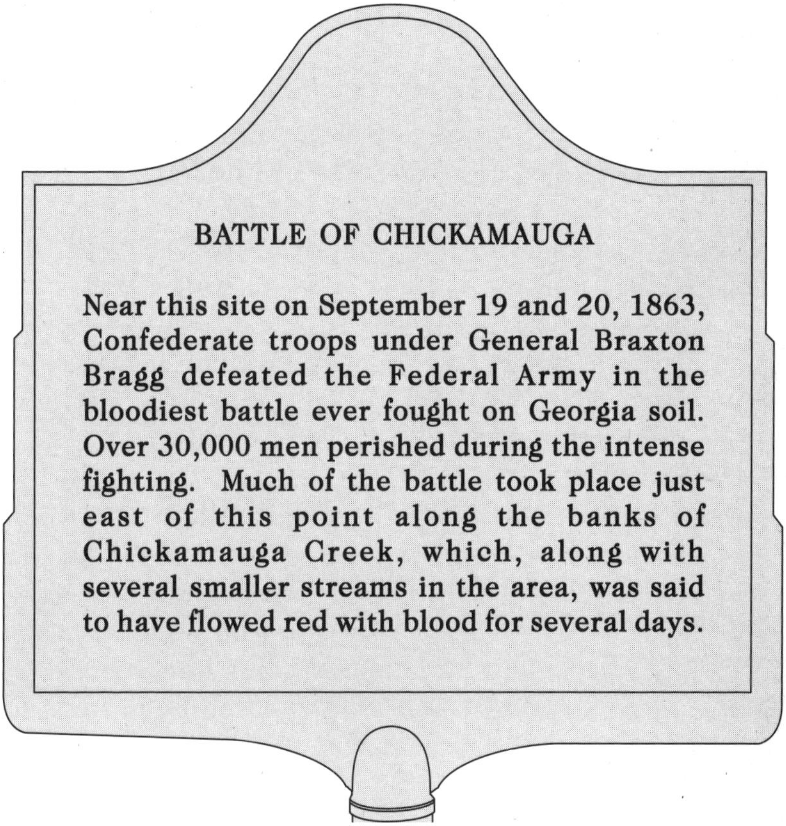


It suddenly dawned on John that he had heard somewhere the old Indian word *Chickamauga* meant *place of death.* In almost a panic, he quickly glanced down at his watch. Cold chills shot down his back. The date was September 19.

# A Turkey Ain't Just a Turkey

## Chapter 3

Dillon Boswell roared into camp with the three dead turkeys in the back of his shiny new Jeep. He jumped out and hefted the birds over his shoulder, holding them by their feet. It was a considerable load, but Dillon was a big man. He grabbed the pistol off the front seat of the open vehicle and started toward the cook tent.

"Hey, Dexter! Hey, Jack!" he hollered across the clearing. "Lookie what I got!"

Dexter Smith and Jack Cadwallon were playing poker on a homemade camp table in the shade of some tall pines. Several dollar bills and some loose change lay on the table next to the deck of cards. Behind them, Dusty Gresham was snoozing comfortably in a hammock strung between two saplings, with the latest issue of *Sports Afield* balanced across his broad midsection. Jess Ferguson was in the cook tent sorting through some boxes and setting up his kitchen in the proper order—as only he could do. These four men were the only hunters left in camp. Cap Sullivan and the others were out in the woods scouting for sign.

"Camp meat, boys!" Dillon stated ostentatiously as he displayed his bounty. "With this much fresh meat in camp, we can hold off on killin' a doe for a few days." He glanced over toward the cook tent. "Hey, Jess, you know how to roast a wild turkey?"

Jess poked his head out between the front flaps of the spacious walk-in cook tent. "I've roasted a turkey or two in my time," he answered dryly.

"Yeah, but have you ever roasted a *wild* turkey before?" Dillon asked, pushing the point.

"A wild turkey oughta' cook the same as a tame bird," Jess said with obvious irritation in his voice.

"I didn't know they was wild turkeys aroun' here," Jack said, looking up from his inside straight. "Where'd ya' git 'em? In town?" He burst out laughing.

"Back down the road about a mile and a half, for your information, Mr. Smarty Pants," Dillon answered defensively. "Just past that run-down farm of old what's-his-name. There was a whole flock of 'em. Musta' been a good fifteen birds in all. They ran across the road into the woods and I nailed 'em as pretty as you please—three shots, three dead turkeys." He proudly held up his long-barrel .22 magnum revolver for everyone to see.

"You sure them turkeys was wild?" Dexter asked.

"You're derned right, they're wild!" Dillon insisted. "Just look at 'em. You can tell by their tail feathers."

"They wouldn't be in season even if they was wild," Jack mused. "We ain't got no fall turkey season aroun' here."

"Who cares?" Dillon responded. "We need camp meat, don't we? Now we don't have to shoot a doe for a while. What's the big deal? A couple of scrawny old turkeys couldn't be any more illegal than a doe deer, could they?"

"No, but we *always* kill us a doe for camp meat at the beginnin' of the season," Jack argued. "It's camp custom."

"And the boys are out lookin' for one right now," Dexter added. "They ain't likely to come in empty-handed, neither. I'll tell ya' that much."

"Well, we got us a Thanksgivin' feast for sure, now," Dillon said. "A doe'll just be icing on the cake. Jess, how 'bout pluckin' and cleanin' these critters for me, will ya'?"

"I'll cook 'em, but I ain't about to pluck 'em or clean 'em," Jess answered coolly. "You shoot 'em, you clean 'em. Rule of the camp." He turned and disappeared back inside the tent, letting the flaps close behind him.

"OK, just be that way!" Dillon yelled. "You don't have to have a hissie fit. I'll do it myself. It's gotten to where a man has to do everything around a deer camp these days!" He continued muttering under his breath.

"How come ya' shot three hens?" Dexter asked. "Wasn't there no gobblers in the flock?"

"A turkey's a turkey," Dillon answered impatiently. "I couldn't tell what they were. They were runnin' full out."

He walked over and placed the dead birds on a plywood table next to the cook tent. "Anyway, a tender young hen is a lot better tastin' than a rangy old gobbler. I thought everybody knew that!"

"Oh, I see," Dexter said, nodding his head. "I reckon fillin' 'em full a' .22 magnums makes 'em taste better, too!" He winked at Jack.

* * * * *

The battered pickup truck drove slowly into camp along the sandy logging road. It rolled to a stop beside Dillon's Jeep. The stranger inside studied the shiny red Jeep for several long moments. At length he opened the door and stepped out. No one noticed the shotgun he was carrying until he had walked all the way around his truck. Suddenly, the entire camp came alive. All heads turned to the unshaven man in the bib overalls. Even Dusty sat up and came to attention, a bit bleary-eyed from his nap.

"Howdy, Mister," Dexter yelled out in a friendly voice as the man approached. "Sump'n we can do for ya'?"

Without speaking, the man gazed about the peaceful camp until his fiery eyes fell upon the three dead turkeys. A heavy silence filled the air. He spat a stream of tobacco juice from one side of his mouth with the calculated precision of forty years' experience.

"Which one a' you gol-derned idiots shot my turkeys?" he demanded. The antique double-barrel shotgun rose menacingly.

All eyes turned to Dillon. Once again, Jess poked his head out of the cook tent to see what all the commotion was about. Dillon stammered and cleared his throat, but he couldn't seem to get any words out.

"Which one a' you blasted fools owns that-there Jeep?" the man demanded in a loud voice. He spat again.

"Oh, boy," Dexter whispered to Jack. "Looks like the gobbler's done come off his roost to collect his hens." He snickered under his breath.

"Ol' Dillon's sure gonna need a coupla' aces up his sleeve to buy his way outa' this'n," Jack whispered back, never taking his eyes off the shotgun.

"Uh . . . I . . . er . . . you mean . . . these . . . wild turkeys . . . belong . . . to you?" Dillon stuttered.

"Wild turkeys! Wild turkeys!" the farmer erupted. "Why Hells-a-fire! Them-there turkeys come from my barnyard flock. They's about as wild as that-there hound dog settin' in the back a' my truck!" He aimed the shotgun squarely at Dillon. "You're the one who done the murderin', ain't you?"

Several rapid glances had been directed toward the droopy-eyed hound standing in the back of the farmer's pickup, but the shotgun and the man holding it quickly reclaimed everyone's attention. Suddenly the empty pistol Dillon was holding, which moments before had been like a proud appendage, felt heavy and incriminating in his hand. In truth, he had emptied the six-shot revolver at the flock of running turkeys. Now the gun was useless.

"I knew sump'n didn't look right about them birds," Jack whispered.

"I didn't know they were yours," Dillon pleaded. "I thought . . ."

"Thought what—that they was wild?" the farmer asked. "Why you consarned city slicker fool! Them turkeys was my chur'ins pets! You city folks don't know didly, do ya'?"

Dillon swallowed with noticeable difficulty. "I'll pay for 'em," he offered. "I'll pay you a good price. Whatever's right with you. How much? Does twenty-five dollars sound about right?"

"Apiece?" the farmer said. His small, beady eyes cut right through Dillon. "Why, that don't even come close. Them hens was breedin' stock."

"OK, OK," Dillon said. "I'll make it an even hundred. That's fair, isn't it?" He swallowed again. "One hundred dollars. Here . . ." He started to reach down into his pocket.

"Don't you move!" the farmer yelled, raising the shotgun higher. "And drop that-there weapon you're holdin'."

Dillon did as he was told. He cringed as his brand-new revolver hit the ground with a sickening thud. He raised both hands slightly.

"I'm not moving! I'm not moving!" he said quickly, trying to convince the farmer.

"I oughta' fill yer' thievin' hide with buckshot, the way you done my turkeys," the farmer said in an ugly tone.

"Look, Mister, I'm real sorry. It was an honest mistake. Those turkeys went runnin' across the road into the woods and I thought they was wild. But I'm willin' to pay you and make it right. Just name a fair price. How much?"

"A hunerd dollars apiece ain't nowhere close, neither," the farmer said. "Them turkeys was special. They's wo'th a whole lot more'n that."

"What? A hundred *apiece*? That'd be three hundred dollars, Mister. Three hundred dollars! I'm willing to pay you a fair price, like I said, but that's ridiculous!"

"You callin' me names after ya' gone and murdered my pet turkeys? Why, I oughta' give ya' both barrels right now, you, you, sorry . . . ."

"He's just about hot enough to do it," Dexter whispered to Jack.

"No. No. I'm not calling you names," Dillon pleaded, holding up both palms in assurance. "If you say it's gonna take three hundred dollars to make you happy, then three hundred it is. A hundred apiece. That's fine with me. Is it OK with you?"

"I said a hunerd apiece ain't nowhere close, you thievin' turkey killer!" the farmer snapped, glancing around camp. "But bein' you're a greenhorn city slicker fool who don't know no better, I'm a'gonna let ya' off light." He looked back toward the parking lot. "Th'ow me over the keys to that-there Jeep!"

"What? My Jeep? What are you plannin' to do?"

"Why, I'm a'gonna settle with ya' like I said. Th'ow me them keys—Now!"

"My Jeep? Are you . . . ? That Jeep's brand-new, Mister. It cost me a lot of money."

"It don't matter if it was give to ya'," the farmer answered matter-of-factly. "It's a'gonna be mine, now!"

Dexter was beside himself. "That feller's got some kinda' nerve," he told Jack in a low tone. "Looks like things're about to get right interestin'."

Dillon could find little humor in the situation. "Why that's extortion!" he declared. "You can't get away with this. . . . It's highway . . ."

". . . robbery?" the farmer finished for him, with an even meaner look in his eye. "There ya' go again, callin' me names. You're jus' askin' for a load a' buckshot, ain't ya'? I flat-out oughta'. . . ."

"But that's not even within reason, Mister," Dillon pleaded.

"'Bout as much reason as shootin' a man's turkeys outa' his backyard, I'd say. Now th'ow me over them keys! I ain't askin' again. And fix me up a deed to that-there Jeep. Quick-like! I ain't got all day!"

Dillon looked around in desperation, as if silently appealing for help from his companions. In the face of the shotgun, however, no one dared to move. Finally, he got up his courage.

"You can't get away with this, Mister. I'll call the law on you."

"Suit yerself, city slicker. You're welcome to call the sheriff if'n ya' got a mind to. . . . Ain't likely to do ya' much good, though. . . . Sheriff a' this-here county just happens to be my stepbrother."

A wicked smile crossed the farmer's face, as if he had been through all of this many times before.

"An' I'm sure the local judge would jus' love to try this-here case in his courtroom," the farmer continued. "Ya' see, he's my wife's daddy, and we're kinda a close-knit family. Fact is, I ain't had no occasion to visit his courtroom since that no-count Davol boy come snoopin' 'round my farm after my fourteen-year-old daughter. . . . I put a screechin' halt to that. . . . He's still in the jail!

"Let's see. . . . Enterin' private property what's been legally posted by the law . . . burglarizin' a feller's backyard . . . murderin' and a'stealin' livestock with a deadly weapon . . . takin' the very food off'n a poor dirt farmer's table. . . . That oughta' be good for a right healthy fine and about six months on the county work gang. Now fix me up that-there deed and have ever' one a' these other slickers to witness to it. And make it legal and proper like you city folks know how to do. I'm a'tellin' ya' for the last time, I ain't got all day!"

Jess produced a sheet of paper and a pen from somewhere inside the cook tent. Dexter and Jack cleared some space on the poker table. Dillon sat down. With a shaky hand, he began to write out a makeshift transfer of title.

"What's your name?" he asked the man with the shotgun.

"Willard Mizell," the farmer answered, emphasizing the *M*.

"How do you spell it?"

"Cap'tal W-i-l-l-a-r-d, cap'tal M-i-z-e double l."

When the document was complete, Dillon signed his name at the bottom of the page. With great ceremony, each of the other four men solemnly witnessed his signature. Mizell kept the shotgun trained on the group during the entire procedure. After everyone had signed, Dillon stood up and approached Mizell. Reluctantly, he handed him the paper along with the keys to his Jeep. Mizell looked it over. Then he folded it up and stuffed it into the top pocket of his overalls. He spat one last time, tipped his hat, and cautiously backed away toward the parking area.

"What about your truck?" Dillon asked weakly.

"Take it," Mizell said almost graciously. "I ain't a'gonna be a'needin' it no more. You can take that flea-bit hound, too. He'll come home when he's a' mind to. . . . Better watch 'im, though. He's bad to run deer."

Mizell got in Dillon's Jeep and carefully balanced the shotgun across his lap. He cranked the engine.

"What about your turkeys?" Jess hollered.

"Y'all can keep them, too," Mizell yelled. A shrewd smile suddenly broke across his sun-wrinkled face for the first time. "They ain't fit to eat, nohow!"

He backed the Jeep out into the road and rumbled off down the sandy trail toward the highway.

Dillon walked over to the clearing where his beloved Jeep had been parked. With legs that felt like jelly, he sat down on the ground and stared down the empty logging road in silence.

"I reckon this is one time when a turkey ain't just a turkey," Dexter said to Jack in a low voice. He and Jack looked at each other and tried to be serious, but they couldn't hold back. Dexter cracked a big smile. Then Jack started to laugh. Dusty and Jess joined in. Soon, all four men were laughing uproariously.

# The Tiger Patrol

## Chapter 4

He arose very early in the morning as was his custom. He began to stir about in the small cabin, first going through the daily ritual of stocking the old wood stove with kindling and lighting a fire, then preparing a fresh pot of coffee—always made very strong and always taken very black. Once these two important chores were out of the way, he stepped outside to relieve himself at the edge of the clearing beside the cabin, deliberately forgoing the comfort of the indoor facilities. Clad only in a T-shirt and a pair of frayed, army-green military gym shorts, he intentionally left his coat hanging in its usual place by the door so that he could feel the sharp sting and sudden shock of the cold night air against his skin. He knew that he could withstand the cold for a short time, and he also knew how much he would appreciate the warmth of the stove once he was back inside, sitting in his chair and sipping on his first cup of coffee.

Outside it was cold and dark. The open, cloudless sky was alive with an immeasurable number of stars. Some appeared to be twinkling brightly. Others gave the illusion of moving slowly across the heavens when they were really not moving at all. Still others were very faint and barely visible to the naked eye. All of his old friends were there: the Big Dipper, the Little Dipper, Orion the Hunter, and the other familiar clusters of stars that had been his constant companions over many years spent outdoors. He had always held great affection for the darkness and the night sky. But he was especially fond of the stars and the great unexplained mysteries that the infinite heavens stubbornly guarded.

The mere act of stepping outside and standing beneath the vast unknown world above automatically elevated his thoughts. It was like walking into a great cathedral from the busy sidewalk of a large city. The transformation that always took place was immediate and very real. It was also very spiritual. He had long ago ceased trying to unravel the complex mysteries of the universe as he had so often attempted in his youth, but he still felt a strong sense of belonging and of being a tiny part of whatever it was that loomed above him. Now, he simply accepted what he saw as a thing of great beauty and awe. And although such sights always moved him, he no longer wasted time or energy thinking about complicated matters that he could not fathom.

*I prefer to think of simpler things,* he told himself as he shivered in the cold. *Things that are more of this earth, such as, Where will my buck be this morning? Will he show himself down in the hardwood bottom near the lake where I have chosen to hunt? And simple things like, I wonder if the 'possum came by last night and picked up the little surprise I left for him. I bet a thousand dollars he did. Probably smelled those fish heads three miles away. If he didn't, I know that family of 'coons did for certain. I'll be sure and check the back porch after I return from the woods. Yes, those are the types of things I prefer to think about. Those are the things I can understand.*

Then, much as a small child might, he raised his chin toward the sky and took a deep breath. He exhaled sharply, deliberately blowing a thick cloud of mist into the night air. He smiled contentedly as he watched it dissipate by the light of the stars overhead.

He turned and hurried back toward the door of the cabin. "Great guns!" he said out loud in a cheerful tone. "It's gonna be a cold one today! No snow, just bone-biting cold!"

He had lived alone for many years. He had separated from his wife so long ago that he seldom thought about her anymore. His two children were grown and lived far away. They had their own busy lives. Although he cared for them deeply, there was little personal contact between father and children. He did have friends, though—good friends. Most of his best friends were close hunting companions with whom he had spent many seasons. They understood his ways, and they respected him for the kind of man he was.

The memories of hunts gone by were among the most cherished memories of his adult life. He loved it when the walls of the cabin echoed with the laughter of those friends, and he loved the various smells associated with a cabin filled with hunters. Soon, those very things would come to pass. For now, however, he had chosen to remain alone.

Today was special. Today was the opening day of deer season. Having no wife, and deliberately having chosen not to share this day with any of his close friends, he had made it an annual ritual to selfishly reserve this day for himself alone. The long-awaited day marked with an *X* on the calendar represented such a significant happening that he did not want to share it with another living human being. Instead, he had purposely turned to the peaceful solitude of the cabin for this time of quiet reflection. On this day, the creatures with whom he shared the woods outside the cabin would be his only company.

He was a hunter, and the excitement of the chase had long been his primary passion in life. Things had not always been that way. In the past, things had gotten clouded for a time, with the usual disappointments and complications of life. But for the past twenty years or so, his love for the outdoors was the only thing he needed to sustain him. He wanted it that way, and he had no regrets. What's more, he blamed no one for the failures of the past. He was perfectly content to live out the rest of his days in this manner. His requirements were simple, and he asked nothing more of life.

People who did not know him well were always astonished to learn that he had not yet celebrated his fifty-seventh birthday. His once blond hair had long ago turned stone white, and the creases in his weathered face made him look much older than his years. It wasn't, however, because of any hard living or the usual overindulgences of youth. Nor was it due solely to the regrettable situation with his former wife. Most of the inward scars he still carried could be directly attributed to the lingering effects of a far-off war that had totally consumed his life for a two-year period more than a quarter of a century earlier.

Amazingly, he had not died in that war like so many others he had known—at least, not in the physical sense. But he always believed that it would have been much better if he had. Instead, he had returned from the jaws of hell to face an equally unpleasant fate—a wife who had betrayed him and left him for someone else because she couldn't stand the loneliness and the constant fear of becoming a young widow with two small children, and an indifferent country filled with chanting protesters who looked upon his service as war crimes instead of the performance of his duty.

He poured himself a cup of steaming black coffee and sat down next to the woodstove. He cautiously tested the rim of the cup by sipping his first taste of the delicious black liquid. He sighed deeply and sat back. Yes, it was opening day once again, a day he always greeted with much anticipation and excitement, a day he jealously guarded for himself alone so that he could savor every fleeting moment.

The time would come soon enough when the cabin would be filled with loud voices and the smell of frying eggs and gun oil. He knew he would savor that as well, but in a different way. There would be much hopeful talk of bagging giant bucks with rocking chair antlers, and considerable homage would be paid to this most regal of big-game animals. There would also be much lighthearted kidding and prank playing. That he loved too, but on this first day of the brand-new season, his thoughts and actions were selfishly reserved for the ever-present memories of what had taken place so long ago—still so very fresh in his mind in many ways, yet so misted and clouded in others that the events of that time seemed as if they had occurred centuries earlier.

Now that another hunting season was finally at hand, all energies in the days and weeks ahead, as always, would be devoted to the quest for a great buck. But before that singular endeavor could get underway, it was necessary to celebrate another anniversary of sorts, one that had taken place long ago and in a faraway land worlds apart from this picturesque cabin in the November woods. Ironically, the exact date of that anniversary corresponded very closely to opening day of deer season. Even more ironically, and through a bizarre twist of fate, the memories of that dark time could also be defined by another regal—yet most unlikely—member of the animal kingdom.

To the man sitting in the chair, the contemplation of, and homage paid to, this other noble creature seemed as reasonable as raising his mug and toasting the trophy deer head hanging on the wall across the room. Yet to anyone else, the differences might seem profound. For this other animal that was now doomed to occupy his thoughts represented not only the sum total of all that had happened to him during those dark days of war but also his personal apocalypse. And now the kinship he shared with this unlikely beast was so deeply rooted that it was equal in stature to the mighty white-tailed deer that he had spent an entire lifetime honoring.

*Perhaps,* he had frequently thought, *we're headed for extinction together.*

In due time his eyes gazed across the room to a pair of framed 5x7 photographs on the mantel above the fireplace. The photo on the left and the more recent of the two was a study in contrast. It depicted a single, bright red rose on a long green stem lying on a black marble edging against a polished black granite wall that bore the names of dozens of men, all of whom had perished in that unspeakable war. He had taken the photo himself after carefully placing the red rose below the countless rows of names during one of several visits to Washington, D.C. One of the names several inches above the red rose belonged to a man who had been a personal comrade.

The photo on the right, somewhat faded and obviously of older vintage than the first, depicted a group of happy, smiling young men—five to be exact. The general mood of the photo seemed typical of the youth it depicted: upbeat and carefree. The photographer had caught these men during an unusual moment. To judge by their faces alone, a casual viewer might guess the picture had been taken on a college campus. But the lush green tropical background and the loose military garb worn by the men would have been strangely out of place in such a setting. What's more, the faded photograph also depicted another strange sight. The five smiling men in the photo were gathered around a most unusual trophy.

Were they hunters? Here were five happy, smiling men in faded green combat fatigues, cigarettes hanging from the mouths of two: bright, young men in the prime of life, M-16s in hand and other equipment strapped over their shoulders. The man on the right was holding up the bizarre trophy—a now slightly rotten trophy after six days of monsoon rains and the sweltering, rotting humidity of the jungle. It was the head of a young tiger.

Indeed these young men were hunters, but their uniforms and equipment did not suggest that their quarry was the unfortunate animal seen in the photograph. To the contrary, these five men were hunters of another kind—man hunters—and they had come upon this unlikely trophy by sheer chance.

Now, after all these years, it was almost fitting that the strongest memories retained by the man in the chair were not of the human beings he had killed in battle, nor of the great human suffering and numerous atrocities that accompany all wars, so many examples of which he had witnessed. Nor were they of the many cherished companions he had lost: Four of the five men in that photo, as well as that "trophy of trophies," had never returned home from the jungle. Two of the men had died in his arms. Only he alone had emerged without a scratch.

Those other things, the concept of war in simple human terms—men being ordered to kill each other by unseen superiors who conducted their battles from the safety of command posts in obscure places, perhaps hundreds of miles away; men killing each other like savages; men, women, and children dying; men living like animals in the jungle; men actually turning into animals—had long ago been permanently blocked out. Even the youthful faces in that faded photograph were no longer visible to him when he looked at them. He had conditioned himself to look beyond the faces. For a long time now, they had merely become nameless images that no longer existed, much like the woman who had betrayed him.

But there was one haunting recollection triggered by the sight of this photo that revived a memory that could never be blocked out. Perhaps that was so because it represented something on a different plane, another dimension, something almost of another world. For this reason, he had carried it with him for all these years, and he knew it would remain with him until the day he died. It came back always, in good dreams and in bad, and in conscious thought during the day at the most unexpected times. It was something extremely spiritual in substance, similar to contemplating the vastness of the universe. It was equal in importance to any other great spiritual experience he had encountered in his life. And on this day especially—opening day, the greatest day of the year for deer hunters—he had for a long time set aside a few minutes to stop and reflect. Now this special remembrance had become a ritual. Like an old home movie, it began with the vivid image of a magnificent tiger moving through the grass.

The man sitting in the chair sipped his coffee and smiled. In his youth they had referred to him as "indestructible." It seemed as if nothing could harm him. No danger was too great. He had developed a reputation for leading a charmed life and for becoming reckless, although he had never intentionally tried to live up to that reputation. Bad things simply never happened to him. He had walked away from several terrible automobile accidents in high school. He had also been a star running back on the football team, and he never so much as twisted an ankle. His reputation for being reckless continued during his college years, and then he attained a lifelong dream: He joined the Marine Corps. Two years later, he went off to fight in a war.

* * * * *

It had not been his choice to fight in this war. Privately, he questioned its validity. But it had been his duty, and he went willingly. He found to his surprise that he was amazingly well suited for the jungle warfare that awaited him. He had always been a natural leader, and he was good at leading his men into battle. He had been a deer hunter all his life, and the conditions of war were amazingly similar to those of deer camp. He was an excellent woodsman. In many ways, sneaking through the jungle seeking out the enemy was much like stalking an elusive white-tailed buck.

So a reputation for being reckless once again became his trademark. He took chances that no one else would take. In the eyes of his superiors, he was the perfect Marine. Outwardly, at least, he was not afraid to die, and that was an attribute that every senior officer looked for and liked in a subordinate officer.

What's more, he never seemed to worry about whether he might get killed. He went to extreme measures to protect the lives of his men, but he seemed to have no regard for his own safety.

Some thought he was deliberately trying to get himself killed, but he knew better. He knew something that no one else knew. He *knew* that he was going to survive this war. After all, he was said to be indestructible, and even he was beginning to believe it. It seemed as if no bullet could penetrate his invisible coat of armor. He was one of the chosen few whose destiny it was to survive every ambush, to return unscathed from every patrol. He was the one who, for better or for worse, was chosen to carry the torch for those who remained behind. He was like a reincarnation of Crazy Horse, the great Sioux leader. Each new day in the jungle became a good day to die, but the easy death that befell so many others eluded him time after time.

Then one day everything changed. It was all because of the tiger, and things were never the same after that. The war was never the same. Before the incident with the tiger, nothing had really mattered. Like a lot of men in similar situations, he had grown cold and indifferent to the death and suffering around him. The great fragility of life and the tragedy of human existence ceased to have any effect on him. He knew in his heart that, in many ways, he cared more for the wild things he had always been around and hunted than he did for people. As a Marine, he became good at killing the enemy. That was his job. He felt no remorse, no feelings of any kind. He was invincible. He was a survivor!—until the day the tiger came, that is, and then everything changed.

It happened on a routine patrol into enemy territory. They were well behind the lines deep in the jungle near the Cambodian border. Because of his woodsmanship and his fearlessness, and because of his great concern for his men, he was usually the "point man" on every patrol. Some said he could smell the enemy long before they appeared. He did have a certain knack, a certain way of sensing things, and he knew it. Long ago, while hunting crafty white-tailed bucks back home in the States, he had developed that knack, and it had been with him ever since. It came in handier than ever in the jungle, for here he was no longer hunting a graceful animal that could not fight back. The quarry he hunted now was the most dangerous game of all—a hate-filled human being who wanted to kill him more than he had ever wanted to kill anything in his life.

K Company had lost three men the day before—one to a land mine, two in a brief firefight. Two others had been badly wounded and evacuated out by helicopter. One of the dead had been his best friend. After the loss of the five Americans, he had personally been responsible for single-handedly killing seven NVA regulars. The patrol had killed nineteen enemy soldiers altogether, scoring a decisive victory as far as headquarters was concerned.

*Three Marines lost and two wounded,* he thought at the time, *none of whom had been a day over nineteen years of age. Three dead American Marines for nineteen slant-eyed, subhuman little gooks. Probably not a bad day's work in some commanding general's book. With that kind of trade-off—one Marine for every six of the enemy—total victory in this Godforsaken land should be at hand in no time!*

Then he became enraged. A hundred thousand gooks weren't worth the price of one of his fellow Marines. He set out on a personal vendetta to kill them all.

K Company was on the move shortly after first light the next day. The men had made a wide circle that took them several miles behind the suspected NVA position, and they were now headed back to the safety of their own lines. There was deep concern that the company of NVA regulars they had encountered the day before might be reinforced and cut them off. He was the point man as usual. All at once he sensed something directly ahead. He got down on his belly and started crawling through the grass. He reached a little knoll on the edge of a small clearing and paused to study the scene in front of him.

The jungle was deathly quiet. There was an eerie silence all around, and he knew something was amiss. Then the hair on the back of his neck stood up. Every fiber of his body told him that something was about to appear directly ahead. Suddenly he saw movement in some high grass a little to his right. With nerves of steel, the one-time master deer hunter now turned U.S. Marine and man-killer slowly raised his M-16 and prepared to put yet another notch on his weapon.

At one time, in the early days, the taking of another human life had held great significance. Now it meant nothing. At one time he had vomited for ten minutes after staring into the glazed eyes of his first official enemy KIA. He had stood there for many long moments and reflected to himself that this torn and lifeless form on the ground before him had once been another living, breathing human being, just like himself; this man probably had a wife or girlfriend back home somewhere that he made love to, and a family who awaited his return. But this man would never return, and he vomited until he could vomit no more.

The killing became routine in a surprisingly short time, and he lost count of the number of men he had killed. He had never tried to keep count from the beginning as some did, but he knew that the number was unusually high. So did everyone else. Very quickly he stopped allowing himself to view what he was doing as the taking of human life. Instead he thought of it as more like eliminating a disease or an infestation of rats or roaches. The killing could be justified, because it was killing something that needed to be killed. It was the law of the jungle—kill or be killed. More important, what he was eradicating might harm one of his comrades.

For a long time, all of his actions seemed justified. But somewhere deep inside his soul, he knew that there would have to be a day of reckoning, a judgment day. However, he never dreamed that it would come in the form of having to live each day for the next thirty years of his life with the guilt and burden of having survived.

*I should have been killed like so many of the others,* he often thought. *I of all people should have ended up on my back in some obscure rice paddy with a bullet through my gullet. Certainly that would have been the easiest way out.*

*Or, if I did have to be one of the chosen few who made it back to the world, at the very least I should have been maimed or crippled for life, armless or without legs like so many others I've seen shipped back to the States. That, too, would have been bearable.*

What he had never counted on, of course, was returning home without a scratch. None of those who made it back alive in any condition were ever the same, but to make it back without a scratch had to be the worst punishment imaginable.

The high grass in front of him moved slightly, and he glimpsed what appeared to be a quick flash of yellow. He fully expected this flash of movement to materialize into a dark-uniformed North Vietnamese Army soldier. And within a few more seconds, he fully expected the enemy soldier to be lying dead in a pool of his own blood. Chalk up one more kill for the American side.

After that an entire brigade of the enemy might erupt from the jungle, and he would kill as many as he could. This might be the day that they would get him, but he doubted it. One way or the other, he intended to make them pay dearly for their great transgression—the transgression of simply being there in that place at that exact moment.

To his great surprise, this anticipated event never came to pass. Instead, to his utter amazement, he realized that this yellow something was a large four-legged animal—not a two-legged man.

"Yellow and black markings. Long, arching tail. My God! It's a . . . tiger!"

He was dumbfounded. He couldn't believe his eyes. He couldn't have been more surprised if old Ho Chi Minh himself had suddenly appeared with a flag of truce. All his life he had dreamed about tigers and tiger hunting. In his youth he had always promised himself that someday he would actually go to the jungles of India on a real tiger hunt. But that boyhood dream was worlds away from the war-torn jungle that now consumed his life.

He had heard stories of tiger sightings near the Cambodian border, but never in his wildest dreams did he ever expect to encounter a living, breathing tiger in the jungle while on patrol. And now he, the great deer hunter, was staring at a live tiger less than fifty yards away. Yet somehow the timing was all wrong! The noble creature seemed strangely out of place, as if it were on another planet in another galaxy, instead of right in the middle of its natural environment.

"What's wrong with you?" he whispered. "Don't you know this is a war zone, filled with land mines and booby traps? A place where men kill each other every day, a place filled with death and destruction? This is no place for a tiger to be roaming around. You shouldn't be here. This is a jungle where NVA and American madmen lurk behind every tree. . . .

"I almost shot you, you crazy cat," he continued. "You'd better get the hell out of here while you can. Go somewhere far away and don't come back for a long, long time. If you know what's good for you, don't ever come back. Do you understand? It's not safe around here. Men have lost all sanity here. This isn't your war. You don't belong here."

The tiger moved through the grass fluidly, unaware that it was being observed. In an instant, it disappeared. All was quiet for the next two minutes.

He rolled over on his back and looked up at the gray, overcast sky. Soon it would rain again. He laughed.

"My God, of all the friggin' things to see out here today, I meet up with a tiger face-to-face. I wonder how many tigers have been killed in this war. How many have been napalmed? No telling. At least, you'll probably make it if you just. . . ."

There was a rapid burst of M-16 fire over to his right. He knew the shots had come from one of his men. He quickly rolled over and studied the scene in front of him. Suddenly he heard talking.

"Damn! Those fools are gonna get themselves killed," he told himself.

He quickly got up and started creeping over toward the sound of the voices. He stopped often to look and listen. The voices got louder.

He sneaked over to another grassy clearing about one hundred yards from where he had seen the tiger. There, fifty yards ahead, standing in broad daylight in the knee-high grass and looking down at something on the ground, were two of his men. They were talking excitedly, as if they didn't have a care in the world. He whistled. Phillips, the young kid from Alabama, looked over at him. He waved to Phillips, who waved back. Then he stood up and started walking rapidly toward the two Marines, wondering what they were looking at.

*It's got to be a dead gook,* he thought. *Maybe a sniper. But why are they standing out in the open like that, talking? Do they have a death wish or something?*

"What the hell are you two doing out here in the open?" he whispered loudly. "Don't you know this place is full of Char. . . ." He looked down. His mouth fell open.

"I got me a goddamn tiger, Corporal," Phillips said excitedly. "Can you believe it? A goddamn tiger, right here in the middle of the goddamn jungle!"

"What the hell did you shoot him for?" Wyatt whispered. "Why didn't you just let him go?"

"Because, man . . . it's a damn tiger. How many times do you see a damn tiger? Not very often. You're a big hunter, aren't you, Corporal? Have you ever shot yourself a real tiger?"

"Hell, no!" Wyatt said harshly. "They don't have tigers where I come from."

He was furious. He was sickened at the sight before him. No dead enemy soldier had ever sickened him as much as this bloodied, lifeless carcass lying in the grass.

"See. This must be my lucky day, Corporal," Phillips said.

"Jeez. I never even seen a f---in' tiger before," the other Marine, named Benson, said in a strong New Jersey accent. "Ain't they getting rare? Man, get a load of those claws. And those choppers."

"They are rare," Wyatt answered. "They're extremely rare. There're only a few thousand of the sons-of-bitches left. Why in the hell did you kill it? You know you're not supposed to be shooting off your weapon. This place is crawling with Charlie. We've probably alerted every gook within five miles. Come on. Let's get back on patrol."

"But Corporal, what about my damn tiger?"

"What about it?"

"We can't just leave him here. I want to take him with me."

"What?"

"I want to take him with me. That's why I shot him. I've always wanted me a tiger skin. Man, can you imagine what this'll look like back home in Birmingham? It'll be one hell of a war trophy. It'll just take me and Benson five minutes to skin him out. Come on, Corporal. Please?"

"What do you think this is? We're not out here on a quail hunt. This isn't a Saturday afternoon dove shoot. Hell, these sons-of-bitches are almost extinct. Don't you know that?"

"Everything's almost extinct in this goddamn hellhole, Corporal," Benson blurted out. "Including us. What the hell difference is one f---ing tiger gonna make?"

"OK. Go ahead and skin him out. But don't do it out here in the damn open. Drag him over into the bushes where you at least have some cover. And hurry up! We've gotta vacate this area fast."

"Corporal Wyatt?"

"Yeah?"

"There's just one thing . . ."

"Yeah? What is it?"

"I ain't never skinned out a tiger like this before. And neither has Benson. Will you show us how to do it?"

* * * * *

The white-haired man got up and poured himself another cup of coffee. It was almost time to start putting on his warm clothes and heading into the woods, but not quite. He still had a few more minutes to sit quietly and ponder.

Phillips was killed six days later, the day after the photograph had been taken. He was shot through the neck by a sniper. He bled to death in less than two minutes. He had strapped the rolled-up skin, along with the tiger's head, onto the top of his pack. In six days' time both the skin and the head were rancid. The skin had started to rot. Phillips had become obsessed with trying to save it, but he knew he was helpless because of the heat and the constant damp. Still he refused to give up his trophy. Everyone started calling the platoon the "Tiger Patrol."

Phillips had asked everyone he saw about saving that hide. Wyatt had not known it at the time, but at some point during that six-day period Phillips had heard about a method for preserving animal skins that primitive peoples used in which the brains of the animal itself were made into a tanning solution. Phillips was desperate to save his tiger skin, and the day before

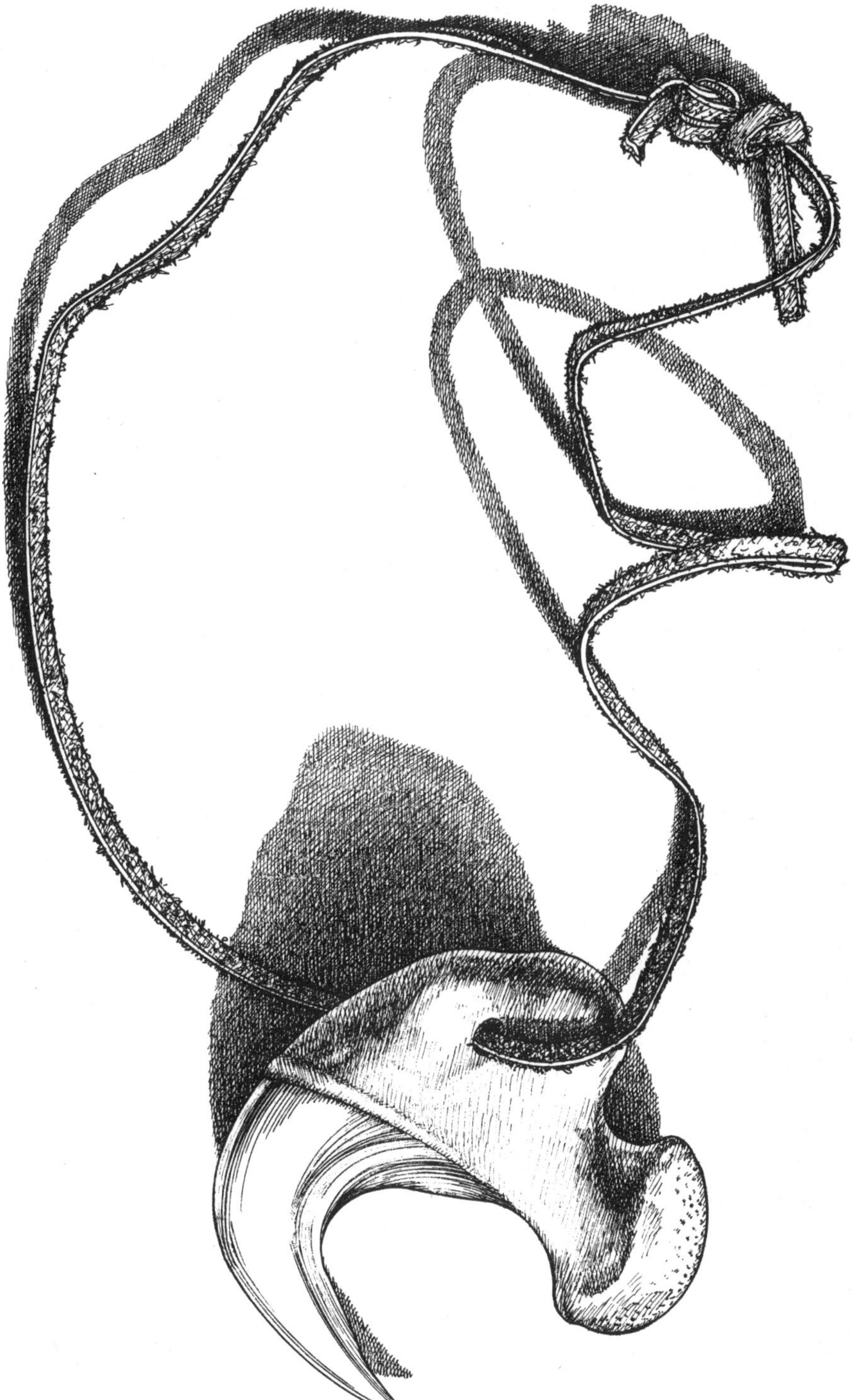

he was shot through the neck, several Viet Cong soldiers had been killed in a brief firefight. Phillips and Benson sneaked out to the dead bodies and relieved one of the corpses of its head. Bringing the man's head back to camp, Phillips opened up the skull and carefully removed the brain with his knife. He then spread the hide out on the ground and started working the mushy substance into the skin. But the skin was too far gone. The next day, the hair started falling out.

Benson inherited the head and skin after Phillips was taken away in a body bag. But after two more days the skin was so rancid that it had to be left behind. Wyatt was furious when he found out about the brain-tanning incident. In memory of Phillips, however, he told Benson to cut off all the tiger's claws before disposing of the skin. He instructed Benson to give one of the claws to each of the men in the squad.

"If we're gonna be known as the Tiger Patrol, we by God better start earning our name," Wyatt told Benson.

Benson did as he was told. Each of the men began wearing his tiger claw around his neck as a good luck charm. But neither Benson nor anyone else could possibly have understood what that tiger had meant to Wyatt, or what its killing had represented in his eyes. To him the claws were much more than simple good luck charms. The living tiger had represented something very special that went far beyond the realm of war and men killing each other. It represented nature in its purest form, without man's destructive intervention. It also represented hope, despite the miserable war, because the tiger had been alive. But all hope was lost the moment that tiger died. Wyatt was superstitious. He had reserved the largest and best claw for himself. It was the "kill claw" from the tiger's right front paw.

Benson wrapped his poncho around the rotten tiger head and carried it with him for several more days. If nothing else, he planned to save the skull. Someone had told him that tiger teeth—mainly the canines—were worth a lot of money. He planned to make some money off this war one way or another. But Benson stepped on a mine in a rice paddy and lost both legs. Sometime during the mad rush to get him out by helicopter, the tiger's head was lost. Wyatt asked around, but no one seemed to know what had happened to it. It took Benson a month to die from his injuries.

* * * * *

"What would have happened to you if you had lived?" the white-haired man asked out loud, speaking to the small photograph on the mantel. He was not speaking to his four dead comrades. He had stopped looking at their youthful faces long ago. He was speaking to the rotting head of the tiger that Phillips was proudly holding up in the photograph. The tiger seemed to have a strange expression on its face.

"Would it have made any real difference if you had lived?" he asked. "Yes, I guess it would have. But if you had, one of the local villagers would have eventually plugged you with some old relic of a muzzleloader, using nails for shot, and you'd have died a slow, agonizing death. Maybe it was the best thing for you, after all—to die in your youth like the rest of us—but you deserved so much better than what you got. No question about that. It wasn't your war. It wasn't your fault that men came into your jungle and started killing each other. But you know what? Even if you had lived to be a hundred, your kind is still headed for oblivion. All because of your cursed skin, and your claws, and your teeth, and your bones.

"You want to know something else? We have a lot in common, you and me. Neither one of us really has a place in this world anymore. We're both antiques and misfits, and pretty soon, we'll both be extinct together. The sad thing is that you really belong here. You've always belonged here. But me and my kind—I'm not so sure. Look at the mess we've made. And it looks like we're gonna keep killing each other until one of these days we'll be extinct as well. Unfortunately, we're probably gonna take you and everything else with us when we go. I just don't see it happening any other way.

"Oh, well. It's opening day! I guess we still have another season or two left in us before we throw in the towel. Since we don't seem to be able to solve the problems of the world, we might as well grab a rifle and go to the woods!"

Wyatt drank his last sip of coffee. Then he reached up and fondly felt the heavy curved object hanging from a leather thong around his neck. It was there, all right, and as always, that knowledge was reassuring. He had never taken it off, except once, to have the sharp point of the claw encased in gold because it was so sharp that it kept scratching his chest. For a long time he had intentionally left the point of the claw uncovered. Whenever it scratched his chest, he liked to think of it as the tiger's spirit coming back to remind him of what had happened that day so many years before, when he saw the most magnificent animal in the world moving through the grass. But then one day he decided to have the point encased in gold.

"I've been waiting a long time for this day," he said out loud. "There's a glow over on the eastern horizon, and it's gonna be cold and clear. I guess I'd better get some clothes on and head on out to my stand. That old buck I hunted last year has got to be carrying a bragging-size rack on his head this season, and I have a feeling I'm going to get a glimpse of him. I guess it's time for the Tiger Patrol's indestructible old point man to get cracking!"

# When It Comes to Deer Huntin', the Good Lord Often Works in Mysterious Ways

## Chapter 5

*When modern deer hunting seasons were first established in Georgia during the late 1950s and early 1960s, it was against the law to hunt on Sunday in many (if not all) Georgia counties. Sometimes those laws were enforced and sometimes they weren't, depending on the sheriff in the particular county. I can remember many a frustrating Sunday in deer camp when boys were not allowed to hunt. Perhaps even worse, they were not allowed to shoot off a firearm because of the noise.*

*That "no hunting on Sunday" rule was seldom broken because most youngsters were led to believe that if they so much as fired a .22 rifle on the Sabbath, the local sheriff, who was no doubt lurking in the bushes waiting for someone to make the slightest transgression, would surround them with a pack of deputies and haul them away to the big house.*

*The laws against hunting on Sunday began to change during the early 1970s. Eventually, hunting on Sunday became an integral part of deer hunting in the state.*

* * * * *

"Why can't we hunt tomorrow?" the teenage boy asked.

"Because it's Sunday," Uncle Buck answered with an air of finality in his voice. He stirred the glowing coals of the dying campfire with a long stick. Yellow flames flared up for several seconds, lighting up a half-dozen sullen faces.

"You boys know they ain't no huntin' on the Sabbath. Why do we always go through this same routine every weekend? You know Sunday's the day we break camp and go home."

"Yeah, but we never break camp on Sunday until late in the afternoon," Logan Collins argued. "At least three or four o'clock. Why can't we hunt till then?"

"Because it's against the law to hunt on Sunday in Talbot County," Uncle Buck answered. "We start shootin' up the woods down here on Sunday and somebody'll call the sheriff and make a complaint. He'll then feel obliged to come pay us a visit, and the first thing ya' know, he's done shut down our entire huntin' operation. That's why!"

"But why is it against the law?" Logan asked. "We've got nearly three thousand acres of woods leased down here to hunt on, and a man could get lost on that much land. Who's gonna know if one measly little hunter is out there in a deer stand mindin' his own business? The sheriff isn't gonna come all the way down here on Sunday morning to see who's sittin' in his stand and who isn't, is he? It would take an army to go through our woods and find everybody's stand. Anyway, if the Good Lord didn't want us to hunt on Sunday, why'd He include Sunday in the weekend? We've only got two days in every weekend, and five days of school in between. That means two days of heaven and five days of. . . ."

"Watch yer' language," Uncle Buck warned.

Logan Collins was not related to Buck Anderson in any way, but like everyone else in the hunting club, he respected him greatly and always referred to him as "Uncle Buck."

"OK. How's this?" the boy asked. "Two really good days of being alive and five days of punishment and misery. But a full half of those two really good days is Sunday, so that means we can hunt only half the time. That means we get punished six days a week instead of five, and get only one day to hunt on the weekend instead of two. It ain't fair! One out of seven ain't good odds."

"Life ain't fair," Uncle Buck said. "But I'm glad to see all that punishment you been subjected to in school lately has at least come to some good. At least you can do some addin' and subtractin', even if you do strike out in the grammar department."

"I know how to talk," the boy said. "But everybody says *ain't* in deer camp, even you."

"I'll have to give you that one," Uncle Buck said, smiling.

There was a long silence. Several older men sat with the two teenage boys, and everyone stared contentedly at the dying coals. After a few minutes, Logan spoke up again.

"You never answered my question," he said to Uncle Buck. "Why is it against the law? Everybody else hunts on Sunday. All those guys down at Mulberry Creek hunt on Sunday. They've even killed some of their best bucks on Sunday. The sheriff never says anything to them."

"For starters, Sunday is the Lord's Day, like I already said," Uncle Buck answered. "'For six days shall ye toil, and the seventh shall be a day of rest.' So that's what we're doin'—restin'!"

"But huntin' ain't toil," Logan argued. "It's fun, pleasant, and restful all in one. That's why we do it."

"I can't argue with that, but there's also that little matter of havin' a large colored church right on the edge of our property, out on Highway 36," Uncle Buck said. "Lots of folks attend that church on Sunday mornin', and it'd be showin' pretty poor manners on our part to start slingin' lead during Sunday services. In case you haven't noticed, deer guns make a lot of noise. It's what's called showing a little bit of respect. That's something they don't teach much of in school these days, but it's still right important.

"As for everyone else doin' it, well, there are a few clubs around that like to bend the rules," Uncle Buck continued. "But we're not gonna be like them! You bend one rule, like huntin' on Sunday, and first thing you know you break another, like shootin' a doe when it ain't doe day. Pretty soon you graduate to shootin' more than the legal limit of bucks. Before you know it, you're a full-fledged outlaw."

The boy was not about to give up. "What if we go to our stands in the morning and sit there, just like always, but promise not to hunt?" he offered. "Instead we'll just look, and if we see anything, we'll promise not to shoot."

Uncle Buck laughed out loud. Several of the other men around the campfire chuckled as well. "Why that's the craziest notion I ever heard," he said. "You mean to sit here and tell me that if I let you and Marty go to your stands in the morning as usual, with your rifles, that you wouldn't be tempted to shoot a nice buck if you saw one? Who in their right mind is gonna hold back from that kind of temptation? We'd have to tie yer' trigger finger behind yer' back with steel cable!"

"It would be better than sitting around camp and wasting the whole day," Logan argued.

"In that case, why would you need your rifles?" Uncle Buck countered. "I'll tell you what. You two are welcome to go to your stands in the morning and do as much deer watching as you like—*without* your rifles! I don't reckon the Good Lord'll frown on that."

"But that wouldn't be fair," the boy argued.

"Why not?"

"Because . . . the woods can be dangerous," Logan reasoned. "If a man is gonna go and sit in his stand, he ought to be armed. What if we run into a pack of wild dogs on our way to our stands? What about that escaped convict that was caught in our woods last summer? Somebody like that could still be out there. What about poisonous snakes?"

"We haven't had any problems with wild dogs in a coon's age," Uncle Buck said. "And ain't no escaped convict in his right mind gonna come blunderin' into a camp full of deer hunters with high-powered rifles during deer season. And if you don't know how to avoid snakes by now, you ought not be in the woods!"

"Maybe we should take up bowhunting," the boy said. "That wouldn't disturb anyone at church. Or maybe we could get silencers put on our rifles."

"It would still be huntin' any way you cut it," Uncle Buck said. "And you'd still be breaking the law. Maybe nobody else would ever know, but you'd know, and if you have half a conscience at all, you wouldn't feel right about it."

"I wish the law would change," Logan said. "If the law changed, I'm sure the Good Lord wouldn't mind. Anyway, where does it say in the Bible that you can't hunt on

Sunday? If Sunday is supposed to be the day of rest, then why can't we rest in our deer stands instead of in camp? It seems to me that this is one of those crazy rules made up by people, not by the Good Lord. I thought that's why we come down to deer camp—to get away from all those crazy city rules and to rest!"

"Like I said earlier, you got a good point, but I ain't about to get into any heavy philosophizin' at this hour," Uncle Buck said. "We can argue till the cows come home, but I think you two know the difference in right and wrong. Times are changin'. Someday I'm sure the law'll change, too. Until that time, we've got to do our best to abide by the rules.

"It's about time to turn in, and you've about worn me out," he continued. "I'll make a deal with you. If you and Marty want to get up early and spend a half a day in your stands tomorrow observing—not huntin'—then it's OK with me. You can take your rifles, and you can do everything you normally do—except shoot a deer, or anything else for that matter. No convicts, no wild dogs, no nothin'! I don't want to hear any shots coming out of the swamp. Understood? If you see the biggest buck to ever grace the woods in south Georgia, you just have to sit there and grit yer teeth. If two Boone and Crockett bucks walk under your tree and start cracking acorns, you can wave to 'em and say hello, but you can't shoot. Understood?"

"Yes, sir."

* * * * *

Logan and Marty were up well before daylight. As planned, they ate a quick breakfast, made some sandwiches for lunch, and headed for the woods. They arrived back in camp around 2:00 P.M. Several of the regular club members had already left for home, and the few remaining hunters in camp were tidying up and packing their gear.

"Well, tell us all about it," Uncle Buck said as he placed an empty five-gallon water container in the back of his truck.

"I'm sure you two saw big-antlered bucks runnin' all around the swamp this mornin', right?"

"We sure did," Marty answered.

Logan nodded in agreement. "We saw two good bucks, just like you said we probably would," he told Uncle Buck. "One was a nice nine-pointer. The other was a good eight. He was just a little smaller."

"Was it hard not being able to shoot?" Uncle Buck asked.

"No, not really," Logan answered. "As it turned out, we didn't have to." He and Marty glanced at each other and grinned.

"What do you mean?" Uncle Buck asked with a puzzled look.

"Well, we got 'em up as far as the creek crossing near where the main trail forks, but that's about as far as we could drag 'em," Logan said matter-of-factly. "They're both field-dressed, but we sure could use some help gettin' 'em the rest of the way back to camp."

Several men who had overheard Logan talking stopped what they were doing to listen more closely.

"What did you say?" Uncle Buck asked, pausing dead in his tracks.

"I said, they're both lying in the trail near the fork, and we'd sure appreciate some help gettin' 'em back to camp," Logan repeated. He spoke with a perfectly straight poker face. "They're pretty heavy. I'd say they each dressed out at around 170 pounds."

The two boys had carefully rehearsed their lines all the way back to camp, and now the words were flowing perfectly.

Uncle Buck puffed up like a strutting turkey. "What? Two bucks? You're telling me you killed two bucks this morning? I told you boys you couldn't hunt. We didn't hear any shots. What's going on here?"

"You didn't hear any shots because there weren't any," Marty said, grinning broadly.

"Then how in the . . . Oh, I get it. It's a joke, right?" Uncle Buck asked.

"No, it's not a joke," Logan said seriously. "We have two nice bucks on the ground, and we plan to get 'em both mounted."

"You're telling me you killed two nice bucks this morning?" Uncle Buck asked again.

"No, we didn't say that," Logan answered. "We said we have two bucks on the ground, but we didn't say anything about killing them. We weren't allowed to shoot anything, remember?"

Uncle Buck sat down on the tailgate of the truck, shaking his head. By now the three or four remaining men in camp had also gathered around to hear what promised to be an interesting explanation.

"I give up," Uncle Buck said, raising both hands as if he were under arrest. "You two got me good. Somehow, I'm thinkin' this might be payback time for all the tricks we've played on you over the past few years, and for all the chores we make you do around camp. That's it, ain't it?"

"This isn't payback," Marty said. "This is serious."

"OK, then let's hear it," Uncle Buck said. "Sounds like it's gonna be a real doozy."

"You can say that again," Logan agreed. "You're not gonna believe it. It's the craziest thing that's ever happened in any deer camp that we've ever heard of. That's for sure!"

Both boys were excited now. They each started talking nonstop at the same time. Within seconds, they were almost yelling.

"Wait a minute! Slow down!" Uncle Buck shouted. "Nobody can understand a word you're sayin'. One at a time, please. Logan, you first. Take it slow and easy, and try to talk in English if you don't mind."

"OK," Logan said, taking a deep breath. "Here's what happened this morning, and it's the honest-to-goodness truth. Since we weren't allowed to hunt, Marty and I decided to go down to the big platform stand on the little peninsula overlooking the swamp so we could sit together."

"Sounds reasonable," Uncle Buck said. "Go on. "

"Well, we saw a couple of does right after daylight, but things were pretty quiet until about 11:00. All of a sudden, this big eight-pointer came bounding through the woods chasing a doe. They disappeared, and then a big nine-pointer came along. He was slightly bigger than the eight. He disappeared, too. A few minutes later, all heck started breaking loose just over the ridge. We heard all kinds of crashing and banging for about five minutes. It sounded like somebody beating on trees with a baseball bat. Then the doe came sneaking back in front of our stand, and the two bucks followed. Just as they got about forty yards out in front of the stand, they stopped and squared off at each other again. It was unbelievable! I mean, they were tearing bushes out of the ground and trying to kill each other."

"That's usually what bucks do when they fight," Uncle Buck said matter-of-factly.

"Yeah!" Marty added. "It was a battle to the death, and we had a front-row seat!"

"The eight-pointer suddenly got in a good lick and horned the nine-pointer in the abdomen, right behind his ribs," Logan continued. "You could hear the antler go in, and when the eight-pointer jerked away, the nine just stood there with his head down and his tongue hanging out. The eight hit him again, and blood was coming out. You could pretty much tell it was all over for the nine. Suddenly the eight got his head down one last time and charged. The nine sort of sidestepped him, and when he did, he sank his antlers right into the shoulder of the eight. One of the tines went right through his heart. Then it was over for both of them. The eight immediately walked over to a large pine and piled up on the ground. Within a few minutes, his head went over and he was dead. The nine staggered off through the woods. We got down and followed him. He made it only about seventy-five yards. He was dead, too. We found him in the middle of the trail."

"The whole thing was unbelievable!" Marty added.

Uncle Buck appeared to be doing some calculating in his head for a few moments. "So, you boys have yourselves two good bucks on the ground, and nobody fired a single shot at either one of them. Is that about the size of it?"

"That's about the size of it," Logan answered.

"Well, if that don't beat all," Uncle Buck said. "You're right. That's about the dangdest fish story this old fool has ever heard coming out of a deer camp. And I've heard some real whoppers! Sunday or not, day of rest or not, I reckon we've got a pair of bucks out in the woods that need to be tended to. Is there anything else?"

"There is just one other thing," Marty said.

"Yeah," Logan seconded. "We learned something pretty important while we were sittin' in our stand today, and we didn't have to be in any church to figure it out."

"Oh, yeah? What's that?" Uncle Buck asked.

"What they say is true: The Good Lord sure works in mysterious ways!"

# A Rite of Passage

## Chapter 6

J. C. Larson and his twelve-year-old nephew had just gotten settled on the wooden platform fifteen feet off the ground when the question came.

"Do you think we're gonna kill one this morning, Uncle Jim?" the boy whispered excitedly.

With each word, mist poured from the boy's mouth. They were sitting on the edge of a large alfalfa field. The cold, gray dawn was just beginning to give way to the light of the new day. At any moment now, the hazy shapes of feeding deer would begin to materialize from the dark shadows.

J. C. was silent for a long moment. Then, speaking in a low voice, he said, "The word *kill* is one of those words we tend to use pretty loosely sometimes, Danny. But it's a mighty strong word, and there's some pretty powerful medicine associated with it. Now I s'pose if you look in the dictionary you'll find a fancy definition. In simple words, *kill* means to end the life of some living creature.

"In deer camp, when everybody starts coming back in after the morning hunt, it's customary for one hunter to ask another, 'Did ya' kill anything this morning?' It's sort of an accepted figure of speech. And living out in the country like we do, killing is much more a part of everyday living than it is in some other places. On hog killin' day, for instance, we'll kill a hog or two so we can have a supply of pork for the winter. But there's a different reason altogether why you and I are sitting here in this deer stand.

"Killin' any kind of animal is a sacred act, especially an animal as beautiful as a white-tailed deer," J. C. said. "With that act comes a lot of responsibility. First off, there's got to be respect for the animal itself and respect for the taking of that animal's life. Next, there's also a deep responsibility to make sure you kill that animal in a quick, humane manner."

"I have a lot of respect for everything I hunt," the boy said.

"I know you do," J. C. whispered. "But it's a sad commentary on our society that in many places around the country, killing has come to take on a whole new meaning. What with crime being the way it is these days—thugs and gang members killing each other on the streets of our cities, murder rates going through the ceiling, motorists shooting each other on the highways, even children shooting other children in schools—some people might say that life is cheap and killing has become commonplace.

"But life is not cheap, Danny. All life on this earth is sacred, and the taking of any life is always a sacred act. When a boy kills his first deer, as you're about to do, a lot of baggage goes along with it. In many ways, the taking of a life helps that boy come to grips with his own mortality, and his own understanding of life and death. If that boy respects the animal he has killed, as our American Indians respected all the living things they hunted and killed, then the act can be justified. That's the real essence of hunting. But if that boy—or anyone else, for that matter—kills for the enjoyment of watching something die, then the animal has been sacrificed for the wrong reason and the act is a wrongful one. It's a sin against humanity and a sin against nature.

"Although most of us try our dead-level best to live by that important set of rules we know as the Ten Commandments, the truth of the matter is that all life on earth lives by killing and eating other life. We humans eat both plants and animals every day in order to survive. Cows eat grass. The deer we hunt eat acorns and alfalfa. Birds eat insects. That eagle we saw last week eats fish. Fish eat other fish. That's the way life on this good earth has always been. Everything in nature is part of a continuing cycle of life and death.

"When it comes to what many consider to be the most important commandment—*Thou Shalt Not Kill*—I guess you could say most people reserve that one for the taking of human life. Humans should never kill other humans, period. Yet, sadly, it seems that even this most important rule has gone by the wayside in many segments of our society today.

"Fortunately, Danny, you've been brought up to know the difference between right and wrong and to respect all people and all living things. And speaking of respect, when an American Indian killed an animal for food, he always thanked that animal for giving its life so that the Indian and his tribe could live. The animal was sacred—whether it was a buffalo, a deer, or a fish in the river—and the taking of that animal's life was a sacred act. To go a step further, everything in nature was sacred to the Indians. Not just the animals but also the trees, the rocks, the sky, the clouds, even a blade of grass—everything in the universe was part of the divine mystery.

"Hunting to all of the primitive peoples of the world was a spiritual experience. There was a covenant between the animal and the human communities that the animal helped to sustain. Early man knew that animals possessed powers he could never have. In many ways, the animals being hunted were his equals or superiors. That's why the Western Indians worshiped the buffalo, the Southeastern Indians worshiped the white-tailed deer, and the Northwestern Indians worshiped the salmon. The animal sacrificed may have varied, but the reverence for that animal was the same. And, by thanking the animal after killing it, and showing reverence for it, early man believed that the animal would come back again and again and continue to give him nourishment.

"To primitive man, the very act of being alive on this earth was sacred, and every minute of every day was a spiritual experience. That's the kind of important heritage we should have inherited from our Indian forefathers. But sadly, a lot of people have lost that respect for Mother Earth and all of her children."

Suddenly it was daylight, and the forms of several deer could be seen out in the alfalfa field. They were all does.

"I didn't mean to give a sermon this morning," J. C. whispered. "But some of this stuff is pretty important. And by the way, to answer your question, Danny Boy—yes, sir, I believe we're gonna kill something today!"

Forty-five minutes later, Danny and his uncle were kneeling over a young Iowa eight-pointer, Danny's very first buck.

After some of the initial excitement had worn off, Danny began stroking the buck's thick winter coat. J. C. stood by silently so that Danny could share a special moment with his trophy. After a few minutes, Danny looked into the buck's glazed eye. A single tear began to roll down Danny's cheek. "Thank you," he said softly.

# Jacobs's Well

## Chapter 7

"I'm gonna kill ol' Red today," Wilbur Adams declared as he and his partner, Candy Johnson, were driving toward their hunting lease in the predawn darkness. "I can just feel it in my bones. Today is gonna be the day!"

"I hope you're right," Candy answered. "I'm sick of hearing about Big Red. I wish somebody would kill that son-of-a-gun so I could finally see what he looks like."

Wilbur and Candy had been hunting together on the old Jacobs place for years. During the past few seasons, a much sought-after buck known locally as Big Red had been seen many times by area hunters and farmers. This trophy whitetail had earned its nickname because the top of its head and much of its winter coat were a distinctly dark rusty-red color—hence the nickname. Although Candy had never laid eyes on the renowned whitetail, Wilbur had seen him twice in the past—once the season before and once only several weeks earlier while he was putting up his tree stand. This second sighting really got Wilbur fired up. Wilbur, like every other hunter in the area, dreamed about putting Big Red on the wall.

It was the second weekend of rifle season, and it was a perfect morning for hunting—cool and clear with no wind. The rut was at its peak. Wilbur knew that bucks like Big Red should be preoccupied with finding does instead of trying to save their skins. Upon arrival at the old Jacobs place, Wilbur and Candy parked in their usual spot and headed out in opposite directions, toward their stands.

Less than thirty minutes after shooting light, Candy heard a single shot. Since he was positive it had come from the vicinity of Wilbur's stand, he immediately climbed down from his tree and headed in that direction. When he reached the hollow where he knew Wilbur had been hunting, he whistled.

"Over here!" came the excited reply from inside a long gully, about fifty yards from Wilbur's stand.

Candy quickly made his way toward the gully. When he got to the edge, he peered over. A few yards away his partner was kneeling over what appeared to be a huge buck. Wilbur was obviously in the finishing stages of field dressing a fine trophy.

"Did you kill Big Red?" Candy asked excitedly.

"I sure did!" came the enthusiastic reply. "I told you I was gonna shoot him today, and I did! And he's every bit as big as everyone said!"

Candy scrambled down to his partner's side. There was no doubt about it. Just as all of the stories and rumors had said, the buck possessed the reddest coat Candy had ever seen on a deer. In addition, the big whitetail had a massive rack with several tines over ten inches in length. The thing that really set the rack off, however, was the buck's unusual eye guards. Each of the long eye guards was split into triple tines, giving the big buck a total of fourteen countable points in all.

"That's gotta' be Big Red, all right," Candy stated. "Congratulations, partner! What was he doin' when you shot him?"

"Thanks," Wilbur replied. "There really wasn't much to it. He just came moseying down the trail right under my stand. It was less than a twenty-yard shot."

"Well, it's about time somebody got this old rascal," Candy said. "If it couldn't have been me, I'm glad it was you. What are you plannin' to do with him? I hate to leave the woods this early. It ain't even eight o'clock, and we still got all day to hunt."

"You're right," Wilbur agreed. "It's too early to go home. I'd like to hang him somewhere till tonight, but it's warming up awful fast and the flies are already starting to buzz. If I hang him in the woods, the flies will be all over him."

"Yeah, and it's gonna be warm today," Candy said. "I don't know where we could put him. . . ."

"It'll take us hours to drag him out of the woods and drive to a cooler somewhere," Wilbur said. "And I don't want to mess up your hunting."

"Hey, I've got an idea," Candy offered. "The old Jacobs home is only about 150 yards from here. Let's drag him over there."

"And put him in that house? Why, that old house is falling down, and there's probably rats and everything else in there. Plus the flies would still be all over him."

"No. That's not what I had in mind," Candy countered. "I was thinking about the well."

"The well? What the heck are we gonna do with a well?"

"Put him in!"

"What?"

"We'll hang him down in the well."

"You must be crazy. Not with my buck! Especially not with Big Red!"

"Why not? It's the safest place around. I've got fifty feet of nylon rope in my pack. We can tie the rope to his antlers and lower him down into the well about ten feet. It'll be cool down there, it's dry, and the flies won't bother him. We can even cover up the top with some boards to keep the varmints out."

"I don't know. . . ." Wilbur said, scratching his chin. "This isn't just any buck we're talking about, you know. This is Big Red!"

Thirty minutes later the two hunters were standing at the edge of a hole in the ground in the backyard of the old Jacobs place, breathing heavily after having dragged the big buck mostly uphill for 150 yards through the woods. The uncovered well had eroded away to a width of about four feet across at the ground level, but it quickly narrowed to a much smaller diameter as it penetrated the black depths of the earth. Candy immediately started tying his rope to Big Red's antlers. The back porch of the old dilapidated house stood about twenty feet away.

"We'll just lower him down about ten feet and then tie the rope to the support on the porch," Candy said. "Then, after dark, we'll bring the truck over here, pull him back out, and load him up."

"Are you sure this rope is strong enough?" Wilbur asked, peering down into the dark hole. "It looks pretty deep down there."

"Heck, yeah," Candy replied confidently. "It's rated at two thousand pounds."

Once the rope was tied securely around the buck's antlers, the two men slowly began to edge the two-hundred-pound carcass over the side of the well. Wilbur wrapped the rope around his right forearm several times for a tighter grip, while Candy walked over and looped the opposite end securely around one of the stout 4x4s that held up the ramshackle back porch.

As soon as the bulk of the deer's carcass had been pushed over the side of the well, it fell freely for some distance until the slack in the rope was gone. At that point, Wilbur's arm was almost yanked out of its socket, and he was very nearly jerked into the well after the descending buck. Fortunately for him the rope around his arm pulled loose first, but not before it had inflicted a severe rope burn and rubbed off most of the hair from his elbow to his hand.

A moment later, the dead weight of the heavy buck easily yanked free the 4x4 support beam from the porch. While the roof of the front porch was caving in on top of Candy, the heavy eight-foot beam skidded across the yard, following the rapidly descending buck. As the beam slid past Wilbur, who was sprawled on the ground next to the well, one end of it raked across his thigh, inflicting a nasty blow to the back of his leg.

Fortunately, the heavy beam ended up straddling the well, checking the descent of the falling buck. By that time, however, Wilbur was lying on the ground alongside the well writhing in pain, and Candy was on the porch nursing a large knot atop his head and trying to dig himself out of the debris. All the while, Big Red dangled some thirty feet down in the well. Then the rope broke. Wilbur cringed as he heard the muffled thump of his once-in-a-lifetime trophy hitting bottom.

Neither of the hunters had counted on the dead weight of the buck putting so much strain on the rope as the heavy carcass dropped down the well. Now they found themselves in a real pickle. For the rest of the day, they plotted and planned on how to get Big Red out. With their flashlights, they could see him way down at the bottom of the well, lodged against the narrow walls like a tiny rat with antlers. At last, about an hour before dark, Wilbur decided to give up and drive into town and hire a wrecker. It would cost him a lot of money, but it would be a surefire way to recover his prize.

Several hours later they returned to the old Jacobs place. The wrecker backed up to the well, and the attendant began to lower a long steel cable with a hook on the end. By the light of several flashlights he was finally able, after considerable effort, to get the hook around one side of the buck's antlers. The wrecker slowly began to pull Big Red up out of the eerie blackness.

"So that's the famous Big Red, huh?" the attendant mused as the buck was slowly being brought up. He was guiding the cable with one hand and shining his flashlight down on Big Red's antlers with the other. As the buck slowly ascended out of the murky depths, the attendant noticed the triple brow tines on top of the buck's head.

"I see how he got his name now," the attendant said.

"Oh, you mean his red coat?" Candy queried.

"No. I mean his funny-looking rack. Looks like two pitchforks on the top of his head. Why, with that red hair and those two pitchforks, it looks like the devil himself rising up out of the depths of purgatory."

It took a second for the comment to sink in. Suddenly, Wilbur's face lit up for the first time during the long evening. "It is!" he agreed, smiling wickedly. "You're absolutely right. That's not Big Red. There never was a buck named Big Red. That's Satan himself, the devil buck—the buck from hell!"

The two deer hunters never said a word to each other all the way home. While Candy nursed the knot on his head with an ice pack, it was all Wilbur could do to drive the truck with his sore arm and badly bruised leg. As they pulled up in front of Candy's house, Wilbur looked over at his partner and finally broke the silence. "If you want Big Red, he's all yours."

"Are you serious?" Candy asked. "You want to give me Big Red?"

"I've never been more serious in all my life. You want him or not?"

"Yes, of course I want him. I'll have him mounted and hang him in my den if you don't want him. He's the biggest buck I've ever seen in my life!"

"That's fine with me. He's all yours. I don't care what you do with him. If you do get him mounted, though, do me one favor. . . ."

"Sure. What's that?" Candy asked.

"Whenever I come over to your house, please put him up so I don't have to look at him. I never want to see that deer again as long as I live!"

# Deacon Campbell and the Dummy Deer

## Chapter 8

It was a week before opening day of deer season, and the excitement was building. Most of the Cook County locals had been feverishly putting up stands, doing some last-minute scouting, and trying to decide where to hunt on Saturday morning. As usual, Deacon Campbell and his sidekick, J. P. Stone, had been out driving around looking for deer. After dark, they pulled into Mel's Diner out on the four-lane to have a beer with the rest of the gang.

"Did you hear the news?" Bobby Perry asked Deacon as he and J. P. walked to the back and sat down.

"No. What news?" Deacon asked.

"The game warden nailed Donny Plunkett yesterday afternoon," Bobby explained. "Son, he's in hot water, now!"

"What happened?" Deacon asked.

"It's the craziest thing you ever heard," Bobby said. "The warden had one of those fake deer set up in a field over on the edge of the state park. You know, one of those mounted dummies—a life-size buck with a real rack. And ol' Donny fell for it, hook, line, and sinker."

"Yeah. What'd he do?" Deacon asked with curiosity.

Deacon really wasn't a deacon at all. In fact, he hadn't seen the inside of a church in many a year. The name was just a nickname.

"He shot it, that's what he did!" Bobby answered. "Three times! Ol' Donny saw the deer as he was driving by. He stopped and got out of his truck right in the middle of the road. He made sure no cars were coming, leaned across the hood, and put three shots into that old buck's boiler room as pretty as you please. Only problem was, the buck didn't go down. He just stood there lookin' at him."

"You're kiddin'!" Deacon said. "Then what happened?"

"After the third shot, Donny thought his scope was off or something. He tried to sneak in for a closer shot, and the game warden jumped out of the bushes and nabbed him. It liked to have scared him to death. To top it off, the game warden had a video camera with him. He got the whole dern thing on film!"

"Man, that's not right!" Deacon complained. "What's this lousy world coming to, anyway? It's gotten to where a man can't even enjoy his huntin' anymore. Isn't that called *entrapment* or somethin'?"

"Not when it's on state park land, and not when it's a week before the season opens," Bobby said. "Ya' better watch out, Deak. You might be next."

"Not me," Deacon boasted. "Never in a million years. Old Amos Culpepper has been tryin' to catch me for years, and he hasn't come close yet. He's not going to, either. But I do have to admit, that's a pretty lowdown trick—usin' a dummy deer as a decoy." He scratched his chin. "How big was the buck, anyway?"

"Accordin' to Donny, he was a nice eight-pointer."

"What'd they do to him?" Deacon asked.

"I reckon they patched up the holes and set him out someplace else so they could catch some other poor fool. I'm tellin' you . . . ya' better keep your nose clean!"

"No. I mean Donny! What'd they do to Donny?"

"He's gonna have to pay a right healthy fine," Bobby said. "They say it could be as much as $500."

"That's downright criminal," Deacon declared. "It's a sad state of affairs when the game warden has to go to those kind of measures to catch someone doin' what's natural."

"Huntin' from the road ain't exactly natural . . . or legal," Bobby reminded him.

It was common knowledge that the game warden had been trying to catch Deacon Campbell for some time. Deacon was a notorious road hunter. He would drive along the back roads looking for deer, usually just before dark. If he happened to see a feeding buck, or even an occasional doe, he would not hesitate to shoot it from his truck. Then he would come back later and pick it up. The practice was highly illegal, as well as totally unethical and unsportsmanlike, but Deacon seemed to get away with it.

"He'll never catch me," Deacon insisted. "Do you reckon he catches a lot of people with that contraption?"

"Just the dumb ones," Bobby mused.

* * * * *

Several days later, Deacon and J. P. were up to their old tricks. They were driving some of the back roads just before dark, cruising for deer. Opening morning was still a few days away. As they passed by a small grown-up field, J. P. suddenly got so excited he almost jumped out of the truck.

"Stop! Back up! Whoa!" J. P. yelled.

"Why? What is it?"

"A deer! A big deer! I'm talking b-i-g! He's a monster!"

Deacon slammed on the brakes and started backing up. As the truck inched backward toward the open field, both of its excited occupants strained to see antlers.

"There he is!" J. P. said, pointing. "Over there behind those fruit trees."

"Where? I don't see anything."

"Over there. Right next to that scrub oak. Don't you see him? He's a monster."

"No. I don't see a dad-blamed thing."

"Quick! Pull up a little bit and let's get out. We can see him better from over there on the bank."

Deacon drove forward a few yards and pulled off the road. He intentionally left the engine running so the buck wouldn't spook. The two men opened the doors of the truck as quietly as they could. Deacon instinctively reached for his rifle on the rack behind the driver's seat, but J. P. grabbed his arm.

"What if it's a trap?" he whispered. "Remember what happened to Donny?"

"Yeah, you're right," Deacon said. "But it sure isn't against the law to look, is it?" He smiled defiantly, leaving the rifle in its rack.

The two men sneaked across the road and crawled up a small embankment. They hid behind some brush on the high shoulder.

From their vantage, they could easily see the entire head and neck of the big buck.

"Man, he is a monster," Deacon observed.

"Lord have mercy! I think . . . it's . . . Old Klondike," J. P. announced. "Go get your rifle! Quick! It is him! It's Old Klondike himself!"

Old Klondike was the biggest buck anybody in the area had ever seen. People had been trying to kill him for years. Every deer hunter for miles around knew about him, but he spent most of his time on protected state park property, and no one could kill him. Old Klondike had huge antler bases, and long palmated tines with numerous odd points.

"He's not moving," Deacon said. "I think this is a setup."

Deacon started looking around nervously.

"He just moved an ear!" J. P. said excitedly. "He's alive, I'm tellin' you! Go get your gun. You can kill him!"

"I didn't see him move his ear. This is a setup if I've ever seen one!"

"No, it's not. I'm telling you, Deak. That's Old Klondike. I'd know him anywhere. Go get your gun. You can shoot him. You'll be famous!"

Deacon couldn't decide what to do. He looked around cautiously in every direction, trying to convince himself that there was nowhere close-by for the game warden to hide. He reluctantly took J. P.'s advice—against his better judgment. He hurriedly tiptoed back to the truck and grabbed his rifle.

"Is he still there?" he asked breathlessly as he crawled back up the embankment.

"Yeah, he's still in the same place. He hasn't moved an inch."

Deacon took careful aim. The antlers looked much larger and much more impressive through the clear magnification of his scope.

"Gaw! He's humongous!" Deacon whispered.

"I'm telling you. . . . It's Old Klondike! Bust him!"

Deacon eased off the safety. He settled the cross hairs right at the base of the big buck's gigantic neck.

"You'd better shoot him!" J. P. whispered anxiously. "He's not gonna stand there all day."

"It's a setup," Deacon insisted, looking up from his scope. "Look at him. He hasn't batted an eye since we got here. That deer is definitely not alive! It's a decoy!"

"Yes he is. I'm telling you, I saw his ear twitch. It's Old Klondike. The game warden wouldn't use trophy antlers like those. For crying out loud, kill him before he gets away!"

Deacon looked up nervously. "Not me. I'm gettin' out of here. I'm not getting' stuck with any $500 fine! This is a setup if I've ever seen one!"

Deacon quickly crawled down the embankment to the road. He sneaked back to the truck and put his rifle in the rack behind the seat. He peered up and down the road. He breathed a big sigh of relief, satisfied he had done right.

J. P. was still watching the buck intently from his hiding place as Deacon rammed the stick shift into reverse and backed up, stopping within full view of the frozen animal. J. P. frantically motioned for him to shoot the buck from the truck.

"Come on, J. P.," Deacon yelled loudly with a twinge of theatrics in his voice—just in case anyone happened to be listening. "Let's get out of here. I'm not about to fall for. . . ."

Just then, the big buck bolted. He ran across the open part of the field, bounding majestically. With his ears held straight back, his enormous antlers looked grossly out of proportion to his two-hundred-pound frame. When he reached the far tree line, he paused briefly to look back. Then he quickly melted into the brush. Now there was no doubt whatsoever in either man's mind about the identity of this great whitetail.

"Dog bust Old Betsy, Deak!" J. P. yelled in disgust as he stood up. "I told you it was Old Klondike! I told you to shoot him!"

Deacon got out of the truck and stood in the middle of the road. His legs began to shake so uncontrollably that he had to grab the side of the truck to keep from falling down.

"But . . . I . . . could have sworn. . . ." His voice failed him completely.

"Let's get the heck out of Dodge!" J. P. muttered impatiently, stepping down off the embankment. "Like Bobby Perry was sayin' the other night . . . only the really dumb ones get caught!"

SEED &
HARDWAR
WANTED:
A Few Good Men
Are you tough enough to take Old Too Tough?
If so, you could win big!
$
$
DISCRIPTION OF "OLD TOO TOUGH":
LAST SEEN •Crossing highway south of the Locust Grove exit
RACK •Heavy, wide beams
•At least twelve upright points
•Club-like double droptines
BODY •A huge body frame
•Pure white hair covers a long horizontal scar on right shoulder
•Right ear is split
$ 10.00 per ticket – shoot 'OLE TOO TOUGH & win the kitty

# The Legend of Old Too Tough

## Chapter 9

He was too tough to kill, and everyone knew it. At least, that was the consensus among a large segment of the population in and around the small community of Locust Grove. Most of the local citizenry adamantly believed that the giant buck known fondly as "Old Too Tough" would never succumb to a hunter. When the time came for him to cash in his chips, Old Too Tough might eventually die of old age or some natural disaster, but anyone qualified to pass judgment on such lofty matters as whitetail lore knew that the big buck was far too clever to succumb to a hunter's bullet or arrow.

Old Too Tough was the most sought-after whitetail in Henry County's history. He was also the most yarned about. No single buck had ever gained more notoriety or more fame. The rolling farmland that surrounded the ravenous deer-hunting community of Locust Grove had been producing big racks for nearly forty years, ever since the first modern season had opened back in the early 1960s. But Old Too Tough had no equal, past or present. He stood at the top of the heap. In the world of legendary antlers, this great, great grandson of one of the original northern giants stocked into the area so long ago stood in a class by himself.

"If he don't die of old age, he'll probably just get run over by a semi out on the interstate," Seth Barger predicted. "When it comes to being outsmarted by a hunter, it'll never happen, 'cause that deer leads a charmed life. Why, he's dodged more lead these past few years than the first wave of Marines on Iwo Jima!"

Seth, a former leatherneck who had fought in Vietnam, was one of at least a dozen hunters who had become obsessed with trying to kill Old Too Tough. Oddly enough, the big buck was often sighted crossing the interstate along a half-mile stretch just south of the Locust Grove exit. Seth had seen him crossing the southbound lanes at least twice. To the buck's credit, Old Too Tough seemed to be able to dodge fast-moving cars and trucks as easily as he dodged bullets.

Although he was seldom seen with other deer, Old Too Tough was easy to spot in a crowd on account of his heavy, wide beams and long drop tines. In addition to his unusual clublike drop tines, he was also said to have at least six upright tines protruding high above each beam. Nearly all of the dozens of reported sightings alleged the old monarch to be alone.

Old Too Tough had two other distinguishing characteristics as well. His right ear was split down the middle nearly its entire length, giving it an oddly floppy appearance. Many insisted that the long tear was from a bullet, and no fewer than six local hunters took the credit. The old monarch also had a long horizontal scar on his right shoulder. Because the hair had turned pure white, that scar was easy to spot.

Even the nonhunting population in Locust Grove followed Old Too Tough's yearly escapades and well-publicized antics. He eluded hunters as no other buck had ever done. As a celebrity in the community, his was a household name. While a respectable majority of local citizens might have had a hard time coming up with the name of their congressman, or even the name of the current lieutenant governor of the state of Georgia, everyone knew Old Too Tough.

The majority of Old Too Tough sightings occurred during the off-season. Most folks believed that at least two-thirds of the sightings were either exaggerations or outright falsehoods. The other third, however, were generally considered credible. With each new report, the deer's reputation swelled. To some folks, Old Too Tough was almost larger than life.

One day he would be seen over at Cherokee Crossing near the river by a housewife taking a group of boys to a Cub Scout meeting. The next morning a farmer would spot him casually walking across a soybean field. Gus Barker, the mailman, had seen Old Too Tough at least a dozen times. And Margaret Lacey, who drove a school bus, had also seen the big buck several times, always on her afternoon run. There seemed to be no particular pattern to the buck's hopscotch roamings. The only place where he was ever sighted more than once was along that half-mile stretch of Interstate 75, as he casually loped across the high-speed lanes.

Despite the fact that he had dodged so much lead, Old Too Tough had been on the receiving end of a number of well-placed shots. Three seasons earlier, Jimmy Wilkins, the son of a local farmer and a first-time hunter, had emptied his semiautomatic rifle at the big buck at less than thirty yards in front of two witnesses.

Jimmy, his brother Sonny, and Hugh Mason, a close friend, had all been walking across a large pasture on the old Rawls Place down by the Towaliga River on Thanksgiving morning. They were planning on making a three-man drive in a dogleg patch of woods that wrapped around the pasture when Old Too Tough came blundering out of the woods chasing a doe. This was one of the rare occasions when Old Too Tough was seen with another deer, and his female companion was almost as big as he was. Old Too Tough came barreling over a grassy terrace less than thirty yards away. Two of the youngsters stood frozen with their mouths open, but Jimmy had the presence of mind to unload his rifle at almost point-blank range.

At least one of Jimmy's bullets connected. The three boys followed a sporadic blood trail alongside Old Too Tough's enormous tracks deep into the Towaliga swamp bottoms. They eventually lost the trail when the knee-deep standing water forced them to give up the pursuit.

Old Too Tough was not seen again for the rest of that season, and rumors began to circulate that he had surely died in the swamp. A year later, though, Dub Haney, a banker and highly credible, swore that he had solidly nicked Old Too Tough in the neck on the opening day of rifle season. Dub had also followed a long blood trail, only to be disappointed when the trail abruptly ended on the banks of White Oak Creek.

Not being one to give up easily, Dub had then solicited the help of Bill Hilsman and his tracking dog Spook. Bill ran the local deer cooler out east of town. Spook was a legendary coal-black German shepherd that had a nose for finding wounded deer. If the trail was fresh enough, he seldom failed to find his quarry. In this case, however, Spook acted as if someone had sprinkled pepper on the trail, and the old buck just seemed to vanish into thin air.

Once again, everyone thought that Old Too Tough might have gone on to his reward. Three weeks later, however, Seth Barker almost ran over Old Too Tough out on Interstate 75 just after dark. Seth was so shaken up that he had to pull off the road to regain his composure. Seth swore that he could see Old Too Tough's gigantic rack so well in his headlights that there was no way he could have been mistaken about the identity of the buck.

Several other reliable hunters also claimed to have put lead into various parts of Old Too Tough's anatomy, and legions of less reliable hunters made similar claims. But no one could produce a carcass or a rack, and the reputation of the big whitetail continued to swell. People not only believed that Old Too Tough was unkillable; they also began to believe that he possessed supernatural powers.

Old Too Tough was frequently a topic of discussion at the grocery store, and he was often mentioned in stories in the local newspaper. Mothers began to threaten their naughty sons by telling them that Old Too Tough was coming to pay them a visit if they didn't behave. Old Too Tough was even the subject of a fiery Sunday sermon one hot summer morning by Pastor Nelson Sawyer at the First Methodist Church.

In fact, it was Pastor Sawyer's sermon praising this great animal's tenacity and dogged ability to avoid hunters that spawned a lot of discussion later on. Pastor Sawyer had touched on the fact that the chances of winning the lottery were significantly greater than the chances of bringing Old Too Tough to bay. Later on, after some of the church elders had pooled their resources and collectively purchased a large block of lottery tickets, it was John Harmon who came up with the inventive scheme. During the Wednesday night church dinner the following week, John proposed the idea of offering a cash prize to any hunter who could bring down Old Too Tough during the upcoming season.

"Here's what we'll do," the inspired parishioner—who also happened to be the community's leading accountant—suggested. "The rules will be simple. Anyone interested in entering the contest can buy a ticket for a donation of $10. If a lucky ticket holder brings Old Too Tough down by fair chase during the regular season, he will be eligible to win the kitty—as long as he can prove that Old Too Tough was dispatched legally. Of course the winner will have to produce Old Too Tough's intact carcass and antlers for inspection, and, just to keep everybody honest, there'll also be a polygraph test.

"If someone who has not purchased a ticket ends up legally shooting Old Too Tough," John continued, "then a random drawing will be made from all those names who bought tickets, and the lucky hunter will split the jackpot 50/50 with the person whose name is drawn.

"And finally," John proclaimed, "since no one really knows if Old Too Tough is dead or alive, if he is found dead, the person or persons finding the buck's remains will be eligible to win the kitty. In order to win, though, they'll have to show at least three witnesses exactly where the remains were found, and those witnesses will have to ascertain the legitimacy of the claim."

The idea of putting a cash bounty on Old Too Tough's thick hide was the biggest thing to hit Locust Grove since the Creek Indians went on the warpath in the early 1800s. Theodore Perkins, owner of Perkins Seed and Hardware, where many of the locals gathered for morning coffee, offered to sell tickets from his store. Someone got the bright idea of printing up posters with an artist's rendering of the big deer and these engaging words: "WANTED: A FEW GOOD MEN. ARE YOU TOUGH ENOUGH TO TAKE OLD TOO TOUGH? IF SO, YOU COULD WIN BIG!"

The posters, boasting several misspelled words, went up all over town, and the amount of prize money began to grow. Eight weeks before opening day, almost everyone in town had purchased a ticket. Because so many local citizens believed that Old Too Tough might be dead, three-fourths of those who bought tickets were nonhunters. Soon it seemed as if everyone in the county was out scouring the woods for Old Too Tough's remains. Nearly 750 tickets were purchased over a span of several weeks, and the jackpot grew to the unbelievable sum of just under $7,500.

Two weeks before deer season opened, Jesse Kilgore, a local building contractor, decided to sweeten the pot. He and some other businessmen offered to match the kitty. That motivated people from outlying areas to begin buying tickets, and soon the pot had reached the whopping sum of $18,350. Because of the amount of the jackpot, and the excitement it created, it was decided to put a time limit on the contest. If Old Too Tough didn't show up dead or alive by the last day of the season, all the money would be given to the charity of John Harmon's choice.

That didn't sit too well with many Locust Grove residents. Everyone knew that John's younger brother was a former TV evangelist who had gone astray—there had been a highly publicized scandal involving the fallen angel's attractive secretary—and people feared that the unclaimed prize might be channeled toward that undeserving faith healer. That fear further motivated young and old alike to get out and search for Old Too Tough. By the time rifle season opened, it seemed as if the entire county had mobilized to hunt for the big buck. Many people seemed to lose their senses. A county map was put up in the drug store, and pins were placed at every point where sightings had been reported during the past five years.

One enterprising hunter began interviewing everyone who had ever claimed to have seen Old Too Tough, including some of the children on the school bus. He then plotted all of the sightings on a computer-generated map and started selling the maps to local hunters. Predictably, the dot-covered map revealed no telltale patterns.

By the second week of deer season, no place in southern Henry County was safe for a big buck to hide. Seemingly every patch of woods was invaded and every rock turned over. It was like a feeding frenzy of hungry sharks. People who had never hunted before bought rifles and licenses and started hunting, even housewives. It was a boom to the local economy—especially for Perkins Seed and Hardware. More bucks were taken into Hilsman's cooler than ever before, and Bill Hilsman had to hire extra help to handle the overflow. Despite all of the excitement, however, no one saw hide nor hair of the legendary whitetail.

The weeks turned into months, and at last the season was almost over. More and more people began subscribing to the theory that Old Too Tough had succumbed the previous year, and there was much negative talk about where the prize money might end up.

Then one cold, blustery day toward the end of December, as a flurry of snow was falling, Pete Scofield was making his way south on the interstate as he had done a thousand times before. Pete owned the local bakery, and he frequently delivered bread and baked goods to several small stores in the southern end of the county. On this particular predawn morning, young Emory Johnson was helping him. Emory was a high school senior who would be graduating the following spring.

Four years earlier, both of Emory's parents had been killed in a freak airplane accident. Emory's father had been a local farmer. Both parents had flown to south Georgia in a small plane to look at some new farm equipment. On the return flight, the plane had gone down in a summer thunderstorm.

Pete had been good friends with Emory's father, and Pete became Emory's guardian. Very little money had been left over after the estate was settled, and as a result, Pete frequently paid Emory to help him out. Sometimes he did odd jobs around Pete's farm or helped with deliveries before school.

Both Pete and Emory were avid deer hunters. They often hunted together on a private farm through which Old Too Tough was known to have traveled. In fact, both Pete and Emory believed adamantly that Old Too Tough was alive and well. Just like Seth Barger, Pete had seen Old Too Tough on two separate occasions as he had attempted to cross the interstate. He would never forget the sight of that enormous rocking chair rack and those unbelievable drop tines.

Throughout his high school career, Emory had excelled in football. As a wide receiver, he had led the Henry County Yellow Jackets to three divisional championships. He had incredible hands, and it was said that he could catch any pass that was lobbed within ten yards of him. He was also extremely fast.

Because of his amazing talent, Emory had been a good bet for a full football scholarship at the University of Georgia, where he hoped to get a degree in wildlife biology. However, all dreams of getting a scholarship were dashed when another tragedy struck. While Emory had been mowing hay on a tractor the previous summer, the tractor had turned over, crushing his left knee. The injured knee healed well enough for him to get around on it, but he would never play competitive football again. And without the scholarship, Emory's hopes of attending the university all but disappeared.

Like most hunters in the area, Pete and Emory often talked about Old Too Tough when they were together. Pete had entered them both in the contest, and they were forever plotting and planning and trying to figure out where Old Too Tough might be hiding.

"All mature bucks develop specific habits and preferences as they grow older, just like humans," the older buck hunter told the youngster. "Discovering their habits is often the key to success. For instance, some bucks'll run a big circle and travel as far as ten miles from their core living area—say every two or three days—using almost exactly the same route every time. Usually they'll be seen every so often at various points along that route. It's sort of like the bread route we run. If you can ever pick up part of that route, and find the exact trails, sometimes it's possible to do some backtrackin' and just about figure out the entire circle.

"Other bucks may travel only two miles," Pete continued. "Also, some bucks'll leave their core areas the first time they're disturbed by hunters, and they may not return until after huntin' season is over. Others'll bed in virtually the same spot almost every day, no matter how many times they're disturbed. Or they may have several safety strongholds where they'll seek sanctuary during the daylight hours.

"Then too, I've read about some bucks that have been known to run a long, straight line from one point to another instead of a circle," Pete added. "Again, it may be as far as ten or twelve miles from point A to point B. They'll be seen at regular places, too, at road crossings and places like that. A lot of times you can find their tracks and backtrack 'em as well.

"But Old Too Tough is the dangest buck I've ever tried to figure out. We know he covers a pretty wide area from all the sightings, and the only thing he's ever done consistently is cross the interstate. So that's gotta be part of his route. But where does he go when he gets to the other side? There's no rhyme or reason to anything he does. He must have himself the best dadgum hideout in the whole county! All big bucks are individuals, but I reckon Old Too Tough is about the consarnedest individual I've ever run across!"

Emory nodded his head in agreement.

The two hunters were headed south on the interstate on the very same stretch of I-75 where Pete had sighted Old Too Tough in the past. Ironically, on this cold day in December, Pete and Emory had just been talking about the legendary buck. As always, they had been trying to second-guess his whereabouts as they watched the snowflakes cut through the predawn darkness. When they were half a mile from the exit that would take them over to their next stop, listening to football scores on the radio, suddenly, out of nowhere, a huge, gray blur filled Pete's headlights. There was a tremendous impact, and the bread truck swerved off the road to the right and up on the grassy shoulder.

Fortunately the shoulder made a steady rise, and Pete was able to maintain control until the vehicle rolled to a stop. Considerable damage had been done to the front of the truck. When the two shaken occupants took a flashlight and went back to investigate the cause of the collision, they saw a large-bodied, antlerless deer lying dead on the shoulder of the road. It had apparently been killed instantly by the impact.

At first, they assumed the dead animal to be a large doe.

"Oh, I hate this," Pete said, having no apparent concern for the damaged truck. "This is the second doe I've hit, and it makes me sick to kill such a beautiful animal with a vehicle."

Emory was the first to notice the two red spots, about the size of a quarter, on the deer's forehead where a set of large antlers had recently rested. The dead animal was indeed a buck, not a doe, and a large buck at that. The buck carried a huge frame. It was obvious he had once been a mighty animal, but his body was now thin and emaciated.

"This is even worse," Pete said, shaking his head. "The truck is fixable, but you can't ever replace the kind of beauty that nature put in our woods in the form of a magnificent white-tailed buck. It sure is odd that he shed his antlers so early. . . ."

"Maybe his poor physical condition had something to do with it," Emory said. "Man, he sure is a big deer."

"Yes he is," Pete agreed in the dim light. "Come on. Let's load him up in the back of the truck. After we make our delivery, we'll take him to the house and see how much meat we can salvage. It'll be OK if you're a little late to school, won't it? I'll vouch for you."

"Oh, sure," Emory told him. "We don't have that much going on this week, and first period is study hall."

Although damaged, Pete's truck was drivable. Pete and Emory loaded the buck in and headed on down the highway. After making their delivery, they drove back to Pete's barn. Emory offered to skin the buck and help cut up the meat. Pete backed the bread truck into the barn and turned on the lights. He walked back and made two slits in the buck's hind legs and attached a steel singletree between the tendons. Tying the singletree to a stout rope, he then hoisted the big deer right out of the truck. In the light of the barn, the first thing they both noticed was the long, white scar on the deer's right shoulder.

"I'll be a yellow-bellied sapsucker," Pete said. "Old Too Tough has a scar like this. You don't suppose . . .?"

"He's a mighty big buck," Emory said. "But he's awful poor looking." Then, noticing a recent wound on the deer's back right haunch, he added, "Look at that. He looks like he might've been shot through his hindquarters."

"Pe-w-w! From the way it smells, it's infected, too," Pete said. "It looks like it's at least several weeks old."

"I can't believe somebody shot a deer like this and didn't find him," Emory said. "What a waste. I wonder if he lost his antlers after he was wounded."

"I don't know, but that's probably the reason he didn't make it across the interstate," Pete reasoned. "He was all stove up in his back legs, and he couldn't run as fast as normal."

"Look at his right ear," Emory said. "It's got a long gash in it."

"I don't think there's any question about who this is," Pete said. Suddenly, he was overcome with emotion. He had to sit down on a stool. Emory had never seen him this upset.

"We're in honored company today, my friend," Pete said, almost choking on his words. "I think we just ran over the most famous buck in Henry County. This shell of a deer was once a magnificent animal, but he's in pretty bad shape now. I doubt if he'd have survived the winter. I'm sure that's why he shed his horns so early—because he's so poorly. I just can't believe we killed him with the truck."

"You didn't do it on purpose," Emory said, trying to console his friend. "It was just one of those things."

Pete tried to pull himself together. A sudden revelation seemed to perk him up. "If this is Old Too Tough," he said, "it looks like we have an interesting problem. With his horns gone, nobody's gonna believe it's really him. And I don't think there's any provision in the contest to present his carcass without the horns attached."

"It's gotta be him," Emory insisted.

"I'm not even sure his meat is fit to eat," Pete added, studying the wound in the buck's hindquarter. "Let's go ahead and skin him out. Let's save his cape, even though we don't have any horns to go with it. He's a beautiful animal despite his condition. Once we have him skinned, we'll leave him hanging for now, until I figure out what to do with 'im. Poor old critter. Maybe after school this afternoon you can come back and we'll take him into town and show everybody what we've got."

As soon as Emory began to pull the hide off the buck's carcass, they found several pellets of buckshot, some old no. 7 or no. 8 bird shot, and a .22 bullet lodged in the deer's neck. They also found an old broadhead encased in gristle in the deer's right shoulder, and there were bullet fragments in the buck's hindquarters. Further investigation revealed that the buck's teeth were worn down to the gums. Several other scars adorned the animal's once huge frame.

"This has to be Old Too Tough," Emory repeated. "If you could win the prize money, at least it would pay the damage on your truck."

"It'd pay a lot more than that, my friend, but I don't care about the money," Pete said. "Insurance will take care of the truck. Nobody's gonna believe this is really him. That's what I'm worried about. Too many green-eyed people out there. And if we can't prove it's really him, the prize money will go to that phony no-account faith healer. Oh, well. I've never won anything in my whole life and probably never will."

"I don't understand how he got away from everybody for so long," Emory said. "He must've really had a special hideout somewhere—just like you've always said."

"He must've had himself a cave to crawl into!" Pete said.

Emory finished skinning the big deer and headed off to school. During his short drive to the high school, he traveled down the same stretch of interstate that he and Pete had gone down earlier in the morning. As he passed near the spot where the accident had taken place, Emory couldn't get Old Too Tough off his mind. The only place anybody had seen the big buck more than once was crossing that interstate. And always, it had been along this same half-mile stretch.

Suddenly, Emory had a hunch. The interstate ran north and south. Along this particular stretch, it was divided by a large, densely wooded island of land about eight to ten acres in size, near the spot where the buck had been hit. This wooded area was thick with pine trees, honeysuckle, and kudzu.

Emory never made it to school. Instead, he exited the interstate as quickly as possible and stopped at the nearest gas station to call Pete from a pay phone.

"Hello, Pete?" an excited Emory said.

"Yes, Emory? What's the matter, son? You haven't had another accident, have you?"

"No, sir. But can you come down and meet me at the BP station at Exit 9? I've got something I need to show you. It's real important. I think I know where Old Too Tough was going. I think I know where his hideout was."

"Don't you think it's a little late for that now?" Pete asked. "After all, he's dead."

"Yeah, but if we can find his hideout, we might be able to find his sheds," Emory insisted.

"That's true," Pete said. "I never thought of that, but what about school?"

"It's OK, Pete. I don't really have any classes till noon. And Old Too Tough is a lot more important than school!"

Twenty minutes later, Pete appeared at the BP station in his pickup.

"Now what's all this about Old Too Tough's hideout?" Pete asked.

"I think I've solved the mystery," Emory said excitedly. "I think I've figured out where Old Too Tough's stronghold might be. It's so simple it's ridiculous. I've studied the map over and over again in the drugstore with all the pins of different sightings, and something just wasn't right about it. Today, after the accident, it finally dawned on me what it was. The interstate runs north and south, right?"

"Yep, that's right," Pete agreed.

"Well, if you look at the map," Emory continued, "there've been thirty-nine sightings of Old Too Tough on the west side of the interstate in this general area in the last three or four years. But only seven of the sightings have been on the east side. Does that tell you anything?"

"It tells me he didn't spend much time east of the interstate," Pete answered.

"What if he didn't spend *any* time on the east side?" Emory offered.

"I don't see how that could be possible," Pete said.

"Think about it, Pete," Emory continued. "We know that a percentage of the reported sightings have to be mistakes, right?"

"I suppose some of 'em were exaggerated," Pete agreed.

"What if roughly 25 percent of the sightings are mistakes? That's possible, isn't it?"

"You're the one in school, not me, son," Pete replied. "Math was never one of my strong points."

"Here's what I'm saying," Emory continued. "What if all seven of the sightings on the east side of the interstate were cases of mistaken identity? What if Old Too Tough never crossed completely over to the other side?"

"He had to," Pete argued. "I've seen him my own self crossing over. Twice! He was trying to cross when we killed him, for crying out loud. If he didn't cross over, where'd he go?"

"I thought you'd never ask," Emory said with a big grin. "That's the revelation I was talking about. Think about it. There's a big island of land between the northbound and southbound lanes on that stretch of interstate."

"And its heavily wooded!" Pete exclaimed.

"Exactly!" Emory said excitedly. "What better place for a buck like Old Too Tough to hide. It's the perfect hideout! What if . . ."

". . . everybody's been looking in all the wrong places!" Pete exclaimed. "We haven't seen the forest for the trees!"

"Think we oughta check it out?" Emory asked.

"Let's go, son!"

The two hunters immediately headed north on the interstate in Pete's truck. They pulled off on the left shoulder and drove right up to the small island of land that divided the interstate. They had no sooner walked into the woods than they found several large rubs on cedars inside the dense thicket. Then, on a little hilltop overlooking the northbound traffic, they discovered a heavily used bedding area in a dense kudzu thicket. It was in that thicket that Pete stumbled upon one of Old Too Tough's recently shed antlers. It was in perfect shape.

Just as he had been earlier in the morning, Pete was overcome with emotion.

"Will you just look at this," he said. "That rascal probably watched me drive by here in my bread truck a hundred times!"

A large single tear rolled down Pete's cheek. A few yards away, he found what appeared to be a small section of main beam from another large shed. This second shed was much older, and the tines had been completely gnawed away.

Twenty minutes later, Emory found the matching shed antler on a narrow trail sixty yards from where Pete was standing.

Pete was so overwhelmed that he had to sit down on the trunk of a fallen tree.

"I'll be a monkey's uncle!" he said, after regaining his composure. He held both massive shed antlers together. "Old Too Tough could hide in here all season long during the daylight hours and be safe. This place is a dadgum fortress!"

"And chew his cud while he watched the cars go," Emory added. "He had everything he needed—good cover, a little food, even a little water."

Pete was silent for a long time. "It's a good thing we saved his cape," he finally said. "Now we can get the old boy mounted so everybody in the county can see him and appreciate him." Pete sighed. "Maybe we can even hang him in the Community Center." Then, after another short silence, he added, "Isn't life crazy? If he'd made it across the road this morning, we never would've known. . . . He ended up getting killed so close to his stronghold. Seth Barker was right. I don't think there's a hunter alive who could've killed that deer."

"And we never would've run over him if he hadn't been hurt," Emory said.

"I reckon we've got all the proof we need for the contest," Pete added. "No one can say a thing now. When all's said and done, I reckon we're both gonna get an education out of this thing."

"What do you mean?" Emory asked.

"Oh, I don't know," Pete answered with a grin.

Once the news was out, everyone in Locust Grove wanted to see the massive shed antlers. Pete and Emory had talked about keeping the exact location of where the sheds had been found a secret, but that proved impossible. Once the cat was out of the bag, dozens of curious hunters drove out to the interstate to see

Old Too Tough's stronghold for themselves. This created a serious traffic hazard along the interstate, and the State Patrol was called in to try to keep people off the right-of-way. As far as the contest was concerned, no one disputed the evidence.

A gala awards ceremony was held the following Friday night at the Locust Grove Community Center. Nearly three hundred people looked on as Hank Carter, the community's leading attorney, presented Pete Scofield with a check for $19,660. Since Emory had been with Pete on the day of the collision, Pete insisted that Emory get up on the stage with him while the check was being presented.

After a short speech by Hank Carter, Pete stepped up to the podium to say a few words. Emory stood next to him.

"It's an honor for me to receive this check," Pete began with a nervous voice. "If Emory and I hadn't ended Old Too Tough's life with the front end of my truck, I don't think any of us would've ever seen him again. Like many great white-tailed bucks that survive beyond three or four years, Old Too Tough seems to have been absolutely unkillable by ordinary means. Many of you have been stating that belief all along. In the end, he was so poorly that he probably wouldn't have made it through the winter."

Pete was once again overcome by emotion. He stood silent for a moment, as Emory rested an arm on his shoulder. "And if Emory and I hadn't hit him with the truck," he continued, "one of the great mysteries of Henry County would've never been solved.

"I've never been one to believe in Fate, until now," Pete added. "After everything that's happened, I believe it was Fate that finally brought Old Too Tough to us. I believe it was meant to be. Fate helped me run over him, and Fate helped me to find his shed antlers. In this case, the Fate I'm talking about had a little help. That help came in the form of a young man that everybody in this community knows and loves. His name is Emory Johnson. Emory was not only with me the day Old Too Tough got killed, but Emory was the man who put all the pieces of this jigsaw puzzle together in the first place.

"As most of you know, Emory's had some tough breaks in his young life," Pete continued. "He lost his parents, and he lost his football scholarship. But through it all, he's always been the kind of young man that everybody in this community can be proud of. Therefore, it wouldn't be right for me to take this prize money today. I don't deserve it. The young man who really deserves this money is standing here next to me. So, with the help of John Harmon, I've decided to place this check in the Emory Johnson College Fund.

"Of course, he'll have to promise us that he'll use it for that degree he wants to get in wildlife biology, instead of going out and buyin' himself a brand-new hot rod. Somehow, I don't think that'll be a problem. And if anyone here wants to add to the college fund by making a little donation, why that would be a fine way of remembering Emory's parents and the most famous buck that ever roamed the woods in Henry County.

"Emory and I are gonna get Old Too Tough mounted, and we plan to hang him right here in the Community Center for the whole world to see," Pete said in closing. "Old Too Tough had a bad time there toward the end, and I feel right sorry for him. But at least he left behind a lot more than the reputation of bein' a deer that was too tough to kill. He left behind a legacy that at the very least is gonna help put a right deserving young man through his first full year of college!"

A few days later, two rabbit hunters from Macon who had not heard about the demise of Old Too Tough swore they saw him as they drove down a dirt road on their way to some land a good fifteen miles from where Pete and Emory had hit the buck on the interstate. Both men insisted that they saw the huge whitetail in all his glory—crossing the road right in front of them—heavy drop tines and all.

When they heard the news, Pete and Emory were elated.

"The legend of Old Too Tough lives!" Pete declared happily. "Or at least, his ghost is still running around out there somewhere."

"I think it's starting up all over again," Emory agreed. "Looks like Old Too Tough will never die!"

# The End of Something

## Chapter 10

Chet Bailey walked into Ed's Gun and Tackle Shop on Monday afternoon with a big smile on his face. He couldn't wait to tell Ed the news. The previous Saturday had been opening day of rifle season, and Chet had connected with a nice ten-pointer shortly after first light. He approached the counter and greeted his friend with a little more bounce in his walk than usual.

Ed's Gun and Tackle Shop was a popular gathering place for local hunters. Like a lot of regular customers, Chet frequently stopped by to chew the fat and see what kind of trade-ins Ed had taken in. Ed, the owner, was a walking encyclopedia of local deer-hunting gossip. If a big buck had been killed anywhere within a hundred miles of town, Ed usually knew about it. Chet loved to catch up on all the latest news. On rare occasions, like today, he had some good news of his own to share.

No customers were in the shop. Ed, who always seemed to be in good spirits, had what appeared to be a troubled look on his face. Before Chet could even open his mouth, Ed greeted his friend and began talking. "Something really unusual just happened a few minutes ago," he said, "right before you drove up."

"Tell me all about it," Chet said. "And then I've got something to tell you. What is it? Did somebody poach a new state record or something?"

"No, nothing like that," Ed answered. "Not more than fifteen minutes ago, this man comes walking into the shop and wants to know if I'd be interested in buying his deer rifle and several other guns. He said he won't need them anymore where he's going. Thinking that was kind of a strange thing for someone to say, I asked him, in kind of a roundabout way, where he was going. He tells me he has cancer, and that he has only about two more months to live. The heck of it is, he doesn't look sick at all. He looks as healthy as you or me—fit and trim like he's never been sick a day in his life."

"How old is he?" Chet asked.

"He says he's fifty-two," Ed answered. "But he looks a lot younger."

"Golly, that's terrible," Chet said, shaking his head. "You just never know."

"He's supposed to be coming right back," Ed continued. "I told him I'd look at his guns and tell him what they're worth."

Two customers came in, and Ed started showing one of them a revolver. While Chet was waiting for Ed to finish, a well-dressed man walked into the store carrying several weather-beaten gun cases under each arm. Chet immediately sensed that this was the man Ed had been talking about. The man had a clean-cut appearance, and he looked fit and healthy, just as Ed had said. The man's hair was just beginning to gray slightly around his temples.

The man walked up to the counter and started uncasing his guns. Ed was still busy, and Chet felt compelled to try to strike up a conversation. He felt certain that this was the same man Ed had described, and he suddenly had a strange desire to try to reach out. Not only did he feel a tremendous amount of compassion for the man, but he also felt a strange sort of curiosity about his condition.

The first rifle to come out of its case was an old Marlin .30-30 lever-action with a Weaver scope.

"I bet that rifle has seen a lot of use in the deer woods," Chet said, trying to get something started.

"Oh, yes," the man said cheerfully. "It's been around in its day. It's been responsible for putting a fair amount of venison in the freezer." He rubbed the stock affectionately. "We've had some mighty fine hunts together."

The man then uncased an old Remington Model 1100 12-gauge shotgun.

"Are you selling these guns?" Chet asked. He felt like an impostor, because he already knew the answer.

"Yes," the man answered. "I don't plan to do any hunting anytime soon, so I thought I'd see what I could get for them."

For a brief moment, their eyes met. Chet sensed a definite tone of sadness in the man's voice, but he also noted an unmistakable sparkle in the man's deep blue eyes and a genuine charm in his soft-spoken expression. Both qualities reflected a great love of life. The man had a contagious, alluring type of charm that immediately struck a chord deep inside Chet's inner being.

Chet wasn't sure whether the man would be willing to talk about his condition. Somehow, though, the man seemed to read Chet's mind.

"I've got an incurable cancer," the man said in a rather casual tone, as if he were talking about the weather. "They tell me I have only a few more months. So I've decided to go ahead and sell my guns. I don't have any children, or anyone special to give them to, so I thought I'd make sure they end up in the proper hands: one less headache for my wife to have to take care of." He smiled.

"I'm really sorry," Chet said. He was almost at a loss for words. "Cancer is a miserable. . . ."

"Oh, don't be," the man replied. "I've had a great life, and I have no regrets. No complaints whatsoever. I've been able to do a lot of interesting things, and at least I've had the blessing of knowing what's going to happen so I could make my plans accordingly. Most people never get that opportunity. Most of us never get the chance to choose where or when our life is going to end, but we do get the opportunity to choose how we're going to live it while we're here. And I'm pretty happy with the way I've lived mine."

"You're right about *where* or *when*," Chet agreed. "And I really don't know too many people who can say they're truly happy with the way they've lived their lives. Most of us end up making a lot of wrong choices. I admire your attitude. Still, it's not an easy thing to face. You're a relatively young man. . . ."

"That's true," the man answered. "I'm only fifty-two. By today's standards, that's still pretty young. It's funny. We often judge a person's time on this earth by how long he's lived. If a man lives to be eighty or ninety, we say he's had a good, long life. But a life should never be judged by longevity. It should be judged by how we spend whatever time we have while we're here. Me? I feel like I've gotten my money's worth. I certainly didn't plan for things to turn out this way, and I wouldn't mind being around for another half a century or so. But I've accepted it now, and I'm planning to enjoy myself as much as I can for the next few months. I've made all of the necessary arrangements, and my wife and I plan to do some traveling for as long as we can."

"I killed my first buck with a Marlin .30-30," Chet said. For some reason, Chet had the distinct impression that this man had not really been an avid deer hunter—at least, not a dyed-in-the-wool fanatic like himself.

*There you go again, being judgmental,* a little voice from within warned Chet. *There are many different degrees of deer hunting enjoyment.*

To Chet's great surprise, however, the man's eyes suddenly lit up, and he began to reminisce.

"I was in the Air Force for over twenty years," the man said. "And I moved around a lot. I got to see a lot of different scenery, and I hunted whitetails in a lot of different states. Western Kentucky, New York State, even South Texas. Also a few muleys." He reflected for a moment. "Ah, yes. I've witnessed some spectacular sunrises, and I've heard the voice of the coyote. I listened to some of the darnedest stories around the campfire that you've ever heard. I've hunted in the mountains in the snow, and I've hunted in the open country of the Midwest. I've hunted in the deserts of the Southwest, and I've hunted in the thick hardwoods of the East. And you want to know something? Every time I watched the sun come up when I was out hunting, it was like I was the only person on earth and I was doing it for the very first time.

"No, I really can't complain," the man continued. "If the truth be known, I never killed all that many deer, but that really doesn't matter, especially now. You know what really matters? What really matters to me are all the memories. I've hunted with some real characters. Looking back, some of the greatest memories in my entire life come from my deer hunting experiences."

Chet's face turned red. He felt embarrassed and ashamed. He also felt a big lump forming in his throat.

*So much for passing judgment, you idiot!* he thought.

Ed suddenly appeared on the scene, and he began examining the man's guns. In addition to the Marlin .30-30 and the Remington shotgun, there was a Mossberg .22 bolt-action rifle and an old single-shot shotgun. None of the guns was of any particular value from a collector's standpoint, but it was obvious that each in its own way held a lot of sentimental value for its owner.

After examining the guns, Ed jotted down some figures on a pad. He made the man an offer. The man accepted, and Ed got out his checkbook and began writing a check.

"Good luck to you," Chet said. "I hope you and your wife get in some great traveling, and I hope you enjoy every minute of it. Somehow, I have a feeling you will!"

"Oh, we will," the man said cheerfully. "No question about that. We're going to head out West and start with the Grand Canyon. I haven't seen the sun set over the Grand Canyon in fifteen years. Then we plan to travel around as long as we can."

Ed gave the man his check. He shook hands with him and wished him the best. The man looked at Chet and smiled.

"I've enjoyed talking to you," he said. Then he turned around and walked toward the door.

Chet looked at Ed and started shaking his head. "I guess we don't know how lucky we are sometimes," he said.

"You got that right," Ed agreed.

"You know, I never even asked him his name," Chet reflected.

The two men were silent for a long while. Finally Ed spoke up. Looking down at the man's meager arsenal of guns, he said, "I don't guess he was much of a deer hunter."

"That's where you're wrong," Chet countered. "That's what I thought at first, too, but, boy, was I mistaken! Oh, he might not be a world-class hunter like some of the guys we read about in the whitetail magazines, but after talking to him, I think he's got to be one of the *best* deer hunters I've ever come across. No, I take that back. *Best* is not a good choice of words. He's one of the *purest* deer hunters I've ever come across. I wish you could have heard what he just told me. I wish I could have written it down on paper or recorded it somehow."

"You could have fooled me," Ed said. "By the way, didn't you say you had some big news you wanted to share? What is it?"

"Oh, it's nothing important," Chet answered. "I'll tell you later. I'd better be getting back to work."

Chet didn't say anything else. He just smiled. Suddenly, the thought of bragging about his ten-pointer no longer held much appeal. Instead, he was thinking about the last incredible sunrise he had witnessed.

# The Phantom Buck of Willacoochee County

## Chapter 11

*Every hunting club in the country probably has its version of the Phantom, an almost larger-than-life trophy whitetail sporting a massive set of antlers and a special name. Invariably, bucks like the Phantom are so wise to the ways of hunters that many have been labeled unkillable. This story comes from the author's novel* Coon Dog Cemetery, *set in the mid-1960s (Coon Dog Cemetery is the name of the hunting club). The Phantom is a legendary buck that has been pursued for so long by some of the various club members that most have come to believe that it will never fall to a hunter's bullet. In this story, Dexter Smith, one of the main characters, decides to go out, on an unusually cold November day in the deep South, after another large buck he has dubbed "Big Foot." As you'll see, the outcome on any given day in the deer woods is never predictable!*

### November 1965

Not a soul was stirring in camp as Dexter Smith scraped the ice from the windshield of his truck in the dark and cranked the engine.

*It's gonna be a cold'un today,* he thought as he sat there, letting the engine warm up.

He reached the edge of the swamp a full hour before daylight. A lone owl greeted him, calling out in the darkness from its nocturnal hideout high in a tree. *Hoo, hoo, hoo . . . Hoo, hoo, hoo, hoo-o-a-h-h!*

*Prob'ly a barred owl,* Dexter thought. *They's a lot of 'em usin' this swamp bottom.*

Dexter smiled as he heard the familiar sound. His mind flashed back to his boyhood days when everyone had called these creatures of the deep forest "hoot" owls, and any youngster who knew anything at all about the outdoors believed the owl was saying, *Who cooks for you? Who cooks for you all?*

Dexter had once seen a barred owl on the edge of the swamp with a water snake in its mouth. On a day like today, though, he knew this owl would have to be hunting for furry game if it expected to find a meal.

"Maybe you'll bring me some luck this mornin'," he whispered affectionately as he quietly passed under the tall pine where the bird was perched.

An unusual and severe freeze had set in. The temperature had dipped into the mid-twenties, leaving the ground as hard as granite. As soon as it was light enough to see, Dexter began to work his way around the east side of the icy swamp. The short, two-week season was almost over. As Dexter slowly still-hunted along the edge of the swamp, his thoughts kept wandering back to all that had happened over the past ten days.

*Lord-a-mercy! It don't seem like so much coulda' happened in just under two weeks' time. It seems more like two months maybe, or two years. . . . An' only a handful a' bucks've been killed so far this season. Thank the Good Lord above the boys each got to fill their tags. . . . With two mighty good bucks, too. Most all the others have been on the small side. I wonder where all the big'uns are hidin' out this year. They're around, but nobody's seein' 'em, that's for sure.*

*Well, at least I know about two humdingers that ain't been shot yet. The Phantom may not be livin' on Coon Dog property any more, but I jus' got a sneakin' suspicion that ol' Big Foot is—somewheres. All I got to do is find 'im.*

To Dexter's way of thinking, that small, sacred piece of real estate that serves as a big buck's regular daytime hideout is as highly valued to that individual buck as is the spot in front of a man's fireplace in his den where his favorite reclining chair sits. Even though Dexter believed that most big bucks are extremely unpredictable, he also believed that they are creatures of habit in many ways, and that could often lead to their undoing.

"As sure as the sun rises in the east in the mornin', most bucks'll go to that special place where they know it's safe to hole up durin' daylight hours—as long as huntin' pressure don't get too heavy," he would often say. "If ya' can just find that special place, ya' got a better'n average chance a' seein' ol' mossy horns an' maybe gettin' a shot."

Dexter frequently referred to this daytime stronghold as a buck's "livin' room." These sacred places always had several things in common. Invariably, a proper "livin' room" was located in a thick, hard-to-reach area that was next to impossible for a hunter to approach on foot without revealing his presence to the bedded buck. In most cases an alert buck would either scent or hear the approaching hunter long before that hunter was anywhere close to the buck's bedding site. But even if an enterprising hunter did manage to penetrate a buck's daytime hideout, a proper livin' room stronghold always had several escape routes leading out in different directions. Hence the local buck-in-residence would simply sneak out and be long gone well before the hunter got anywhere close.

Once a big buck bedded down for the day, only two things could make him leave his haven of safety—being disturbed by a hunter who happened to wander a little too close for comfort, and who probably had no idea a buck was there, or the need to search for a receptive doe during the peak of the rutting season. Otherwise, an educated buck would normally hold tight in his hidden sanctuary from well before the first light of day until well after dark, safe and secure from all would-be intruders.

Frequently, a buck's hideaway was located near one or more fresh scrapes. Most of the major trails in the neighborhood would be marked with a number of large, freshly rubbed trees as well. Large cedars were often the trees of choice. But for some reason on Coon Dog Cemetery property, holly trees seemed to be favored over cedars. Dexter would often find a large holly tree—five or six inches in diameter—near a big buck's stronghold. The outer bark of this tree would always be freshly worked over. In the case of a truly big buck, like the Phantom or Big Foot, these trees would often show signs of having been rubbed by the same buck for two or three years in a row.

Once he located a suitable buck to go after, Dexter had several tried-and-true methods for hunting the elusive animal. If it happened to be during peak rutting times, he would often scrape hunt. Or, if he got lucky and discovered the approximate location of a buck's stronghold, he might station himself near one of the main trails leading in or out. He would take a position and wait patiently for hours at a time, hoping to intercept the buck as it moved in or out. Here infinite patience, as well as an eye to the wind at all times and absolute silence, was critical in helping to avoid detection.

By far, Dexter's favorite method of hunting was to slip quietly through the woods near a suspected buck stronghold, pausing often to look and listen. However, that type of hunting could be attempted only when conditions were just right—usually during the morning hours, when the wind was steady and the ground was still damp with the early-morning dew. Dexter seldom attempted to sneak deliberately into a known hideaway. The chances of spooking the bedded buck were far too great, and once a big buck knew he was being hunted, he might move out of the area permanently.

Over the years, Dexter had discovered some of these daytime sanctuaries in the most unlikely places. In more populated areas he had located several carefully concealed bedding areas directly behind someone's house, practically in someone's backyard, only a few yards from screaming children, barking dogs, and clotheslines full of drying laundry. More than once he had found a daytime hideout on the knoll of a hill overlooking a busy four-lane highway. There a resourceful buck could while away the dangerous daylight hours in complete safety—chewing his cud and leisurely watching the cars pass—only a rock's throw away from the pavement. In deep woods with a lot of swampland, the job of locating a buck's living-room stronghold was often extremely difficult and frustrating. Since that was the case at Coon Dog Cemetery, Dexter knew he had his work cut out for him.

"Ol' Big Foot's gotta' be aroun' here somewheres," he told himself as he skirted around the edge of the swamp.

The standing water along the edge of the swamp had frozen into long, thin sheets of ice, and with every step, Dexter made too much noise.

"This ain't gonna work," he said out loud in a low tone. "I'm gonna have to get to higher ground where the ice ain't as bad, or else ever' deer in the swamp is gonna know I'm here."

An hour after good shooting light, Dexter had circled around to the back side of the swamp to a piece of high ground that formed a long, thin peninsula. This elevated area stayed dry nine months out of the year. There the going was quieter. For some reason, few hunters from Coon Dog Cemetery ever ventured back into this area. The high ground was surrounded by standing water on three sides. In milder weather it was a haven for snakes, mosquitoes, and an occasional alligator.

Dexter suspected that he was getting close to the back boundary of Coon Dog land. Quite unexpectedly he walked up on a newly built wooden platform in a branching maple tree about fifteen feet off the ground. The sturdy-looking deer stand was a mystery. He was sure it did not belong to any Coon Dog hunters.

*Somebody musta' slipped in here from the back side,* he thought. *But I wonder how they carried all that wood in here. It musta' been a right sizable job. . . . I reckon they didn't know this was Coon Dog land, since the boundaries ain't marked too well back here.*

Dexter had always hunted on the ground. Despite that lifelong preference, however, he was quick to recognize the advantages of hunting from an elevated position up in a tree. During the past few seasons, some of his companions had started using wooden platforms, and some of the more industrious Coon Dog hunters were even beginning to use those lightweight, newfangled, "portable" climbing tree stands they made out of aluminum and plywood. The benefits were obvious. A portable tree stand could be placed in a strategic location by being chained to the trunk of a tree. And everyone agreed that a woods-wise buck could not scent a man fifteen or twenty feet up in a tree nearly as easily as he could if that man were on the ground.

Being from the old school of deer hunting, Dexter had never had any desire to climb up into one of these tree-stand platforms. But now his curiosity was aroused. For one thing, this particular stand had not been put here by accident. Dexter immediately noticed a large, open scrape about thirty yards away, directly under the overhanging limb of a medium-size holly tree.

He walked over to the scrape for a closer look. The strong and unmistakable smell of musk hung heavily in the air. The scrape had been visited recently, probably within the hour, Dexter figured. The rich, black earth had been pawed vigorously, and leaves and dirt had been slung five to six feet away. A large wet spot in the center of the opening—dotted with small bubbles that were still plainly visible—indicated that a buck had left his calling card a short time earlier. Dexter studied the woods around him. He counted half a dozen fresh rubs on four- to five-inch saplings within a fifty-yard radius.

"Yep, this ol' boy's been usin' this area right regular," he said in a low tone. "Looks like a fair-size animal, too. . . . I wonder if this could be some a' ol' Big Foot's doin's."

Dexter walked back over to the maple tree. He contemplated the wooden tree stand for several moments. The trunk of the tree branched into three sections, and a triangle-shape platform had been nailed between those sections. Heavy railroad spikes had been driven into the tree for steps.

*H-m-m,* Dexter thought. *If somebody went to all the trouble to build 'em a good stand on our land, the least I could do is oblige 'em by checkin' it out. I ain't climbed up in a tree like this since I was a boy!*

Dexter instinctively glanced around as if to make sure no one was watching. Leaning his old Savage Model 99 rifle against a nearby sapling, he grabbed one of the cold spikes and pulled himself up. He went up the tree with surprising agility. Even though he was wearing wool gloves, he could still feel the sharp coldness of the steel spikes. He climbed up onto the platform and stood up, grabbing a limb for support. A small wooden seat had been built against the largest section of the maple, and he sat down.

*This ain't really all that bad,* he thought.

Visibility was good. Over to his left, he could see the tops of the tall cypress trees out in the swamp. Directly below him on the right, he could see the faded blue markings that had been painted on a line of trees, indicating the property boundary. A pulpwood company owned land that bordered the back boundary of Coon Dog land, and Dexter now for the first time realized that this mysterious tree platform had been built right on the property line.

Dexter was enjoying the view so much that he forgot all about his rifle on the ground below. It was a rare occasion, indeed, that he would ever separate himself from his rifle for any reason while in the woods hunting. Even when he napped on the ground during the middle of the day by sitting down and leaning back against a tree, his rifle always rested comfortably across his lap. Many were the sad stories told around the campfire each season about some foolish hunter who had left his rifle in the truck or leaning against a tree while going to check on some fresh deer sign or while stepping away to answer the call of nature, only to have the buck of a lifetime suddenly appear within easy range.

The sharp crack of ice breaking seventy five yards away brought Dexter back to reality with a gut-wrenching start. He knew that he had violated one of the most fundamental rules of deer hunting the moment he had leaned his rifle against the sapling, and now it was coming back to haunt him. Even as his trained woodsman's eyes searched through the trees to pick up movement, he knew that the sound had been made by a large-bodied deer. Immediately his eyes zeroed in on the heart-stopping sight of long tines glistening in the morning sun.

The buck was walking across a narrow slough, with his head down and his huge antlers swaying from side to side, crunching ice and splashing water with every step. As the big deer jumped up out of the slough onto higher ground, it paused, raising its head majestically for a careful look around. A steady stream of mist poured from both nostrils. Dexter was offered a perfect view of the buck's extraordinary antlers.

"Lord-a-mercy! It's the Phantom!" he whispered in a panic, quickly glancing down at his rifle. "I've really done it now. Great Aunt Jemima!"

Dexter had known right away that the buck carried an enormous rack. The moment the big animal paused and raised its head, however, the long drop tines that hung down like clubs from the bottom of each beam immediately separated this deer from any other whitetail in the area. The long tines, the wide-spreading beams, and the thick mass, as well as those unmistakable drop tines—so unusual for this part of the country—distinguished this great buck from all others in Coon Dog Cemetery history. Dexter knew that he was being given the rare privilege of staring at a living legend. But he was helpless to do much more than stare.

He had glimpsed the Phantom only once before, two years earlier. The giant buck had jumped across the road in front of his truck at night while Dexter was returning to camp. Then, too, there had been no mistaking those huge antlers, illuminated in the headlights. Even though the sighting had lasted for only a few brief moments, a picture of that incredible whitetail had been permanently etched in his mind. Over the years, others who had seen or missed shots at this seemingly charmed buck always described the one-of-a-kind rack in the same meticulous detail.

"Looks like ya' got me dead to rights this time, ol' buddy," Dexter whispered solemnly as he slowly shook his head in disgust. "I reckon ya' can chalk up another vict'ry in yer' favor. Oh, Lordie. How could I do such a stupid thing? I'm sure I ain't the only hunter you've caught with his pants down. They's prob'ly a couple a' dozen. Maybe even a couple a' hundred, huh?" Dexter glanced down at his rifle again. "I'll tell ya' one thing, though. If you'll jus' turn yer' head and look the other way for about fifteen seconds, I'll shinny back down this tree and grab my rifle so fast it'll make yer' head spin!"

The big buck continued to look around.

*Dang!* Dexter thought. *Dang! Dang! Dang! Ya' hunt as hard as ya' can, an' ya' try to do ever'thing jus' right, but the first time ya' slip up an' make one little mistake, the bull-a'-the-woods steps out an' makes a monkey outa' ya'. It happens ever' time!*

*That's buck huntin' for ya', I reckon. They's a hundred different things ya' gotta' do jus' right. Ya' can do ninety-nine of 'em perfect, without a hitch, but if ya' mess up on even the last little thing, ya' might as well forget it, 'cause that's gonna' be all she wrote. Of all the stupid, gol-derned positions to get myself in. What would the boys think if they saw me now? I reckon you've really got me up a tree this time, ol' buddy!*

The Phantom took several steps forward. He glanced over toward the scrape as if he knew it was there, but he made no attempt to go to it.

*I wonder if that's his scrape,* Dexter thought. *He knows it's there, but he ain't payin' no attention to it. It must belong to another buck.*

Quite unexpectedly, the Phantom put his head down and began to feed. Several large white oaks grew on the peninsula, and the ground was littered with acorns.

*I ain't believin' this,* Dexter thought. *Now he's gonna rub salt in the wound by paradin' aroun' in front a' me while I'm stuck up in this dad-burned tree! He must know I'm up here!*

The buck was facing directly toward the maple tree, less than forty yards from Dexter. Looking down on such a magnificent animal was a stirring sight.

*Thank goodness the wind is right,* Dexter thought.

Dexter's breath misted heavily every time he exhaled, and he tried to control his breathing so that the smokelike mist would not give him away if the Phantom happened to look up.

*You prob'ly ain't gonna hang aroun' for long, but if you keep on feedin' for a few more minutes, they's an outside chance I might be able to climb down and get my rifle. No . . . that's about the most harebrained idea I've come up with yet! The chances a' climbin' down this tree without bein' seen're a million to one!*

The buck seemed to be in a hurry to eat as fast as he could. He was making a lot of noise, crunching the cupped, woody ends off the big oval nuts and allowing them to drop out of his mouth as he swallowed the acorns whole.

*Turn aroun' ol' buddy. For cryin' out loud, please jus' turn aroun' an' look the other way. That's all I'm askin'!*

As if in answer to a prayer, the Phantom gradually began to turn and feed in the other direction. Dexter was beside himself. This was the chance he'd been hoping for. He knew he had to go for broke. The instant he thought the buck's eyes were looking the other way, Dexter quickly stooped down and swung his body over the side of the platform, placing a foot on the closest spike. The Phantom looked up. Dexter froze. The big buck crunched the cap off an acorn between his powerful back molars. It fell to the ground. After a few seconds, he twitched his tail and lowered his head. Dexter moved down a step, hugging the tree for all he was worth. His free leg was groping to find the next spike when the Phantom looked up again. Dexter paused once more, holding his breath. He was in a very awkward position, with his leg poised in midair. The Phantom appeared to be looking right at him, cupping his ears forward and staring. At length, the big buck twitched his tail again and returned to feeding. Dexter breathed a sigh of relief and calmly lowered himself down to the next spike.

This went on for several nerve-racking minutes. Inch by inch, Dexter eased down the tree. Fortunately, the trunk of the maple was large enough to hide most of his body. Dexter was only two spikes away from the ground, still hugging the tree like a squirrel, when the Phantom suddenly raised his head, turned, and started walking directly toward him.

*Oh, boy!* Dexter thought. *He's fixin' to walk right over here an' kiss me on the cheek!*

The Phantom stopped less than thirty feet away. Dexter held his breath. The big buck raised his nose and inhaled deeply. He glanced over toward the scrape. Apparently, something in the air momentarily got his attention. He turned and casually walked to the scrape, and once again Dexter breathed a sigh of relief.

"Thank you, Lord! Thank you!" he whispered, looking up.

The big whitetail sniffed the urine in the freshly pawed earth. He began to nuzzle and lick the broken branch of the tree that hung out over the scrape. He did this for several long moments, totally absorbed in what he was doing, while Dexter slowly lowered himself to the last spike. All at once the Phantom raised his head as high as he could and began to strike his antlers against several of the higher limbs of the tree, thrashing wildly and making a lot of noise. He was now facing completely away from Dexter.

Dexter silently lowered himself to the ground. Never in his life had he been so glad to place both feet on solid earth. He swore a quick oath that he would never climb another tree again as long as he lived. He reached for his rifle, keeping one eye on the buck. In his haste, the back of his open, gloved hand brushed against the barrel, pushing it away from him. Before he could catch it, the rifle fell to the ground with a loud thud. Dexter cringed and held his breath, hugging the tree for all he was worth, knowing this had to be the last straw.

The Phantom whirled around, staring directly toward the maple tree, trying to pinpoint the source of the noise. Then he bolted—bounding through the woods in a dazzling burst of speed, going back the way he had come, his long white tail bouncing from side to side like someone waving a large white handkerchief. Dexter quickly grabbed his rifle up off the ground and brought it to his shoulder, but there was no way possible to get a shot at such a fast-moving target.

Just as the big buck reached the elevated piece of ground where he had paused after he had stepped up out of the slough, he did something that Dexter would have bet anything in the world against. The Phantom stopped to look back. Perhaps the sudden noise had been more startling than alarming. Whatever the reason, this was the one chance that all hunters spend a lifetime waiting for, the one potentially fatal mistake that big mature bucks like the Phantom seldom, if ever, make.

The big whitetail stood absolutely motionless for several long minutes, studying every leaf and twig within his field of vision in an effort to discover the source of the startling noise. The cross hairs of Dexter's scope were trained on the deer's body, but a large clump of brush prevented a shoulder or neck shot. Dexter's arm began to quiver. The old .300 Savage lever-action that he was now holding in an offhand position had brought down many a fine buck over the years, but he knew he couldn't maintain this stance indefinitely.

Suddenly the Phantom put his head down and took a short step forward. The buck was just stepping down into the icy slough when the rifle roared. The huge whitetail dropped in his tracks with a broken neck. He rolled down the short incline and came to rest in the icy water on the edge of the slough. Dexter quickly chambered a fresh round and started walking rapidly toward the fallen giant. By the time he reached the slough, the Phantom was dead.

Dexter stood at the top of the hill looking down at the big buck for several long moments. He couldn't believe his eyes.

"Great Scott!" he stammered, almost apologizing. "If you had jus' kept on runnin', I never woulda' been able to get off a shot."

Dexter made sure the Phantom was dead. Then he laid his rifle on the ground and pulled the massive deer out of the water. Dexter's legs were still trembling from the long minutes of being cramped on the side of the tree. He knelt down beside the huge animal and stared at the incredible rack.

"I don't deserve you, ol' timer," he said out loud, stroking the buck's thick winter coat. "This is the craziest thing that's ever happened to me in my whole life." He shook his head in utter disbelief. "I do ever'thing wrong that a hunter can possibly do, an' I still end up killin' the biggest buck that's ever been seen in these parts. It jus' don't make sense, but I reckon they's a lot a' things in this life that don't make much sense. . . . I'll tell ya' one thing, though: I'd rather be lucky than good any day a' the week."

Dexter had seen some outstanding antlers in his time, but nothing he had ever witnessed compared with the buck that now lay before him. The massive rack contained five long upright tines on each side. Several of the tines were split, including the thick brow tines. At least four of the primary tines were between ten and twelve inches in length. Dexter figured the spread to be somewhere around twenty-two inches, and he could barely get his hand around the thick antler bases. But the two distinguishing features that really separated this deer from any other buck Dexter had ever seen were the amazing drop tines that hung down from each of the heavy beams.

"These things are unreal," Dexter said, grabbing one of the thick, clublike drop tines. "They look like they've been carved out of polished ivory."

Dexter sighed.

"This is unbelievable," he said, staring down at the old buck's gray muzzle. "I reckon it's fittin' that you're still carryin' such a big rack, too. Why, you must be six, seven years old by now, maybe older. Ya' wouldn't a' had too many seasons left, that's for sure."

Dexter counted eighteen points on the huge rack. The Phantom's massive body equaled his oversize antlers in every way. Dexter guessed that he weighed at least 275 pounds on the hoof.

Dexter's breath still misted heavily. He noticed the small clumps of ice that were clinging to the buck's long white guard hairs on its belly and underside. He shook his head.

"I go an' make two of the most idiotic mistakes anybody could ever think about makin'. I climb up a tree an' leave my rifle on the ground, and then, like a plumb greenhorn, I go an' knock my rifle over. And what do ya' do? Ya' stop to look back, an' ya' stand there gawking at me like a dumb little yearlin'. Ya' coulda' been in the next county by now. Don't ya' know that?" He continued to shake his head. "I slap don't deserve this."

Then Dexter did something he had never done before. He leaned down and kissed the ground.

* * * * *

Dexter rolled back into camp an hour later. He could hardly hold back his excitement. Dillon, Jack, and several other men were standing around a crackling fire, drinking coffee. Dexter parked the truck and casually walked over to the fire circle.

"Got any more a' that coffee?" he asked.

"What's the matter? Cold get to ya'?" Dillon asked. He still had on all of his heavy hunting clothes. He had obviously just gotten back in from the morning hunt himself.

"Yeah, as a matter a' fact, I got right chilly out there this mornin'," Dexter admitted. "It was flat cold out there."

"You musta' left out awful early," Jack said.

"Yeah, I did," Dexter replied. "Couldn't sleep. So I got up an' left. Anybody see anything?"

"Naw," Dillon responded. "It must be too cold for 'em to be movin' around much today. I always thought deer liked cold weather, but I swany, I never even saw a squirrel this mornin'. How about you?"

"Yeah. I saw a pretty fair buck," Dexter answered matter-of-factly.

Jess ducked out of the cook tent holding a large, fire-blackened aluminum coffee pot and a mug.

"Here. You look like you could use this," he said.

"I sure can," Dexter said gratefully. He smiled as he took the cup. "Thanks, Jess."

"Anybody need a refill?" Jess asked, looking around.

Several of the men held out empty cups. Jess filled Dexter's cup first, then he began refilling the others.

Dexter sipped the steaming black coffee and smiled cheerfully.

"U-m-m, um!" he said. "Ain't nothin' like a cup a' Jess's strong black coffee to thaw out a man's innards an' melt the icicles in his veins on a day like this!"

"Tell us about the buck you saw," Dillon said impatiently. "You're the only one who saw anything today. What happened? Couldn't you get a shot?"

Dexter put his mug down on one of the upright logs used as a seat around the fire circle. He slowly pulled off both of his weathered wool gloves and held his fingers out toward the fire. Everyone immediately noticed the dried blood still caked on his hands.

"Yeah, I got a shot," he answered happily. "This has been the craziest day I've ever spent in the deer woods."

"What do you mean by that?" Dillon asked, staring down at the blood on Dexter's hands. "Did you kill something?"

"Yeah, I did," Dexter said. "I jus' killed the Phantom."

Dillon's mouth fell open. "What? You're kidding!"

"No. It actually happened," Dexter stated. "I ain't believin' it myself, but it's the gospel truth!"

"Why, you old son of a gun!" Jack yelled out. "That's great news! Why didn't you tell us sooner?"

"I was gettin' aroun' to it."

"How big is he?" Dillon asked excitedly. "Gosh darn it! I just don't see how you do it every year!"

"I reckon he's big enough that I'm gonna' need plenty a' he'p totin' 'im outa' the swamp," Dexter answered. "He's one heck of a deer, all right."

"How many points does he have?" Dillon asked. "Did you count them?"

Dexter picked up his mug and took a sip of coffee. Everyone waited expectantly for his answer.

"You ain't gonna' believe this, but I think he's gonna' be some kinda' record. He's a real hoss. I ain't never seen a set a' horns like he's wearin'! He looks like he's got a couple a' trees growin' outa' his head."

"How many points, for crying out loud?" Dillon asked again.

"Eighteen in all. He's got 'em growin' ever' which-away!"

"Eighteen? You gotta be kiddin'!" Dillon exclaimed. "I gotta' see this with my own eyes!"

"You're welcome to he'p me tote 'im out," Dexter said. "It's gonna' be a right good piece."

"Let's go," Dillon said. "I'm ready. I've been hearing stories about the Phantom ever since I joined this crazy club, and I've never even seen one of his tracks. I always thought he was just a figment of someone's imagination."

"No, he's real," Jess said. "Too many people have seen 'im and shot at 'im."

"How do you know it's really the Phantom?" Dillon asked. "Does he have drop tines like everyone says?"

"Yep. He's got 'em, all right," Dexter answered. "His bases look like Coke bottles, an' them drop tines look like baseball bats. They ain't no question about who he is!"

"Ye-e-e-e, Hi-i-i!" Jack yelled. He slapped Dexter on the back with such force that some of his coffee splashed out onto Dillon's coat. Dillon jumped back like he'd been bitten by a snake.

"Would you mind watchin' out?" he yelled.

Jack ignored him. "This is the best thing that's happened down here all week . . . all season! Man, I'm glad you didn't kill anything on that stupid hunt with Shady Holler."

"Me, too," Dexter said. "I reckon this makes it all worthwhile."

"It sure as shootin' does!" Jack agreed.

Jess reached into his pocket and pulled out a leather-covered flask filled with Southern Comfort. He looked at Dexter.

"Here. You look like you could use a good slug of this," he said. "You've had a long mornin'. Put some of this in your coffee. It'll warm your insides. Anyhow, it's time to do some serious celebratin' around here!"

He poured a generous amount of the brown liquid into Dexter's mug.

"I reckon I need to get the Phantom outa' the woods b'fore I start celebratin'," Dexter said.

"Aw, we got all day to do that," Jack said. "He ain't goin' nowhere, an' ever'body here'll help out. B'fore we do a thing, though, I wanna' hear the whole story. I wanna' hear ever' detail, from start to finish!"

"It's the craziest deer huntin' story you're ever gonna' hear," Dexter said, "I'll tell ya' that much. In fact, it's so crazy, you're gonna' think I made it up. It was stupid, dumb luck. I don't deserve to be standin' here talkin' about it."

"Isn't that the way it always happens?" Dillon asked.

"Not always," Jess said. "Let the man talk."

"This time it sure did," Dexter responded modestly.

"Luck'r no luck, I wanna' hear all the gory details," Jack said again. "Then I wanna' go see if that ol' bruiser's half as big as ever'body says he is!"

"He is!" Dexter affirmed. "I'll guaran-dang-tee ya' that!"

Everyone crowded closer to the fire circle. Dexter propped one boot up on a log and reared back. With his usual animated expression, he began narrating the humorous, exciting, nerve-racking account of the most unforgettable buck-hunting adventure he had ever experienced. He tried his best not to leave out a single detail.

# Tracking the Elusive "Horned Canecutter"

## Chapter 12

*This story is one of two in this volume taken from the author's popular column "The Misadventures of Arnold and Waldo," which ran in* North American Whitetail *magazine from 1997 to 2003. In the magazine, the stories were written under the author's pen name, D. A. Deerslayer.*

* * * * *

The American Legion meeting hall was packed with a capacity crowd when the illustrious out-of-town guest arrived. It was time for the annual Piney Woods Rooter Roast, sponsored jointly by the Women's Auxiliary of Ludowici and the Altamaha Fur, Fins, and Scales Hunting Club. This year, there was an added bonus at the much-anticipated wild pig cookout. Buck Hurricane had secured as the keynote speaker none other than W. Philpot Osborne IV, worldwide hunter extraordinaire and noted Wall Street tycoon.

From the moment he arrived, Mr. Osborne played the part of the big-game hunter like a Broadway ham. Dressed in expensive khakis and calf-high leather boots, he also sported a wide-brimmed Stetson hat—complete with a synthetic leopard-skin hat band—pinned up on one side in the tradition of the legendary Rough Riders.

Eager to hear every word spoken by this big-game guru, Waldo, Arnold, and Doc Bragg made sure they had front-row seats as Buck Hurricane introduced the famous guest.

"Folks, it's a special honor to introduce our speaker tonight, Mr. W. Philpot Osborne IV, who has just arrived from the Big Apple. Mr. Osborne, or Bwana Bill as most of his admirers call him, has been on numerous African safaris. He owns one of the finest trophy rooms in the world.

Without further ado, I give you that great American hunter, Bwana Bill Osborne!"

Everyone clapped as Bwana Bill strutted up to the podium.

"It's a pleasure to be with you," he began. "Most people think I'm some kind of super hunter because I've traveled the world in search of superior trophies. But even though I've taken numerous species of African and North American big-game, including two grand slams of sheep, all the big bears, and every species of North American deer, that certainly doesn't mean that I'm anything special. . . ."

"It just means he's got more money than Methuselah," Doc Bragg whispered.

". . . And just because I shot a record *chui,* a ten-foot croc, and thirty-two pieces of meat on my most recent safari to the Dark Continent doesn't put me in any special category," Bwana Bill continued.

Waldo was outraged.

"Why would anybody want to shoot a perfectly good piece of meat, let alone thirty-two pieces of meat?" he asked Arnold. "Why, that's the biggest waste of game I've ever heard of. Hasn't this Banana Phil fellow ever heard of using paper targets? Doesn't he know there are starving people in China? And what in the Sam Hill is a *chewy?* Some kind of fortune cookie? If you ask me, *he's* a croc!"

"Don't you know anything, you fool?" Arnold hissed. "That's African lingo. He means he shot thirty-two animals for camp meat while he was on safari. And his name is *Bwana Bill,* not *Banana Phil!*"

"*Chui* is Swahili for leopard," Doc Bragg added.

"Well, it sounds like some kind of acid reflux tablet to me," Waldo said. "Anyone who shoots thirty-two pieces of meat oughta be strung up on the meat pole! That's gotta be way over the legal limit. If we shoot one doe for camp meat down here, it lasts us near about the whole season."

"It's different in Africa," Doc Bragg explained. "When you're on safari, you've got to feed everyone in camp."

Bwana Bill continued to rattle on about his hunting exploits. Waldo started to get up and leave.

"Hold your horses," Doc Bragg whispered, grabbing his friend. "After all, there are times when we have to take the agony with the ecstasy. I reckon this is one of those times."

"That man ain't agony," Waldo said. "He's pure misery! He may have an office in the Umpire State Building and he may dress in Ambercrumby and Finch duds, but he don't impress this ol' boy one bit!"

"It's the *Empire* State Building!" Arnold whispered impatiently. "And it's *Abercrombie* and *Fitch,* you nitwit. Don't you know anything?"

"I know that somebody needs to give this big city game hog a little dose of south Georgia comeuppance," Waldo whispered to his two companions. "Just 'cause the Yankees squeaked by the Braves in the World Series a few years back doesn't mean he can come down here and talk down to us like we're a bunch of uneducated half-wits."

"You're right," Doc Bragg agreed. "Something tells me this man is a phony. But teachin' him a lesson might be easier said than done."

"Not if you're an old swamper from south Georgia!" Waldo whispered with a sly grin. "We start by giving him back a good dose of his own medicine! Only I plan to use a little *Southern* lingo instead of big foreign words you can't even pronounce. I may need some help."

"You can count on me," Doc Bragg whispered.

"Me, too," Arnold said. "Just don't do anything that'll embarrass us too awful bad . . . please? After all, I am supposed to interview him on our radio show."

As soon as Bwana Bill had finished speaking, Waldo zeroed in on him like a buzzard dropping down on a kill. Arnold and Doc Bragg sidled closer so they wouldn't miss out on any of the action.

"Banana Phil, could I have a word?" Waldo asked the famous hunter.

"It's Bwana Bill," the celebrity answered, obviously irritated.

"You say you have every species of North American big-game including all the various grand slams, plus a lot of other critters from around the world. Is that right?" Waldo asked.

"That's exactly what I said," Bwana Bill answered, eyeing Waldo suspiciously. "I've even taken a jaguar with a spear."

"Ever hunted any gnarly bucks in the swamp country?" Waldo asked.

"Can't say that I have," Bwana Bill replied. "When I'm stag hunting, I only go for the biggest and best animals in the world."

"Oh, I'm not talking about stags," Waldo said. "We've got plenty of them around these parts, too, including some pretty hefty Black Angus steers. What I'm talking about is trophy whitetails."

"My dear fellow, I've hunted *muy grandes* in south Texas and Mexico, and four-hundred-pound brush-busters in Canada. But I've never had any desire to hunt any of those grasshopper-size *Key* deer you boys grow around these parts."

"The racks on some of our little *Key* deer, as you call 'em, might surprise you," Waldo said. "But since you've never hunted here before, I reckon there's one kind of slam you couldn't possibly have."

"My good man, I own every kind of slam recognized by the Rowland Ward's record book!"

"In all due respect, Banana Phil, I don't reckon you have *a swamp slam,*" Waldo stated matter-of-factly.

"A what?"

"A swamp slam," Waldo repeated. "Down in our neck of the woods, if a man ain't got a swamp slam in his double-wide, he's not considered to be much of an outdoorsman."

"My good man, I've hunted all over the world—except in certain places where it's beneath my dignity to tread," Bwana Bill stated. "What in heaven's name is a *swamp slam?* And what is a *double-wide?*"

"Simple," Waldo said. "A swamp slam consists of four of the toughest critters in the South to come by—a twelve-foot gator, a piney woods rooter . . . er, wild boar, that is, with at least five-inch stickers. . . ."

"Tusks," Doc Bragg offered. "And er, a *double-wide* is a kind of south Georgia trophy room."

"Next comes a 450-pound honey marauder . . ." Waldo continued.

"Er . . . black bear," Doc Bragg translated.

"And by far the hardest trophy of all . . ." Waldo leaned over and began whispering, ". . . a genuine, south Georgia horned canecutter!"

"A *what?*" Bwana Bill screamed.

"Most out-of-towners call them *jackalopes,*" Doc Bragg translated.

"With at least six points to the side," Waldo added, smiling.

"That's right," Arnold said. "Because of all the snakes, ticks, mosquitoes, leeches, chiggers, quicksand, swamp gas, and other strange happenings in the swamp country, a genuine south Georgia jackalope—er, horned canecutter—is considered by many to be one of the toughest animals in all of North America to put on the wall. Even tougher than a gnarly swamp whitetail."

"What do you boys take me for, some kind of idiot?" Bwana Bill stated. "I've heard of jackalopes in Texas, but they're not real."

"Of course they're not real in Texas," Doc Bragg offered. "That's because their range is restricted to certain parts of south Georgia. That's also why they've never been recognized by the Boone and Crockett Club as a separate game species. Because they're found only in Georgia, other states like Texas have gone to extremes to keep them from being recognized. Why do you think taxidermists make replicas with antlers and rabbit skins and sell them for so much money?"

"But there's no substitute for the real thing," Arnold added. "Kinda like those fake whitetail antlers certain people have been makin' lately. They try to pass 'em off as world records, but the experts can always tell the difference."

Bwana Bill was beginning to take the bait.

"I'm an expert in my field," Bwana Bill stated. "But I always thought jackalopes were the product of someone's imagination. Tell me, do you have one of these er . . . swamp slams in your, uh . . . double-wide?"

"Not just one," Waldo answered proudly. "I have two!"

"Do they actually have six points to the side?" Bwana Bill asked.

"The small ones do," Waldo said with a straight face.

Bwana Bill suddenly put his arm around Waldo as if they were long-lost buddies. He turned away from Doc Bragg and Arnold. "Tell me something," he said. "You look like a man who might be interested in a sound business proposition. Since you have two of these slams in your possession, would you consider selling one? I'd be willing to make it well worth your while. It'd be quite a novelty in my trophy room."

"Why, Banana Phil!" Waldo said. "If I sold you one of my swamp slams, and you were to put it in your trophy room back home, folks might start thinking the wrong thing."

"Oh, no. I'd never let that happen," Bwana Bill said. "I'd tell everyone that I got it from my good friend, er . . . what'd you say your name was?"

"Maybe you oughta come down here during huntin' season and try to collect one for yourself—provided you're not too superstitious," Waldo suggested. "Huntin' the swamp country really ain't so bad—as long as you don't run into any screamin' swamp painters."

"Any what?"

"That's local lingo for wildcats," Doc Bragg translated. "They're ten times more dangerous than an African *chui*. Why, they can defeather a thirty-five-pound turkey gobbler quicker than a six-foot south Georgia diamondback can coil!"

For some reason, Bwana Bill never took Waldo up on his offer. Chances are he was too busy planning his next African safari.

# The Three-Legged Bet

## Chapter 13

The green pickup truck slowly pulled into the graveled parking lot of the pulpwood yard, noisily crunching small rocks under its wide, knobby tires. Mike Fletcher cut the engine and stepped out, grabbing a brown Manila envelope off the seat beside him. He slid the envelope under his arm and walked briskly across the yard lot toward the trailer office. The clear, strong odor of pine resin and freshly cut wood permeated the crisp fall air.

Across the yard, the loader-operator was busily loading a long, flat railroad car with large bundles of pine pulpwood. He waved at Mike from high atop his tall machine. Mike pretended to look the other way and did not respond. He walked across the truck-weighing scales, stepped up the high, single step, and entered the front door of the small office. Inside, the woodyard manager hailed him with a cordial greeting from behind his bare wooden desk.

"How ya' doin', Fletch?"

"Doin' great, Jimmy," Mike answered. "How about you?"

"Oh. I can't complain," the man answered. "We never seem to get enough wood these days, but then, you can't have everything."

Jimmy Green, the woodyard manager, always greeted Mike with a friendly smile. He was a hard worker to boot, and Mike enjoyed doing business with him.

"Well, maybe I can help solve that problem," Mike said. "Jeff Banks has a large block of pulpwood he wants to thin." Mike opened the Manila envelope and pulled out several timber maps and charts.

As the two men sat side by side behind Jimmy's desk drinking coffee and reviewing the timber estimates a few minutes later, the red-faced loader-operator, Grover McGibony, stepped through the doorway. He pulled off his bulky work gloves and threw them down on the table beside the door.

"Git one yet?" he asked Mike.

"No, not yet," Mike replied. Mike never looked up from the colored timber map he and Jimmy were studying.

"I got me another'n yesterdee evenin'," Grover volunteered. "That's three fer me so far, and they're all bucks, too . . . two cowhorn spikes and a big three-pointer."

Mike looked up at Grover.

"In case you can't add, that's one over the legal limit," he said with a definite sting in his voice. "If I spotlighted deer at night the way you do, I'd probably have at least a dozen by now, but I don't hunt that way. That's not even hunting!"

"I didn't shine that'n yesterdee," Grover said defensively. "I kilt him fair'n square yesterdee evenin' in a field over at Mansfield." As he spoke, the black chewing tobacco remnants caught in Grover's gums showed between his yellowed teeth.

By nature Mike Fletcher was usually very even- tempered. For some reason, though, this misfit of a man named Grover McGibony always seemed to rub him the wrong way.

"You've never killed anything fair and square in your entire life," Mike said bluntly. "I oughta turn you in to the game warden. If they could make a case, I would—so fast it would make your head swim."

"Come on, Mike," Grover said. "I hunt 'em fair an' square plenty. I just needed me some meat's the reason I shined them first two."

Grover walked over to the small refrigerator in the corner of the trailer and took out two cans of beer.

"Here, have a beer on me," he said, holding a can out toward Mike.

Grover had been told not to drink beer during working hours. But it was just about quitting time, and he was trying to impress Mike.

"I swear to God, I kilt that'n yesterdee legal and proper," he repeated.

"Keep your damned beer for yourself!" Mike said. "I'm drinking coffee."

Grover backed away and put the rejected can down on the table, a trace of hurt showing faintly in his bloodshot eyes. Mike knew he could push Grover to the limit and that Grover would always back down. In a way, Mike almost felt sorry for the man. Grover was one of those hopeless souls who always looked dirty and soiled. His clothes were eternally wrinkled and grease stained. He was short, standing about five feet, seven inches tall, and his large belly, which always bulged out over his belt, and his round, double-chinned face highlighted the fact that he was at least forty pounds overweight.

Grover's only positive attribute seemed to be his clear, blue eyes. Mike Fletcher had often wondered about those misleading eyes. If Grover shaved and washed up, he might look like any other clean-cut, decent human being. And if he combed his hair and put on some clean clothes, he might easily pass himself off as a rising young man who was going places in life.

But Mike Fletcher had never seen Grover McGibony in clean clothes, and he doubted if he ever would. Grover's eyes seemed to be the only salvation to his sad condition in life. They appeared to be the dark blue, penetrating eyes of a knowing, intelligent man. Yet there was a serious flaw somewhere back in the recesses and hidden depths of bright color, because Grover could tell a lie, or cheat his best friend, or steal from his employer without the slightest hesitation. And his method of killing deer—by spotlighting them in the dark with powerful lights when they were blinded and helpless—thoroughly enraged Mike Fletcher.

Yes, this arrogant, boastful little runt of a man always rubbed Mike the wrong way. Mike vowed to try to hold back his rising temper. Grover wasn't worth the effort.

Grover popped open his can of beer and took a long, greedy gulp.

"We got five hundred acres leased up the river, Fletch," Grover said. "If you wanna git one fer sure you can hunt with us some this comin' weekend."

"No, thanks, Grover," Mike said. "I have my own place to hunt. Anyway, you wouldn't know what it's like to hunt a buck during daylight hours, the way most people do. You oughta try it some time. You might find some real sport in it."

Mike was seldom confrontational, but the words seemed to flow from his mouth before he could even think about what he was saying.

Grover was undaunted. The put-down didn't seem to bother him one bit. "Shoot, Mike. I'd bet you my Browning automatic against yer bolt-action out there in yer truck that I could kill a buck anytime, faster'n you could."

Mike looked up and stared at Grover in disbelief. He looked over at Jimmy, then back at Grover. He knew Grover would frequently make a bet, then try to weasel out of the wager if he lost. But the challenge had been made. It could not go unanswered.

"You don't know what you're saying, Grover," Mike said. He looked at Jimmy and shook his head.

"Yeah, I do," Grover insisted. "I'm sayin' I could go out anytime, anyplace, durin' the day and kill me one 'fore you could."

"And you're willing to bet your rifle on it?" Mike asked doubtfully. Grover had come to own the expensive Browning automatic .270 under mysterious circumstances. It was a safe assumption that the gun had been stolen.

"That's right. Mine against yers."

Mike Fletcher thought for a minute. "I tell you what, Grover. Today's Wednesday. What're you doing Saturday?"

"Nothin'. Huntin' maybe."

"You're on, then," Mike said. "Here's the deal. We both go out on Saturday and hunt all day, in a place we both agree on. If neither one of us kills anything, we'll call it a draw and set up another day and keep hunting until one of us scores. But I'm warning you, no games."

"Suits me," Grover said, smiling. "Where ya' wanna hunt?"

"Somewhere neither one of us has ever hunted before," Mike said. "So it's fair." He looked over at Jimmy. "You know any good places close-by?"

Jimmy looked up at the large aerial photograph on the wall. The photo showed all of the local farms in the area.

"How about Farley's place?" Jimmy said. "He's got 300 acres with a lot of big hardwood stands, a swamp bottom, and a forty-acre soybean field. He said we can hunt on his farm anytime. And it's crawling with deer. Nobody hunts on it much." Jimmy knew Grover had never been there—at least legally—during daylight hours.

"Sounds good to me," Mike said. "Can you take us over there and show us around?"

"Yeah, tomorrow afternoon," Jimmy said. "I'll call Mr. Farley and set it up."

"Is that OK with you?" Mike asked Grover.

"I'd ruther hunt on my lease," Grover said. "But it really don't matter all that much."

"Good," Mike said. "We need to agree on some ground rules. We'll meet at 5:30 A.M. at the crossroads in Newborn right before we go into the woods. We'll meet again just after dark. The first man to kill an antlered buck is the winner. I'm not talking about shooting any spikes, now. I'm talking about a grown buck with antlers. If we both get one, the larger rack wins. And if neither of us gets anything, we'll set up another day. OK?"

"It's OK by me," Grover said. "Be sure and bring that sweet-shootin' little bolt-action."

"I will," Mike said.

* * * * *

By late Saturday afternoon, Mike Fletcher had hunted hard all day without seeing a single deer. He had met Grover at the designated time before daylight. He had told Grover that he planned to hunt on the north end of the property, mostly around the large swamp. Now he could kick himself for taking on this challenge with such a worthless adversary and for wasting almost an entire day in the woods.

The Farley land was divided almost in half by a dirt road. Grover had gone into the southern portion of the property where the soybean field was located. Mike Fletcher had found very little buck sign where he had been hunting, so he decided to spend the last hour of daylight hunting over the soybean field. He half expected to find Grover there, but when he reached the large opening, he found no sign of the man anywhere.

About thirty minutes before dark, Mike took a stand on the edge of the field on the downwind side. He sat on the ground Indian-style and leaned back against the trunk of a large pine, concealing himself just far enough inside the tree line to be well hidden yet still have a good view of the field.

He had been there only a short time when he heard a distinct noise in the woods over to his left. He instinctively raised his rifle and waited. Almost immediately, he saw the unmistakable profile of a walking deer. It was a large doe, headed out to feed in the uncut field. The doe stopped cautiously just inside the tree line about fifty yards from where Mike was sitting. She studied the field for several minutes. Then she looked back into the woods. As if on cue, two half-grown, six-month-old fawns tiptoed up behind her.

The wind was perfect. Mike knew the deer could not scent him. They walked out into the field single file and began nibbling on the tasty, uncut soybean shoots that were now eighteen inches high. Mike was totally engrossed in watching the three deer as the sun dipped down beyond the trees.

Only a few minutes of shooting light remained. Suddenly Mike heard another rustling sound coming from the same direction as before. Once more he raised his rifle in readiness. This time, he saw the antlers of a nice buck before he saw any part of the buck's body. His heart began to pound, but he forced himself to remain steady and wait.

The buck was following the same trail the doe had taken. In a matter of seconds, he would be in the opening. Mike decided to wait until the buck was completely in the clear before firing. The buck was walking at a steady pace, totally undisturbed. Yet he seemed to walk with a strange, jerking gait unlike anything Mike had ever seen before.

The buck paused for a long time on the edge of the field—just as the doe had done—while the few remaining minutes of precious daylight slowly ticked away. He scrutinized every tree and bush as Mike tried to bide his time and wait patiently for the perfect opportunity to shoot. His arms were trembling slightly as he held up his rifle, and he made every attempt to control his excitement. It would be an easy shot at less than fifty yards. What more could he ask for? And this was some kind of nice buck! He had to be at least an eight-pointer, and his back tines were easily nine or ten inches long.

The big buck finally stepped into the field, walking toward the doe and fawns in his strangely jerking gait. Mike carefully centered his scope on the buck's shoulder and took a deep breath. He was just about to squeeze the trigger when he did a double take. The right front leg of the buck was completely gone, just above the knee. That explained the strange gait.

Apart from the missing leg, the buck appeared to be perfectly healthy in every way. He was large in body, and his neck was thickly swollen. His antlers were even larger and wider than Mike had originally assumed. Without question, this was the finest buck Mike Fletcher had ever seen in the woods.

The buck shuffled out across several rows of soybeans in his peculiar, three-legged gait, totally unaware of any danger. Mike's mind was suddenly filled with mixed thoughts. This magnificent animal had probably been shot in the leg the season before. By some miracle, though, the sleek-coated deer had survived the ordeal. He had lost a leg, but he had survived. And now Mike Fletcher was going to put an end to him.

The buck was broadside to Mike, still fifty yards away. Mike silently eased the safety forward. The bet was his for the taking. He'd show old Grover, that miserable excuse for a human being. Mike didn't care about winning a rifle.

He just wanted to beat Grover. Right over wrong. Good defeating evil. He was the white knight, and he would ride away on his white horse as all white knights are supposed to do.

He began to squeeze the trigger of his deadly .30-06. Then he stopped. He had executed many similar shots in the past, killed many a smaller buck. But now, something deep in his soul would not allow him to go through with it—even though this was the best buck he had ever had in his sights. This amazing whitetail was a survivor. The buck deserved to live. He had earned that right. He had suffered enough.

Mike Fletcher took his finger off the trigger and lowered his rifle. He watched the buck for several more minutes in the fading light. Then he quietly stood up and silently eased back into the woods.

"There'll always be another day," he whispered as he walked toward his truck in the darkness, paraphrasing a familiar saying that his grandfather had often used when Mike was a boy. He smiled. "It was the right thing to do."

Mike waited at the crossroads for over an hour, but Grover never showed up. Since he had not heard any shots during the day, Mike was satisfied that Grover had gone home empty-handed as well. After an hour and a quarter had gone by, Mike got in his truck and drove off.

The next morning, the phone rang bright and early while Mike was still in bed. It was Grover.

"Well, how'd ya do?" Grover asked in his insolent tone.

Mike was half-asleep. "Where were you last night?" he demanded. "We were supposed to meet after dark."

"I got sorta tied up," Grover said. "Did ya' kill anything?"

"No . . . I . . . didn't do so good," Mike answered. There was no point in telling him about the buck.

"Well, I did!" Grover said victoriously. "I got me a nice'n . . . a big eight-pointer!"

"Where?" Mike asked. "What time?"

"Down at the soybean field where I was huntin'," Grover lied. "I got 'im late yesterdee evenin'. . . about a half-hour 'fore dark."

Mike Fletcher was silent. His blood pressure was on the rise.

"Looks like you owe me a rifle," Grover continued. "When can I come get it? Oh, yeah, by the way, guess what?"

"What?"

"The buck I killed . . . he only had three legs. You oughta see 'im. His front leg is clean gone just over his knee. Somebody musta' done shot it off last year! Don't that beat all!"

# The Gift of the White Deer

## Chapter 14

### Part I

"Can we keep hunting just a little while longer, Grampa?" the boy asked. "Ple-e-ase? It's such a great day to be in the woods. Can we try to find just one more squirrel before we have to go in?"

"I wish we could," the old man told his grandson. He looked away from the boy's pleading brown eyes and pretended to be looking up in the trees. "You see those black clouds rolling in behind us, don't you? That rain's not gonna hold off much longer. It's already startin' to sprinkle. If we go home wet, your grandmother'll skin us alive!

"Anyway, we've had a humdinger of a morning," the man continued. "Eight bushytails. More than enough for some good fixings. Gotta leave some for next time. This is about all your old grandma can handle at one time. They'll be plenty more days ahead to hun. . . ." His voice broke slightly.

"You mean if we're not out deer hunting, right?" Scotty Riley asked his grandfather. He grinned broadly. "After deer season starts, there won't be much time to do any squirrel hunting. I'm planning on hunting every single day over the Thanksgiving and Christmas holidays unless we luck up and get Old Ironsides early."

Gus Riley fought hard to keep the tears from welling up in his eyes. A lump was forming in his throat, making it difficult to speak. He continued to look up in the trees so his grandson wouldn't notice. If the boy did notice, he was doing a good job of not letting on. Suddenly Gus saw movement in the top of a tall pine tree about forty yards down the ridge from where they were standing.

"I think I see one," Gus said, pointing to the top of the pine. "Tell you what. You stay here, and I'll go down and circle around the other side of the tree and try to get his attention. If he shows on your side, you know what to do. But we have to hurry. This'll have to be the last one of the day."

"OK, Grampa," the boy said. "I'll hide behind this tree so he can't see me."

Gus hurried off down the hill, making a wide detour around the pine tree. Scotty stepped behind a small oak and started searching the top of the pine for movement. He immediately saw the quick jerking motion of the squirrel's tail high up on a limb in the canopy of the tree. The squirrel had flattened itself on the top of the limb the moment it saw Gus walking down the ridge. Scotty could not see its body. All he could see was the methodical twitching of the long *S*-shaped tail. The boy propped his .22 rifle against the side of the tree to help hold it steady as Gus had taught him. Then he waited. Ideally, if their strategy worked, the moment Gus got around the tree, the squirrel would edge itself around the limb and offer Scotty a shot.

Gus was nearly out of sight when Scotty heard something moving through the leaves directly behind him. It sounded just like a person walking through the woods. The noise was unnerving because it was so close. Scotty whirled around without thinking. His mouth fell open in disbelief. Standing ten feet away was a four-month-old fawn frozen in its tracks. With huge round eyes, the small deer was staring nervously at the thing before it that had made such a sudden and unexpected movement. The fawn's much larger mother was standing thirty feet behind it, also poised like a statue.

To see a live deer in the woods at this distance was an amazing piece of luck for a boy just learning how to be a hunter. Even more amazing, though, was the fact that this was no ordinary fawn. The half-grown deer was solid white! For a brief instant, Scotty's eyes and the big brown eyes of the fawn—the only color Scotty could detect on the deer's body other than white—locked together. Then, without warning, the alarmed doe snorted loudly and crashed off through the woods.

The fawn was right on her heels. As the doe ran, she continued to snort in quick, loud nasal outbursts every time she exhaled. Scotty's heart was pounding like a drum. He could see bright flashes of white weaving through the trees as the fawn chased after its mother.

Scotty was still shaking when Gus walked back up the hill.

"What happened?" Gus asked. "Didn't you see the squirrel? He came around on your side of the limb and sat there for the longest time. Then he disappeared. Must be a cavity up in that tree."

"Grampa, have you ever seen a white deer?" Scotty asked excitedly.

"No, can't say that I have," Gus answered. "Why?"

"I just saw one, Grampa! He was solid white, and he was standing right there. I mean, he was solid white all over!"

"Is that a fact?" Gus said. "I thought I heard a deer snorting up above you."

"That was his mother," Scotty said. "He was with his mother. They walked right up behind me. That close! He was so white I thought he was a goat at first. But then I saw his mother, and I knew he was a deer."

"Was there another fawn with the doe?" Gus asked. "They usually have two little ones, you know—twins."

"No, sir. He was the only one I saw."

"Something probably happened to the other one," Gus said. "If it was white also, something probably got it. Something will probably get this one, too. By the way, what makes you so certain he was a *he?*"

"I don't know. I just thought he was, that's all. He could have been a doe fawn, but I'm pretty sure he was a little buck."

"Well, I'll be," Gus said. "That's a real unusual sight around these parts. Pete Barkley swore he saw a piebald yearling down by the river a year or two back. Pete said it was standing behind a bush, watching him. The pitiful little critter thought it was completely hidden from sight, but because it was almost all white, it stood out like a sore thumb. I've never seen a solid white deer around here, or a piebald."

Then, as an afterthought, Gus added, "Actually I did see a white squirrel in the backyard one time. Poor little rascal. He didn't have a chance. A hawk got him. Took him right off the side of the tree near the feeder one morning. A big redtail. Your grandmother was horrified. But white things generally don't do well in nature. The survival rate isn't very good. Tell me, was this fawn white all over, or did he have any patches of gray on his body?"

"He was white all over, Grampa. He was as white as the sheets hanging on Gramma's clothesline."

"Could you tell if he had pink eyes and ears?" Gus asked.

"He had big brown eyes, for sure. He was only ten feet away, and he stared right at me."

"Then he couldn't have been an albino," Gus said. "Albinos have pink eyes and pink hoofs."

"What's the difference?" Scotty asked.

"Well, a true albino has a color deficiency in the pigments in its body," Gus explained. "That's why an albino always has pink eyes. Albinos occur in just about every kind of animal. Humans, too. But a piebald is different. A piebald has a genetic mutation—bad genes, that is—and that's what causes him to be either white all over or partially white. Also, since it's basically bad genes that cause the problem in the first place, a piebald deer usually has a lot of other things wrong with it, too: curvature of the spine, a bad overbite, things like that. They're genetically inferior, and they usually don't last long in the woods. Most hunters shoot 'em on sight."

"Why do they do that?" Scotty asked. "I couldn't have shot that little fawn for anything."

"Some people consider them a real trophy," Gus answered. "Unfortunately, anything rare or different in nature is a trophy to a lot of hunters. And a piebald deer is definitely different, so it's an automatic trophy."

"That doesn't seem fair," Scotty said.

"You're right," Gus agreed. "There's an old Indian saying that I'm right fond of that sort of hits the nail on the head. It goes like this: *Whatever the white man is afraid of or doesn't understand, he destroys.* We've been destroying things we don't understand for centuries, especially predators like wolves and mountain lions. We're just now reaching the point where we're showing animals like wolves a little respect."

"Now that they're almost gone," Scotty added. "The Indians worshipped unusual things in nature like the white buffalo, didn't they?"

"Yes," Gus answered. "The Indians worshipped everything in nature. Even a blade of grass was sacred to them."

"But we kill normal deer all the time," Scotty said. "On purpose."

"That's different," Gus said. "We eat the deer we kill, and we hunt 'em to keep their numbers down. It's called *good management*. But I understand what you're saying. It does seem like there's sort of a double standard somewhere. But at least we know that deer numbers are in good shape. We're not hurting 'em when we hunt 'em; we're actually helping 'em. But it was different with the buffalo. They were slaughtered by the thousands—on purpose. The government figured that if it could get rid of the Indians' food supply, they'd be forced to come into the reservations. And it worked."

"It almost wiped out all the buffalo, too," Scotty said. "And no one really cared about that."

"What's even worse is that it starved a lot of innocent human beings," Gus said.

"Grampa?"

"Yes, boy?"

"Do you think I'm like a white deer?"

"What do you mean?"

"Well, I'm different, too."

"No, you're not. Just because you've been a little under the weather lately doesn't mean you're different. Don't let me hear you talk like that anymore."

"I'm sorry, Grampa."

"Apology accepted," Gus said. "Come on, let's head to the truck. I think the bottom's gettin' ready to fall out. Do you feel like walking fast? Here, I'll carry your rifle. I'm afraid we're gonna get wet if we don't hurry."

"Grampa?"

"Yes, boy?"

"Do you think that little white deer could have been a guardian angel?"

"You never know about things like that," Gus said with a big grin. "If he is, he's probably *your* guardian angel—sent down here to keep an eye on you!"

Scotty smiled broadly. Gus put his arm on the boy's shoulder and they started walking toward the truck.

## Part II

Scotty's grandmother was standing in the doorway of the screened-in porch with her hands on her hips as the truck pulled up behind the two-story farmhouse and rolled to a stop. It was pouring rain. Scotty jumped out and ran up the steps and through the screen door that she was holding open.

"We got eight squirrels, Gramma!" he said excitedly, giving her a big hug. "Four apiece. And I saw a white deer. It was a fawn, and it walked right up to me. It was so neat. Grampa and I decided he had to be a guardian angel. Also, we found Old Ironsides's tracks down by the creek crossing in the mud. Grampa's gonna build us a stand down there in that big grove of oaks near the river. We'll get him for sure in a couple of weeks! Can we have squirrel stew for dinner tonight?"

"I don't see why not," she answered. "You're not wet, are you? I told your grandfather not to let you stay out in the weather and get soaked. Go inside by the fireplace and warm yourself. I don't want you getting a chill."

Gus grabbed the brim of his hat and pulled it down tightly. Then he, too, jumped out of the truck and made a run for the porch. He ran up the steps and through the doorway, carrying both .22 rifles under his arm. Hazel Riley looked at him without speaking. He walked past her, across the porch, and into the house. Scotty was hanging his wet camouflage jacket on a wooden hook in the hallway.

"Do you want me to clean the rifles now, Grampa?" he asked.

"That's a good idea," Gus answered. "I'll dress the squirrels out on the porch so your grandmother can start on the meat.

Why don't you grab a ramrod and run some oil through both guns. They're really not that dirty, but they did get a few raindrops on 'em. It's OK to clean 'em by the fireplace."

"Will you save the skins for me?" Scotty asked. "I'll salt 'em down later."

"All eight of 'em?"

"Yes, please."

"How many squirrel skins do you plan on keeping?"

"Every one we shoot. You know how the Indians were; they didn't waste a thing."

"Yeah, but what are you gonna do with all those squirrel skins you've been accumulating? You must have a hundred."

"I don't know. Maybe make a fur coat someday. I like squirrel skins. They tan easily, and I like the way they smell. And squirrel tails are great for tying flies."

Hazel Riley helped her grandson find the box of gun-cleaning gear in the closet. Then she went back into the kitchen and started cutting up some vegetables for the squirrel stew. Later on, after Gus had brought her the meat, and after a big pot of stew was simmering on the stove, she walked back to the parlor in the rear of the house and sat down at her writing desk by the large bay window. Gus and Scotty were still in the den.

She stared out the window for several minutes, noticing the way the last rays of the setting sun were highlighting the spectacular orange-red leaves of the slanting sassafras tree in the backyard. The rain had stopped as suddenly as it had begun. Already, most of the sky had cleared to a dull blue. She sat motionless for a while. Then she picked up a pen and reached for her journal. During the past months, she had gotten in the habit of writing in her journal two or three times a week.

"Friday, September 24, 6:30 P.M.

"The rain has stopped now, and in its place, a steady sprinkling of bright yellow maple leaves float gently to the ground outside my window in the backyard as if they don't have a care in the world. What a beautiful sight! This is one of the most colorful autumns I can remember in years, and the leaves have changed so early. Never have they changed this early before! Everything is aglow with color—the oaks, the maples, the sassafras; even the poison ivy leaves on the fence out near the shed are a brilliant red.

"Gus and Scotty just came in from squirrel hunting during a drenching rain shower. I was so mad at Gus for taking such a chance with our precious little boy. Scotty's blood counts have been dangerously low all week, and his resistance to infection is practically nil. Life is so terribly fragile. I fear we could lose him so easily. He has gotten very thin and pale, but he is so full of spirit. Hunting with Gus is the most important thing in the world to him right now. How could anyone deny him that one little bit of pleasure?

"At this very moment, he and Gus are in the den by the warmth of the fire watching a new deer hunting video that Gus just bought for him. Gus has always made him clean the rifles out on the back porch, but today, after they came in, he made an exception. He let Scotty clean them in the den by the fireplace. I know they had a glorious time together. They brought home eight squirrels, and I've never seen such radiance in a boy's face! He saw a white deer in the woods today, and he was so excited. Just think—a white deer in our woods. How unusual! It was a fawn. Scotty told Gus he thought the little deer might be a guardian angel because it slipped right up on him before he saw it.

"Scotty asked me to cook the squirrels for supper. I am in the process of doing that now, gladly! It's been three full weeks since he's been well enough to go out with Gus, three long weekends since he's been able to spend any time with us. God bless his wonderful parents for sharing him with us. Time is so precious now, and it means everything for him to stay with us.

"Dear God, he's so excited about deer season. He can't wait! In addition to seeing the white deer, they found the tracks of the big buck he and Gus plan to hunt this year. 'Old Ironsides' they call him—so named because Gus and our closest neighbor, Pete Barkley, have taken shots at him during the past few seasons. Both men swear the buckshot just bounces right off that invincible animal, exactly as the cannonballs did a long time ago off the sides of the ship of the same name during the war with the British.

"'Between the two of us, I reckon Pete and I have slung more lead at that ol' buck than the British did at Old Ironsides during the Revolution!' Gus often tells anyone who will listen.

"Everyone in our part of the county is talking about this buck. They say he leads a charmed life. They also say he is the largest buck seen in these parts in many a season. And to think, he lives on our farm! He must have a magnificent set of antlers. Gus, bless his heart, and Pete, too, each admit they probably never came close to hitting the big buck because of their intense excitement. I'm sure the real culprit behind those missed shots was buck fever. I'm really glad they did miss, though, because hunting Old Ironsides is all Scotty talks about now.

"Try as he might, Gus has never brought home a truly big buck, although there are plenty of them on the farm. He sees bucks all the time in late summer and late winter, but never during hunting season. I know he would give his eyeteeth to bring down a deer like Old Ironsides. More important, though, I know he'd give an arm and a leg to see that Scotty gets a chance to hunt him. Scotty is so excited about spending opening day in a tree with Gus. He lives for that day, just under a month away now. Oh, dear Lord, please grant him that one request. Please give him some time to enjoy deer season. Is that too much to ask?

"I don't know how Scotty's parents do it. My blessed daughter is so willing to share him with us—unselfishly. If I were in her shoes, I don't think I could ever make that kind of sacrifice. Each day is so precious to all of us now. I don't think I could give him up for an entire weekend as they do so willingly. Yet they gladly make the sacrifice week after week when he is well enough, knowing how important it is to him, while also knowing just how uncertain and short the future could be. Truly the Good Lord has blessed us all. What lucky grandparents Gus and I are to have such a grandson!

"A month seems like such a long time, particularly with so many uncertainties ahead. Yet I know the time will pass in the blink of an eye. The weather is already turning cold. He is so pale. Judging from the sparkle in his eyes and the excitement in his voice, though, you'd never guess in a million years that the terrible cancer that has ravaged his small body has taken such a heavy toll during the past few months. Except for his unusual paleness, you would never know that he had ever been sick a day in his life. He handles it so well, and he has such a marvelous attitude.

"Oh, God, I still believe in miracles, and this family needs a miracle so badly. Why my little boy, of all people? Why not one of us? Gus and I have both lived long lives. He is so young and caring, so innocent, so full of goodness. Couldn't you please take someone who is rotten to the core and no good, instead?

"The yellow leaves outside continue to float downward in slow motion as if in a dream, as though the maple trees will always provide an endless supply. The leaves now blanket the yard under the trees and give warmth to the earth like a bright yellow quilt. Only the hand of a true Master could paint such a splendid scene. But I know this is only a temporary illusion. What will happen after all the leaves have turned brown?"

## Part III

"Blow! Take a deep breath and blow as hard as you can! But make a big wish first!"

Quincy, Scotty's eleven-year-old sister, was yelling excitedly. All of the lights had been turned out in the kitchen. The entire family was crowding around the big kitchen table. Scotty was the only one sitting, and a large chocolate cake had just been placed in front of him. The family began to sing "Happy Birthday." The glow of fourteen burning candles atop the cake gave Scotty's face an eerie look. Following Quincy's advice, he took a deep breath and blew. All fourteen candles were quickly extinguished in a large puff of smoke. Everyone clapped and yelled. The lights came on, and Hazel put a stack of small plates on the table.

"That means your wish is going to come true!" Quincy said loudly. "What was your wish? Please tell us."

"He can't," Scotty's mother said. "If he tells what his wish was, it may not come true."

"Oh, yes it will!" Scotty stated. "I *know* this one is going to come true. My wish is that either me or Grampa will get a shot at Old Ironsides. And I just know it's going to happen!"

Hazel handed Scotty a flat cake knife. "Would you like to do the honors?" she asked.

"Yes, Gramma," he answered. "I want to cut my birthday cake."

"Can I have a big piece?" Quincy begged. "Gramma's chocolate is my favorite."

"Everyone can have a big piece tonight," Scotty declared. "Because it's not just my birthday we're celebrating. Only two more weeks until opening day! And then, Old Ironsides had better look out! The woods will no longer be safe. Grampa and I plan to hunt him from now till the cows come home if necessary! Right, Grampa?"

Scotty's mother and father glanced at each other. The anguish clearly showed on their tired faces.

"If that's the way it's gonna be, I reckon you might better have this with you when you head to the woods," Gus stated, opening the pantry door and reaching inside. He grabbed a long, heavy package wrapped in camouflage wrapping paper that he had carefully leaned against the inside pantry wall earlier in the afternoon. "Happy Birthday, boy!" He handed the long package to Scotty.

Scotty knew right away that it was a rifle. "Oh, Grampa . . ."

He tore the paper away. The scoped rifle was inside an expensive, padded leather case. Scotty unzipped the case and carefully let the rifle slide out. "Oh, Grampa. A Remington Mountain Rifle. And . . . let me guess . . . a .280?"

"You got it!" Gus answered. "Now there won't be any excuse for missing like your old Grandpa has been known to do once or twice in the past with his antique shotgun."

"Wow! Your very first deer rifle," Quincy said. "I sure hope you'll be well enough to use it."

Quincy's mother glared at her daughter.

"You better believe I'll be well enough to use it!" Scotty said happily, ignoring his sister. "This is just what I've been wanting. A lightweight Remington .280 with a Kevlar stock and a 3X to 9X scope. Thanks, Grampa! This is the best present I've ever gotten in my whole life!"

Scotty paused from his cake-cutting duties to open his other presents—all hunting-related items. In addition to an insulated camouflage coat and a pair of insulated, calf-high rubber boots from his parents, there was a how-to book about deer hunting from Quincy, a new rifle-cleaning kit from Hazel, and two boxes of bullets and a package of cardboard targets from Gus. All of his presents were wonderful, but he couldn't take his eyes off the new rifle. The cake-cutting quickly passed to Scotty's mother as he sat in his chair caressing the rifle affectionately and looking through the scope.

"You'd better cut yourself a piece of cake and get some of this vanilla ice cream before it disappears," Quincy warned. "Gramma's chocolate cake doesn't last long around this family!"

Scotty sat in his chair without speaking. Chocolate cake had long been one of his all-time favorites, but despite the special occasion, he was unable to eat a single bite. The medication he was currently taking made him feel nauseated around most foods. He knew that if he tried to eat a piece of cake now he would probably get sick to his stomach. But that didn't dampen his spirits. On this special night, there were more important things in the world than chocolate cake.

"Can we go shooting first thing in the morning, Grampa?" Scotty asked.

## Part IV

"Saturday, October 9, 10:30 A.M.

"We celebrated Scotty's fourteenth birthday at our house last night because Gus wanted to give Scotty his new rifle. It was supposed to be such a happy occasion, and it was, in many ways, but much of the time I found myself feeling as if I were riding in the front seat of a speeding, out-of-control roller coaster. How can that be? How can a person's emotional state reach such a high plateau one moment and then sink to the bottom of the well the next? It's a mystery to me. I always thought life was supposed to be one way or the other—with peaks and valleys at certain intervals—but never this crazy dash to some unknown and terrifying destination.

"God, how he loves his new rifle! He and Gus are out back shooting right now as I write these words. So far, I've heard six shots. He has done remarkably well for the past two weeks, holding his own, but how long will this last? From all indications, his treatments have been going very poorly.

"Scotty lives to hunt and fish with Gus. He has grown to be a dedicated outdoorsman just like his grandfather, a chip off the old block. He's spent the last three weekends in a row with us, and he has completely taken possession of the downstairs bedroom, which was once a guest room. Gus says it's just like having one of our own children back in the house again.

"Scotty's room is filled with his most treasured possessions—deer posters, outdoor magazines, books about Indians, fishing tackle, bullets, animal skins, arrowheads, and his beloved new rifle, hanging on the wall on a special deer-hoof rack that Gus made for him. Oh, how I love to go in there and sit on the edge of the bed and look at his treasures when he is not around. He reads and saves every outdoor magazine he can get his hands on. He ties his own flies now, having learned from Gus, and Gus says they all are tiny works of art, better than anything he has ever produced himself.

"It seems so ironic now that he killed his first deer with Gus two seasons ago, when he was twelve, the very same week he was diagnosed with leukemia. I'll never forget that horrible time as long as I live. It all started out so happily but ended in such a nightmare. He was not feeling well that day. Nevertheless, he insisted on dragging his first buck out of the woods all by himself. It was a fine six-pointer. The world was sunny and bright on that crisp Saturday morning. But things quickly changed, and the dark clouds rolled in so unexpectedly.

"When he and Gus finally reached the house, Scotty was pale and exhausted. His once strong little arms, so tanned and well muscled from the previous summer, were badly bruised and sapped of strength. Then came the benumbing news, after two days of testing at the hospital. Our precious little boy had been stricken with leukemia. The treatment started immediately. His only comment was, "Well, at least I got to go deer hunting with Grampa before I got sick." Oh, how I wanted to sit down and cry when he said that, and I did, later that night, in the darkness as I lay in my bed.

"The remission that everyone prayed for lasted only six short months. And now, after nearly two years of fighting a valiant battle, Scotty's parents have been told that the situation is virtually hopeless.

"Oh, dear God, how can anything in this magnificent world be beyond hope, especially as we approach that special time of year when we celebrate the birth of our beloved Savior? Our little boy is so full of promise, with so many dreams, and he is so sure about hunting with Gus over the upcoming Thanksgiving and Christmas holidays. Despite everything, he still insists on attending school on days when he is able, and he does not want or expect any preferential treatment from anyone.

"Gus has suffered horribly throughout this thing, as we all have. He knows all too well that Scotty may not be here for Christmas. This knowledge eats away at him. With every day that passes, the toll seems to grow heavier in his sad eyes. Gus has always had such handsome eyes, but now they are so full of sadness and pain.

"Another shot was just fired. I'll bet anything my little boy just got a bull's-eye!"

## Part V

"Well, whatdaya' think?" Gus asked in the chilly predawn darkness. "All the comforts of home, ey?" He shone the small flashlight around the inside of the six-by-six foot enclosed tree blind that he had built fifteen feet off the ground in a sprawling white oak. The light illuminated two cushioned chairs and a small propane heater in one corner.

"It's fabulous, Grampa!" Scotty replied, looking around as he climbed up through the trapdoor in the floor. "It's the best stand I've ever seen, but then, it has to be since you built it! Tarzan himself would be jealous of this. He never had a tree house half this nice. It's like a small hotel in a tree."

"Well, in that case, maybe we should call her the Marshallville Hilton!" Gus said kiddingly. "As soon as it gets light, you'll be able to see the river. It's only about sixty yards out in front of us through the trees. Can you hear the water?"

"Yes," Scotty said. "Barely."

"Better go ahead and get some bullets in that rifle," Gus said. "It'll be light before you know it."

Gus held the light on Scotty's rifle as the boy deftly opened the bolt and slipped four shiny .280 cartridges into the magazine. He then slipped a fifth into the chamber of the rifle. He quietly closed the bolt and made sure the safety was on. Gus nodded in approval.

"Do you think we'll see him, Grampa?" Scotty asked. "Do you think we'll see Old Ironsides today?"

"You never know," Gus answered. "The rut is going full blast right now, and if he's gonna slip up and make a mistake, it oughta' be during the next two weeks while he's out doing his courtin'. And since the Marshallville Hilton is located right slap-dab in the middle of his favorite stomping grounds, and since I did a fair job of camouflaging it on the outside, if I do say so myself, it's just a matter of time before he comes by here.

"Whether or not that'll be today, though, who knows?" Gus continued. "But we do know he's living in the area. One of his primary trails runs between us and the river, and there're plenty of acorns on the ground everywhere. The acorn crop has been good this year, especially the white oaks, and the deer have been tearing this place up. I predict we'll see some deer today for sure, even if we don't see Old Ironsides. I suspect one or two of them will probably have horns. If you decide to take a smaller buck, you know it's OK with me."

"Thanks, Grampa," Scotty whispered. "But there's only one buck I'm interested in, and there's no mistaking who that is! We have a brand-new rifle and a brand-new tree stand to break in, and it's not going to be on some little scrunthead if I can help it. I've been waiting all summer for deer season to get here, and I'm not settling for anything less until one of us gets him—especially since we missed opening weekend. I *would* go and get sick on the most important weekend of the year!" He paused for a moment. Gus knew there was more coming.

"I'm sorry I made you miss opening day, Grampa," Scotty continued in the darkness. "You should have gone ahead and hunted without me over the weekend."

Gus's eyes welled up with water. He was thankful it was still dark. He cleared his throat quietly. "What? Bring in the new season without my favorite huntin' partner? How could I do that?"

"Easy," Scotty said. "I've tried so hard to stay well until deer season, but it seems like I've been sick all the time lately."

Gus put his arm around Scotty's shoulder. "You didn't miss anything over the weekend," he said. "Like I told you, that cold front coming through on Saturday messed up the hunting, anyway. It was awfully windy. So it's just as well we didn't hunt. Conditions are much better now than they were a few days ago."

There was a long silence. Then Scotty spoke.

"Grampa?"

"Yes, boy."

"Can we name our tree stand the Flint River Hilton instead of the Marshallville Hilton? There's something about the river that's always been special to me."

## Part VI

"Wednesday, November 24, 3:30 P.M.

"I am so worried. Twice now, during the past month, I thought we were going to lose him. He has grown so weak. He is in the hospital now and will probably spend the entire Thanksgiving weekend there. He is so disappointed. He had his heart set on hunting with Gus over Thanksgiving.

"I suppose this latest turn for the worse began back in October, only three days before deer season opened. Scotty developed a severe case of pneumonia and had to be hospitalized then, too. He made an amazing recovery, though. I think it was the result of his sheer determination to go hunting with Gus. But he missed opening day on Saturday, and he was so upset. He and Gus were finally able to go hunting the following Wednesday. They saw two small bucks, but Scotty would not shoot either of them. He insists on holding out for Old Ironsides. This really has Gus worried, because he says that Old Ironsides always seems to disappear every year as soon as hunting season begins. Gus thinks the chances of seeing the big buck are very slim. He hopes that Scotty might decide to shoot a different one.

"Back in early October, Gus began building a wonderful tree blind in a large white oak tree down by the river so that Scotty can be completely out of the weather whenever they go deer hunting. It is enclosed on all four sides, with a special trapdoor entrance in the floor. Gus even put a small heater in it for cold mornings. It has long, narrow shooting windows on all four sides and a fine roof.

"Gus is so proud of his handiwork. It is such a wonderful monument to Scotty. He drove me down to see it, and he tried to get me to climb up into it, but I refused. I probably would have broken my neck if I had tried. Gus went to great lengths to stain the wood the color of the trees around it, and he even draped the sides with camouflage netting and Spanish moss. The tree it sits in looks more like a live oak than a white oak. The blind itself is built between several thick limbs that grow upward like the outreaching tentacles of an octopus and help hide it very well, particularly from the ground. Gus says it has all the comforts of home. Scotty can even sleep in it if he wants to. Gus is convinced that it is *just what the doctor ordered* for our precious boy. They have fondly named their stand the *Flint River Hilton.*

"Scotty's one and only desire now is to get well enough to leave the hospital so that he and Gus can hunt for Old Ironsides. Oh, precious Lord, please grant him that wish."

## Part VII

They arrived at the stand about 10:30 A.M., against Scotty's bitter protests. Scotty had been up since 5:00 A.M., wanting to go to the stand before daylight. But the weather had turned unseasonably cold for mid-December, and Gus had insisted on waiting until midmorning. He assured his grandson that reaching the stand later in the morning, after it had warmed up, would not matter.

"Deer movement will still be good," he had argued.

Now he hoped and prayed he would be right.

Scotty had dreamed about Old Ironsides during the night. While he and Gus were eating the bacon and eggs that Gus had fixed for breakfast, Scotty declared unequivocally that, on this day, they were going to encounter the legendary buck.

They had been sitting in the stand less than an hour when they heard a loud commotion in a dense thicket over by the river. As they watched, a large doe suddenly stepped out of the thicket and started walking toward the stand. Moments later, a dark-antlered, eight-point buck appeared and began to follow the doe. The buck had his nose to the ground, and it was obvious that all of his attention was focused on his chosen mate.

"He's a mighty good deer," Gus whispered. "Take him when he gets out in front of those trees if you want to. We may not see another buck this good anytime soon."

Scotty calmly put the cross hairs of his scope on the buck's shoulder and slowly swung the rifle with the deer as it moved from left to right. Even though the peak of the rut was technically over, having occurred back in mid-November, almost a month earlier, the buck still had a thickly swollen neck. Every few seconds it would stop and lift its nose up into the air to test the wind, but Gus was confident that the wind was in their favor.

"I think I'll wait for Old Ironsides," Scotty whispered with deliberate determination, steadily following the buck in his scope until it finally disappeared.

"I figured you might say that," Gus answered.

"I hope you're not disappointed with me, Grampa," Scotty whispered.

The words were no sooner out of Scotty's mouth than they both heard another disturbance in the same thicket. Before Gus could respond to what Scotty had said, he looked over in time to see a massive buck stepping out of the thicket into the open. The buck paused to survey the scene in front of him like a stately king looking over his royal domain. There was no question about the identity of this great animal. It was Old Ironsides in all his glory!

"That's him!" Scotty whispered. "I knew he was going to come!"

"Go ahead and ease off your safety," Gus whispered excitedly.

With nerves of steel, Scotty released the safety catch for the second time in less than five minutes. He slowly swung the rifle around and settled the cross hairs on the white throat patch of the giant whitetail. It would have been an easy straight-on shot at less than forty yards, but Scotty hesitated. The huge deer began to tiptoe across the oak clearing, passing broadside in front of the stand just as the first two deer had done. The buck was completely unaware of any possible danger.

"What a rack of horns!" Gus whispered. "His back tines must be thirteen inches long! Go ahead. Bust him!"

Indeed, the buck's rack was so large and out of proportion to the deer's body that it seemed to rock from side to side like a heavy basket as the animal walked. Scotty followed the deer's progress while Gus held his breath, waiting for the inevitable shot that would shatter the morning calm. The shot never came. The huge buck at last walked off into brush and disappeared, just as the smaller buck had done.

After a few moments, Scotty looked up from his rifle and smiled.

"Looks like he gave us the slip!" he declared. "Wasn't he a sight?"

He looked over at his grandfather. Gus was stunned. The two hunters sat quietly in the stand without speaking. At length, Gus broke the long silence.

"Just tell me one thing, boy," he said. "Why? I don't understand. For months, all you've talked about was getting a crack at Old Ironsides. You passed up several smaller bucks, and then you had him dead to rights. You had him on a gold platter. You know you might not ever get another chance like that. Why didn't you shoot?"

Scotty's eyes continued to search the woods in front of him as if he were waiting for Old Ironsides to return. Another long silence passed before he spoke.

"I don't want you to get upset with me, Grampa, but there's something I need to tell you," Scotty began. "I really wanted to shoot him—more than anything in the world. For almost two years now, almost as long as I've been sick, I've been hearing about Old Ironsides, the legendary buck in Macon County. You and I found his tracks and all those big rubs he made, and I wanted to kill him so bad I could taste it. Especially with my new rifle. I could just see him hanging on the wall in my room.

"But when I got him in the scope, something came over me. I was calm and steady, and I was all ready to squeeze the trigger. I knew I had him, and I knew I couldn't miss, and I knew he was mine forever. But then I started hearing this little voice inside. The little voice kept asking, 'If you shoot him, then what?'

"This is hard for me to say, Grampa, and it's hard for you to have to hear, but I know that pretty soon, I'm not going to be here to enjoy Old Ironsides and give him the respect he deserves. Oh, I could have given him to you, and you could have gotten him mounted for me, but what would you and Gramma do with him after that? Would you want to hang him in the house as a constant reminder of me? Would you want to tell people that I killed him during our last few days together?"

"Don't talk like that, boy," Gus said.

"I know this is upsetting to you, Grampa, but it's OK," Scotty continued. "The minute I saw him, the minute I knew it was him for sure and I knew he was mine, I really didn't want to shoot him. I didn't have to shoot him anymore. Seeing him in my scope was enough. Killing him wasn't important, Grampa, because I knew I didn't have the right to shoot a buck like Old Ironsides if I wasn't going to be here to enjoy him.

"I started thinking, *My grandfather's been hunting deer all his life, and he's the one who really deserves a buck like Old Ironsides, not me.* I really wanted *you* to shoot him, Grampa. But everything was happening so fast, and so many things were going through my brain. . . Then he stepped back into the brush before I had time to tell you to shoot.

"It's like you always say, Grampa . . . there will be another day. You and Old Ironsides will meet again. I know it in my heart, just like I knew we were going to see him today!" Scotty's voice had reached a high pitch in his excitement. He looked back at his grandfather.

"There's more, Grampa, and this is the most important part. For the longest time now, I've really been scared about what's going to happen. For a while, I was so scared that I couldn't sleep at night, and I'd stay awake all night long thinking about it. I've always tried to be a fighter like everyone wanted me to be, and I tried to have a good attitude. I didn't want this thing to happen any more than anybody else did, and I was determined to beat it. So I fought it as hard as I could."

"I know boy," Gus said softly. "No one could have fought any harder or more bravely than you have."

"But do you want to know why I fought it so hard, Grampa? It's not because I'm so brave or courageous; it's because I didn't know how to do anything else. I didn't know how to throw in the towel, Grampa, do you understand? I've been so scared because I didn't know how to give up. I've never been afraid of what might happen, but I've always been afraid of giving up—of losing the fight, because I didn't want to let anybody down. So I fought it as hard as I could. But just now something happened. The moment I put my scope on Old Ironsides, I knew everything was going to be all right. I knew that, at last, it was all right for me to give up. Something changed inside me, Grampa, and now, I'm not scared anymore—at least for myself.

"But I am still scared for you and Gramma and Mom and Dad and Quincy. I know *I'm* gonna be all right, but I don't know that the rest of my family will be all right, and that's what's been worrying the hell out of me for so long now. That's what I need to know, Grampa, and then I'll be ready for whatever happens. I need to know that everybody's going to be all right. That's why I couldn't shoot Old Ironsides today. He's not rightfully mine to shoot. He's yours, and if you shoot him, it'll mean that you're gonna be OK in the future, no matter what happens."

Gus had to look away. The unswayable old woodsman, the man who had shed very few tears during his entire life, could not hold back. He was speechless, and the tears were flowing freely down his face. Scotty leaned his rifle in the corner of the blind and reached for Gus. The two hunters held each other for a long time.

"Since when did you get old enough to start cussing, young man?" Gus finally asked, trying to be lighthearted and serious at the same time.

"About two years ago," Scotty answered softly.

*Oh, God in heaven,* Gus thought. *We've been sitting around all this time feeling sorry for ourselves while you've been carrying the weight of the world on your small shoulders.*

## Part VIII

"Christmas Day, December 25, 5:45 P.M.

"It's getting dark outside now. I've been sitting here for nearly three hours gazing out the window and watching the snow fall. Can you imagine? A white Christmas in Georgia! I'll bet this hasn't happened in a hundred years! We seldom get snow this far south, but they're predicting at least four inches tonight from a freak storm that has blown up from the Gulf of Mexico. The ground is covered with snow, and the stark, bare trees against the gray winter background are truly a beautiful sight. While the birds and squirrels have been sparring with each other out on the feeder, trying to claim a prize of bread and sunflower seeds, I've been staring at a blank page, trying to make appropriate words flow from my pen, and trying to make sense of all that has happened over the past few days.

"Until a little while ago, no words would come, and no sense could be made of anything. But about thirty minutes ago, Gus came tearing up the driveway honking his horn wildly. Pete Barkley was with him, along with Pete's nephew, who is visiting over Christmas. Gus had a huge buck in the back of his truck. From the sheer size of its antlers, I knew immediately that it was Old Ironsides. Of course, I had to go outside for a few minutes to look at him and congratulate Gus. Pete says he is definitely a record of some kind. His antlers are simply enormous! Can you imagine? My Gus finally got Old Ironsides!

"We lost our precious little boy four days before Christmas. He passed away peacefully in his room here in our home, with all of his beloved family around him. Gus took it as hard as he's ever taken anything in his life.

"I find it strangely ironic that Scotty's entire two-year illness seems to have been so closely linked to deer season. He got sick just over two years ago, right after he shot his very first buck with Gus on opening day. Things went poorly from the start, and Scotty relapsed six months later after an all too brief remission. But what kept him going that first year was the promise of deer season ahead and the hope of being able to hunt the buck that he and Gus called Old Ironsides. The two of them never did see Old Ironsides last season, but they had a wonderful time just being together.

"Then came this year and all of the trials and tribulations that go with any serious illness. Scotty's one and only goal this year was to be well enough to hunt this season as well, particularly over the Christmas holidays. That was his single-minded objective, although he seemed to know that Christmas might be an impossible goal to reach. As summer ended and September drifted into October, he seemed to will his tired little body to continue the battle throughout November and the early weeks of December.

"Looking back now, I suppose the beginning of the end started just before the opening weekend of deer season this year. Again, how ironic! Scotty had been growing continuously weaker since the end of August. He insisted on trying to attend school, just as he insisted on staying with us whenever possible on the weekends. He felt so miserable much of the time, but he lived to be with Gus. His condition was so unpredictable. One day he'd be fine; the next he'd be dangerously ill. Several times he became so sick that the doctors offered little hope. But each time that happened, he somehow bounced back, as if by a miracle, and within a few short days he'd always be ready to go hunting with Gus again.

"After he became too sick to attend school, he wanted to stay with us all the time. That was terribly hard on his parents, but they understood the special relationship he and Gus had developed. How could they deny him something so important to him? Even though they knew that time was getting short, they unselfishly allowed him to spend most of his last two months in our home. They came by to see him whenever possible, often spending the night themselves.

"Then, when it was clear to everyone that the end was near, Scotty refused to go to the hospital. He wanted to remain in his room in our home. That was a big shock to his parents, but it may have also been a blessing in disguise, because it spared them a great deal of pain. And even though it was torture for Gus and me, we wouldn't have had it any other way. During the last three weeks, we had a wonderful lady from hospice who stayed all the time, and her presence made all the difference in the world. She was so caring, and she and Scotty hit it off right away. She read to him, mostly deer hunting stories.

"Gus and Scotty hunted together for the last time on December 12. It was on that day that Scotty saw Old Ironsides and refused to shoot him. Right after that our precious boy took another turn for the worse. But, as always, he made one of his miraculous recoveries. By the 19th he had bounced back, just as he had done so many times before. There was even renewed talk of being well enough to go hunting over the Christmas holidays. But things got bad again, and suddenly he was gone—just like that. He was so unafraid, so sure of where he was going. His foremost concern was knowing that his family would be all right after he was gone. Of course, Gus took it the hardest. He immediately proclaimed that he would never go deer hunting again.

"Everything happened very rapidly after that. Scotty's service was held two days ago. I suppose it went as well as could be expected. Once that hurdle was overcome, everyone in the family decided to do everything possible to try to have as normal a Christmas as we could under the circumstances—primarily for little Quincy's sake. So the children came back over this morning with Quincy, as is their usual custom on Christmas Day, to open presents and have lunch. That's when Gus's great revelation took place.

"Scotty wanted very badly to give Christmas presents to everyone in the family. He'd always been such a thoughtful young man, and he always gave special presents every year. But this year time simply ran out for him before he could do any shopping. Ever since his birthday party back in October, when Gus had given him his new rifle, however, Scotty was determined to do something extra special for Gus for Christmas. He was full of grand ideas, but he eventually settled on taking ten of his best squirrel skins and making Gus a squirrel skin handwarmer. I must confess that when he came to me for help, I was less than enthusiastic. But he needed my help in sewing the skins together, and how could his old grandmother say no?

"Scotty's furry little handwarmer turned out to be a work of art! It's about twelve inches long, and it's attached to a nylon belt that clips around the waist. The inner lining is filled with goose down that we took out of an old pillow, but the very inside itself is lined with more than two dozen bushy squirrel tails, an idea that was Scotty's entirely. Because of those squirrel tails, it is very warm and cozy inside where you place your hands. When Gus opened it, he was deeply affected. Perhaps it was the handwritten card on the outside of the package that got to him the most.

The card simply read,

> Merry Christmas to Grampa—
>
> Since Old Ironsides belongs to both of us, please use this while you are hunting for him on cold, frosty mornings. When you do, think about all the great times we had together!
>
> Love always,
> Scotty
> P.S. My new rifle is now yours!

"After he opened the package, Gus had to leave the room. He said very little during lunch, but every once in a while he would get up and go over by the Christmas tree and pick up the handwarmer and hold it in his hands.

"The children finally left around 2 P.M., and it started to snow lightly. That's when Gus came into the kitchen where I was cleaning up. He was holding the squirrel skin handwarmer in one hand and Scotty's rifle in the other.

"'I'm going to the woods for a while,' he announced. 'Conditions are perfect, and I think that's what Scotty would want me to do on Christmas Day.'

"Gus went on to say that whenever it snows in the South, the deer do crazy things because they're not used to seeing snow on the ground.

"'This might be just the thing that'll make a buck like Old Ironsides slip up and make another mistake,' he told me.

"For the first time in many days, there was a new glimmer of life in my Gus's eyes. Gus put on his old coveralls, got in his truck, and drove off. I don't think for one minute that he ever expected to see Old Ironsides. I think he simply wanted to be by himself for a while, and no place on earth seemed more appropriate or more special to him than the tree stand he had built for Scotty. Apparently, though, the hunting gods had other ideas for Gus on this holy day. And he was right about the snow. He said he saw deer playing in the white stuff everywhere as he drove to the stand.

"Gus said he had been sitting in the stand for about thirty minutes, watching the snow fall and enjoying the unusual scenery around him. By then the snow was beginning to accumulate on the branches of the trees, and Gus said it looked like a postcard from New England. Gus said he happened to be looking at one spot in the snow-covered woods in particular, where everything was solid white, but there was really nothing there—nothing alive, that is. Then all of a sudden, that patch of nothingness began to move. It was a white deer, as pure white as the snow itself. It had been standing there all along, but because it blended so well with the whiteness around it, Gus had not seen it.

"Gus knew at once that it was the same little white fawn that Scotty had seen back in September while they were squirrel hunting. The fawn stood there for some time. Its mother was nowhere to be seen. Gus finally raised Scotty's rifle and started looking at it through the scope. Lo and behold, he could see two little nubbins on the deer's head. It was a button buck! Gus said it was an amazing sight to see a pure white deer standing in the pure white snow.

"Gus started feeling sorry for the little creature. He was thinking, *You poor little thing. If it snowed like this all the time, you'd be in great shape, always safely camouflaged, but it seldom snows in Georgia. What's going to happen to you after the snow is gone?*

"Gus said he was having all sorts of crazy thoughts. He must have gotten preoccupied, because he looked again and the white deer was gone. He never saw it walk away. It seemed to vanish in front of his very eyes. One moment it was standing there, the next it was gone.

"Now Gus was really confused. He thought his eyes were acting up. He continued searching the whiteness in front of him, thinking the little fawn must still be there, somewhere. Perhaps it was so well hidden that he couldn't see it, he thought. Then, all at once, Gus saw movement back in the trees. Another deer was coming. At first Gus thought it might be the fawn's mother. This new deer had the normal, deep gray coloration of a deer in winter coat, but as it got closer, Gus could see that it also had something else—a large set of antlers. It was Old Ironsides! The huge buck walked right up to the spot where the fawn had been standing and paused. Gus said it was really bizarre, because Old Ironsides was standing in almost the same, exact spot where he and Scotty had seen him two weeks earlier.

"At this point, instinct must have taken over. Gus said he doesn't remember aiming or firing the rifle. He simply remembers hearing a loud explosion, and then Old Ironsides was down, kicking in the snow. After Gus pulled himself together, he climbed down and walked over to the spot where the huge buck lay. He could see Old Ironsides's tracks in the newly fallen snow, zigzagging through the trees.

"Gus was beside himself with an excitement that he hadn't felt in a long time. He immediately drove over to Pete Barkley's house to get help. Pete was just sitting down to the family Christmas supper, but he and his nephew excused themselves and left to help load the buck. Old Ironsides is hanging in the barn now, and the three of them have just started taking off the hide. From my vantage here at the window, Old Ironsides looks more like a young steer than a white-tailed deer.

"Gus is already planning to have him mounted. And he refuses to take credit for what he has done. He told me that all the credit should go to Scotty. He wants to hang

Old Ironsides in Scotty's room, just above the deer hoof rifle holder. I know that would make Scotty very happy, and it will also please Gus.

"One more thing, and then I must get to the kitchen to fix some leftovers for supper. As I just mentioned, when Gus walked up to the spot where Old Ironsides lay, he could clearly see the buck's tracks in the snow. He said he could see the heavy drag marks that big bucks always make in the snow. But strange as it may sound, those were the only tracks he could find. Gus said he looked everywhere, but there were no tracks from the white deer. My Gus is a good woodsman. If there were any tracks to be found, he would have seen them.

"Because of this curious circumstance, Gus is thoroughly convinced that seeing the white deer today is some type of sign. Scotty had jokingly told both Gus and me that the white deer was his guardian angel. Now, I think Gus almost believes it. Personally, I don't know what to make of any of this. I do know that Gus has finally rounded the corner. What's more, I think he's going to be all right now. None of us will ever get over the great loss we have suffered, but at least we can once again begin to look toward the future. After all, I believe that the white deer was a gift to our entire family, a gift that we can draw from and hold onto and cherish for a long time to come!"

# The Toss-Away

## Chapter 15

Being the baby of the family, it was Tommy Green's sad lot in life always to wind up with his brother's hand-me-downs. And since Tommy had three extremely active older brothers who properly broke in everything new, most of the toss-away items Tommy received had long since seen better days. From shoes, to winter coats, to sporting equipment and toys, little Tommy always ended up with everyone else's worn-out junk.

When Tommy showed promise for playing second base at the age of eleven, he was given an ancient leather glove that looked like it might have been used by Shoeless Joe Jackson. When he started playing hockey a few years later, his worn skates and marred hockey stick bore the marks of three previous owners through cracks and crevices in the failing leather and dents and battle scars in the warped wood. It wasn't long before Tommy's schoolmates began referring to him as the "Toss-Away Kid."

At times Tommy felt deep resentment, but he tried to take these things in stride. Some day, he vowed, when he grew up, everything he owned would be the best he could afford.

Tommy started deer hunting at the age of fifteen. He eventually inherited an iron-sighted Model 94 Winchester carbine. Although badly neglected, the old rifle boasted two distinguishing features: The dark stock was made of cherry rather than walnut, and the lever-action rifle was chambered for the Winchester .32 Special instead of the standard .30-30.

At some point in the past, however, one of Tommy's brothers had actually dropped the rifle from a tree. The stock had broken into two pieces near the lever and had never been properly repaired. Instead, it had been roughly glued and wrapped with black electrical tape. By the time Tommy received the battered old rifle, much of the bluing had worn off, and large areas of rust covered the barrel. Tape still held the stock together.

"This may not be much of a rifle to some people," Tommy's father explained. "But it's rich in tradition and history. The Model 94 has probably brought down more deer over the years than all other rifles combined. Sure it's nice to have good equipment, but in hunting it's the man behind the rifle that's important. Always remember that a $200 rifle can be just as effective as a custom gun that costs $1,500—if you know what you're doing. Take this rifle and practice with it. Learn how to shoot it, and it'll serve you well in the woods. Someday you'll be able to buy a more expensive gun with a scope. But right now, you'll have to make do with this."

Despite the rifle's worn appearance, it had been fired very little. It was extremely accurate, and Tommy was thrilled to get it. What's more, Tommy had a special affinity for lever-action rifles. The only other gun he had ever been able to call his own was a .22 lever-action Winchester that he had purchased with his own money from a high school friend. Because he was accustomed to shooting the .22 lever-action, he readily adapted to the feel of the Model 94.

When Tommy was twelve, he'd had an opportunity to see the classic 1950s movie *River of No Return* with Robert Mitchum and Marilyn Monroe. Like many movies seen by impressionable youngsters, the film left an indelible mark. He never forgot one scene in particular, in which Robert Mitchum was teaching his son—a boy of about Tommy's own age—to shoot with a lever-action Winchester similar to the one he now owned.

"It's important to hit what you're shooting at with the first shot, son," Robert Mitchum had told the boy. "Otherwise, you might not get a second chance."

Of course, Tommy knew it was one thing for a nineteenth-century wilderness pioneer to be shooting at rampaging Indians who could shoot back, and it was something else for a modern-day hunter to take aim at a big-game animal like a white-tailed buck. Despite the differences, though, Tommy never forgot the important advice about hitting his target with the first shot. He had always tried to follow that advice with his .22. Now he took his father's advice to heart as well. Two weeks later, he killed his first buck with the Winchester—an acorn-fattened seven-pointer.

Tommy did a lot of deer hunting with his beloved rifle in the Minnesota woods where he grew up. He fittingly nicknamed the rifle Old Toss-Away. He found Old Toss-Away to be a perfect companion during or just after a fresh snow. Tommy loved to track bucks when there was new snow on the ground. Most of his shots were at less than fifty yards. He quickly found that the open sights on Old Toss-Away never let him down by fogging up the way scoped rifles were sometimes prone to do in bad weather.

Tommy spent hours during the off-season practicing his shooting. Eventually, he took the rifle to a gunsmith. He had the wooden stock properly repaired and refinished and the metal reblued. When Old Toss-Away returned home, the rifle looked almost new.

As Tommy grew older he acquired a large gun cabinet brimming with fine rifles and shotguns. Ironically, many of those rifles—such as a much cherished Savage Model 99—were classic lever-actions. And even though Tommy had more than fulfilled his father's prophetic words about someday owning at least one expensive deer rifle, Old Toss-Away always held a prominent spot in his gun cabinet. Tommy still enjoyed shooting the carbine whenever he could find time.

As luck would have it, Tommy was offered an opportunity to go to south Texas on a trophy whitetail hunt with several business associates. By now Tommy was on the rise financially. The men who were going on this hunt were all seasoned veterans, and the hunt was to take place on a renowned trophy ranch in the heart of the Texas brush country. Tommy felt honored to be going. He spent weeks organizing his gear and making plans.

On the night before his departure, Tommy packed his rifle. He had decided to take a bolt-action .270 topped with a good scope. As he was placing the rifle into a metal traveling case, he couldn't help but think about the old lever-action rifle and the years of service that Old Toss-Away had provided. He reached for the .30-30 carbine and caressed it fondly.

His memory took him back to that cold, snowy morning almost twenty-five years earlier when he had made a perfect sixty-yard shot on his very first white-tailed buck. Tommy had jumped the seven-pointer from a windfall as he was walking back to the truck in the snow to meet his uncle, and he had been forced to make a quick, instinctive snapshot as the buck dodged through the trees. The buck had dropped in its tracks with a broken neck.

Tommy smiled at the memory. He wiped off the old carbine and placed it in the metal traveling case beside the bolt-action .270.

*They say south Texas is full of wild hogs and javelinas,* Tommy thought. *If I tag out on a nice buck early on, I might just try my hand at a little hog hunting.*

Tommy's trip to south Texas was a dream come true. In addition to the group he was with, several other hunters from various parts of the country had booked hunts at the ranch. Each man brandished an expensive rifle with an expensive scope. Upon their arrival in camp, the first order of business was to walk out to the rifle range behind the lodge and fire a few shots at a fifty-yard target to make sure that everyone's scope was properly sighted in. Tommy grabbed his metal case and walked out to the range with the other men. When he opened the case to take out his .270, however, everyone looked at the old lever-action Winchester as if it were infected with a contagious disease.

Several of the hunters began smirking and making comments behind Tommy's back. "Who is that greenhorn?

Certainly he's not going to hunt in south Texas with that thing, is he?"

Tommy was outraged. He knew times had changed. The art of hunting whitetails had become a very refined business since he was a boy—especially on a renowned trophy ranch in south Texas. Apparently, though, Tommy had violated some kind of unwritten rule regarding the proper way to go about the business. Nowadays, he quickly learned, if a man didn't own a $1,000 binocular and a custom rifle costing twice that much, he was not regarded as much of a hunter by his peers.

Despite the ridicule, however, the Toss-Away Kid had always marched to a different drummer. Now it was time to jump back into action. The belief that anything could be accomplished with the right kind of attitude had been one of his long-standing hallmarks. Determination and a stubborn streak as big as the Lone Star State itself were also a part of Tommy's makeup. He made a decision right then and there. Despite the lack of snow on the ground in this almost tropical climate, all of his trophy hunting in Texas would be done with Old Toss-Away.

Tommy hunted for four glorious days from sunup to sundown without firing a shot. He saw numerous bucks chasing does. He saw hogs and javelinas. He even saw two rattlesnakes and a bobcat, but he opted not to shoot at anything until he first brought down a worthy buck.

Tommy's guide rattled in several good bucks, but none was large enough to take home. Several of the hunters in camp shot average bucks. On the fifth and final day of the hunt, the weather changed drastically. A cold front had pushed through during the night. By morning the biggest bucks on the ranch suddenly seemed to come out of the woodwork.

Thirty minutes after daylight, Tommy shot a massive 24-inch-wide *muy grande* that had never been seen by anyone on the ranch. Numerous sticker points protruded from the buck's rocking chair rack. The one-shot kill was later paced off at 135 yards. The giant buck had come charging in to the sound of the horns. Then, when it was still more than a hundred yards away, it had gotten suspicious and started sneaking off.

Just as with his very first buck taken twenty-five years earlier, Tommy dropped the Texas brute in its tracks. One well-placed shot from Old Toss-Away had broken the big deer's neck. Not only was Tommy's buck the biggest whitetail taken during that particular hunt, but his wide-spreading trophy also earned the distinction of having been the largest nontypical buck ever taken on this south Texas ranch.

Everyone marveled over the shot and the trophy. Some of the hunters who had ridiculed Tommy were dumbfounded at his success. Typically, one or two of the men attributed Tommy's good fortune to blind luck. In truth, the shot had not been easy. For years, though, Tommy had practiced shooting the open-sighted Winchester at paper targets at distances of one hundred yards or more. Now all of that diligent practice had paid off.

As they were packing to leave, the hunter who had been most vocal about Tommy's choice of weapons approached him when no one else was around.

"You know, I used to hunt with an old Winchester carbine like yours," he admitted. "Only mine was a .30-30, and it didn't have a cherry stock. You wouldn't be interested in parting with that gun, would you?"

"No," Tommy answered. "That's one rifle I'll always keep."

Inwardly, Tommy smiled. Once again, Old Toss-Away had proven its invaluable worth.

# Rendezvous at Sheriff's Knob

## Chapter 16

It was one of those strange premonitions that veteran hunters sometimes feel when they are alone in the woods. It came to the man all of a sudden, and it was so powerful that it made the hair on the back of his neck stand up. Someone or something was following him.

*Perhaps it's another deer hunter*, the man thought. *Or perhaps it's some type of animal. White-tailed bucks are sometimes known to follow lone hunters through the woods. Maybe it's Old Slingshot himself, pulling one of his usual tricks on me.*

The home range of the old ridgerunner the man fondly referred to as "Slingshot" included the long, flat-topped mountain known as Sheriff's Knob. The man had jumped the big buck from its bed the year before, just below the top of the mountain at very close range. The buck had a large basket rack with long, white tines and a spread of nineteen or twenty inches.

The most striking thing about the trophy rack, however, had not been the size of the antlers. Instead, it had been the buck's forked brow tine on the left side. Unlike the right brow tine, which was perfectly normal and much shorter, both sections of the split left brow tine were at least six inches long. What's more, they were perfectly forked in a *V*-shape—much like a boy's slingshot.

The man had not been able to get off a shot. But as the buck disappeared over the top of the ridge, he had gotten a good going-away look at the unusual split brow. From that day on, he had referred to the big buck as Old Slingshot. Now, a year later, the man knew that a buck as crafty as Old Slingshot was perfectly capable of shadowing him across the mountain terrace. Somehow, though, the man's instincts told him it was not a deer. That left several other possibilities.

*It might be some kind of four-legged mountain varmint, like a bear,* he thought.

Black bears were fairly common in these mountains, and a curious bear might follow a man's trail from a safe distance. It was mid-October, still early for the bears in these mountains to be in total hibernation. The second possibility was a wildcat. The man knew that a family of bobcats denned somewhere on the ridge near the top of the knob. On several occasions in the past, he had seen a female with three half-grown kittens.

Again, though, the man's instincts told him otherwise. That special sixth sense—developed to such a high degree by humans eons ago when they lived and died so close to nature, that almost animal-like sixth sense that had become so dulled in more recent times as humans became "civilized"—told him that it was no bear or wildcat. That left only one other possibility. It had to be one of those two-legged varmints—probably another hunter. Whatever it was that had made the hair on the back of his neck stand up, Dr. Roscoe McCoy aimed to circle uphill, take a stand behind some good cover, and wait for the intruder to appear.

Doc McCoy had been still-hunting across a series of rolling hardwood terraces just below the top of Sheriff's Knob since daybreak. In four years of hunting this remote mountain top he had never seen another living soul. He always saw plenty of wildlife, but never another hunter. As a result, Sheriff's Knob had become his private little deer-hunting haven, although he knew that sooner or later things would have to change—as they always do. The top of the mountain was ripe with good buck sign, and eventually someone else would blunder onto it as he had done four years earlier. It was only a matter of time.

Reaching the top of the knob was a real chore, especially in the predawn darkness. An old switchback logging road led up from a paved road to the south. A similar logging road came partway up the mountain on the much steeper northern slope. Neither road led all the way to the top, and both roads had been abandoned years earlier. They had been built during the early 1900s as the virgin timber in the pristine north Georgia mountains was being logged out.

Each of the old roads went about two-thirds of the way up the mountain. The rest of the climb had to be made through dense laurel and rhododendron thickets. At times these thickets were quite steep, and it was no easy trek for the faint of heart. The last few hundred yards near the top leveled off into a series of wide, gently rolling terraces that were ideal for stalking. For a man like Doc McCoy, who loved to still-hunt, that made the difficult climb worthwhile.

The top of the mountain had long been a favored refuge for big bucks. Doc McCoy was convinced that more than one gnarly old mountain ridgerunner with a rocking chair rack on his head had lived out his allotted years on this remote mountaintop, relatively free from serious hunting pressure. Doc McCoy always made his approach from the southern side. Reaching the top of the mountain before daylight required a two-hour climb in the dark.

During his first year of hunting the knob, Doc McCoy had killed a superb eleven-pointer on opening day. A sudden Arctic blast had dropped the temperature to a bone-chilling 5 degrees, but despite the cold, that memorable hunt had been ridiculously easy. The only tough part had been getting the 180-pound deer back down the steep slope. Doc McCoy had been forced to quarter the big buck right where it fell. It had taken three grueling trips to get the head, hide, and quarters back down the mountain to his truck.

Doc McCoy had discovered the knob by accident during the winter of 1991. In February of that year, he had been invited on a grouse hunt by a surgeon friend who owned a well-trained German shorthaired pointer. Doc's friend had insisted that the area just below Sheriff's Knob was one of the last strongholds in the north Georgia mountains containing a huntable population of grouse. Sure enough, the two hunters had seen plenty: By the end of the day, they each had their limit of two birds apiece.

The pair of hunters had returned to the mountain two more times that season. Each time, Doc McCoy noted the unusually large tracks of what he knew had to be a large trophy buck. The tracks always led up the logging road toward the top of the knob. When he suggested to Jack, his companion, that they venture up to the top of the mountain to see what they might find, Jack had waved him off and answered, "Not me, friend. It's way too steep, and there are no trails for the last half a mile. A man could get lost up there."

Being the determined old cuss that he was, however, Doc McCoy came back in late spring by himself during turkey season and climbed to the top of the mountain to do a little prospecting. The gold he was seeking was of the white variety. He was hoping to find a good buck carrying a big set of ivory-tipped antlers, and he found the mother lode. On one of the long, flat terraces just below the top of the knob, Doc McCoy found a huge, weathered shed antler that tallied up a gross score of 75 Boone and Crockett points.

The partially gnawed antler had five normal tines, the longest of which was ten inches. The G2 and G3 tines were both split like the rack of a mule deer. Doc McCoy also found a series of old scrapes and numerous rubs on several well-used trails on one of the winding terraces just below the top of the mountain. There were plenty of fresh tracks, and he had no doubt that they had been made by the same buck whose tracks he had seen on the logging road while grouse hunting.

Doc McCoy made two more scouting trips to the knob in early fall as the leaves were beginning to change. Then he came back to hunt the knob on opening day. Precisely one hour after daylight, the big main-framed 5x5 with forked tines came sneaking down the trail to visit one of his scrapes, and Doc McCoy was there to greet him with his Remington .270. The intense cold had not been much of a deterrent, and the hunt for the trophy buck had been one of the easiest he had ever made.

"It could have been 50 below today," Doc McCoy jubilantly told his wife that night, "and I still would have been sweating by the time I got up to the top of the knob!"

"You shouldn't be up there alone," she responded, in typically female fashion. "It's dangerous to be hunting by yourself in such a remote area."

After deductions, Doc McCoy's buck scored an impressive 158 B&C points. For a mountain deer, that was big!

Doc McCoy enjoyed hunting alone, although his good fortune was short-lived. Much to his disappointment, he didn't see an antlered buck on the knob the following year. It was during the third season of hunting the mountain that he had jumped Old Slingshot from his bed. After glimpsing the buck's rack, he went back several more times that year to hunt Old Slingshot, but the wise old buck gave him the slip on each occasion.

Now, on his first outing of the fourth year of hunting the knob, Doc McCoy suddenly had a strange premonition that someone was following him. He circled in an uphill direction around some thick mountain laurel and came out on one of the wide terraces just below the top of the knob. He removed his daypack and sat down on the ground, leaning back against an ancient chestnut tree that had succumbed to the blight more than a half-century earlier. He grabbed a piece of venison jerky from his coat pocket, put it into his mouth, and started chewing. He began his wait.

Completely unaware of Doc McCoy's presence, the lone hunter had been ghosting across the ridge just like his predecessor. He had come all the way around the mountain from the northern slope, and it was his intention to make a complete circle around the oblong mountain top and eventually end up where he had started. Naturally, he was startled when Doc McCoy spoke out.

"Howdy, neighbor," Doc McCoy said.

The man froze in his tracks. When he finally zeroed in on the stranger leaning back against the huge chestnut log, he said, "I thought I was the only deer hunter in the world dumb enough to make the long climb up here."

"No, there's two of us, I reckon," Doc McCoy said, smiling.

Doc stood up and held out his hand. "People call me Roscoe," he said.

"Is that a fact?" the man asked. He extended his hand and smiled. "My name's Hutch," he said.

"I was just gettin' ready to sit down and break out some lunch," Doc McCoy said.

"Oh, yeah? I've got a couple of sandwiches and an apple or two myself," the man offered.

"Let's break out the vittles on our chestnut log table here and partake in a feast, then," Doc McCoy said. "What do you say?"

"Sounds mighty good to me," Hutch agreed.

The two hunters began talking and eating. It was a cordial luncheon. Each man talked about how he had found the mountain and about how long he had been hunting in the area. Doc McCoy told Hutch about his eleven-pointer, but he was careful not to say anything about Old Slingshot. Nor did Hutch, who was also on the trail of what he believed to be a large trophy buck, ever offer a word about the abundant big buck sign he had discovered on the north side of the mountain. The two hunters never got beyond first names, and neither man was prone to volunteer too much privileged information.

When they had finished eating, Doc McCoy pulled out a small flask of Jim Dickel* bourbon whiskey.

"I think we oughta drink a toast to our meeting," he suggested. "And to all the big bucks we plan to drag off this mountain."

"I'll drink to that," Hutch said.

Doc McCoy handed the flask to Hutch.

"Here's to our health, to our future, and to big bucks everywhere!" Hutch said.

"Here, here!"

After the toast, Hutch said, "Well, I guess I'd better be getting back around to my side of the mountain. If I hear any shots, I'll come back over here to see if you need help."

*George Dickel bourbon made by Jim Beam.

"Sounds good to me," Doc McCoy said.

The two hunters shook hands and went their separate ways.

A month later, on the last day of the season, Doc McCoy was back on the top of the knob, making a last-ditch effort to find Old Slingshot. It was another cold and clear day. Around noontime he decided to work his way over to the chestnut log to rest and eat lunch where he and Hutch had met four weeks earlier. As he topped a small rise, he immediately spotted the bright blaze orange of another hunter's coat. The hunter was sitting on the chestnut log facing away from Doc McCoy. As he got closer, Doc McCoy could see that the other hunter was his friend Hutch.

"Well, look what the cat drug in," Doc McCoy said as he stepped up to the log.

Hutch turned around and smiled. "It's about time you got here. I've been sittin' here for almost an hour, and I'm gettin' right famished. Hope you brought the dessert."

"I have it right here in my jacket," Doc McCoy said. "I always keep a little Jim Dickel on hand for a real emergency. You know—heart attack medicine." Doc McCoy tenderly patted the small flask he always kept in his coat pocket.

"That climb alone is enough to give most men a heart attack," Hutch replied.

"I can think of a lot of worse places to cash in my chips," Doc McCoy said.

"Me, too," Hutch agreed. "This is one of the most beautiful places I know of."

Once again the two hunters broke out some sandwiches and began to eat. This time, something moved them to become more open in their conversation.

"I might as well tell you, I'm huntin' a pretty good-size buck," Hutch admitted. "He seems to be crossing over from my side of the mountain to yours on a regular basis."

"There must be several big bucks up here, then," Roscoe said. "I'm huntin' a real giant myself. I call my buck Old Slingshot because he has split brow tines on the left side. They look just like a boy's slingshot."

"That's odd," Hutch answered. "We seem to have quite a bit in common. I have a name for my buck, too. I call him Old Whitey because he's got a lot of gray hair on his face and a double throat patch. I got a good look at him once at about twenty yards. He was standing in a laurel thicket, but danged if I could get a shot."

The conversation soon turned to other topics.

"Wonder what the poor folks are doin' today," Doc McCoy said as he started on his second ham and cheese sandwich.

"One thing's for sure," Hutch replied. "We have the whole place to ourselves."

There was a small opening in the trees that offered a perfect view of the wide valley below.

"Wonder where the name Sheriff's Knob came from," Hutch asked.

"Probably had something to do with moonshiners, if I had to guess," Doc McCoy said.

"Maybe the sheriff himself had a still down in one of those draws," Hutch offered. "There are several good springs coming out of the ground on my side of the mountain."

"Speaking of spring water and mountain dew, isn't it about time we had a little shot of heart attack medicine?" Doc McCoy said.

"You've got it," Hutch replied with a big smile. "I even have a can of peanuts we can open."

Doc McCoy was just reaching for his flask when both men heard something approaching on the trail that led through a thick wall of mountain laurel. It sounded exactly like a man walking through the woods.

Suddenly a huge buck walked out of the thicket not twenty yards from the chestnut log. The deer immediately spotted the two hunters sitting on the log and stopped dead in his tracks. Both rifles were leaning against the log several feet away.

"My gosh! It's Old Slingshot!" Doc McCoy uttered.

"No, it's Old Whitey!" Hutch insisted.

The buck wasted little time in making his escape. He lunged to his left and bounded down the open terrace in several heart-stopping jumps. When he was about fifty yards away, he did something totally unexpected. He paused briefly to look back, behind the cover of a large white pine. Hutch was the first to reach his rifle. He grabbed his scoped .30-06 and fired two quick shots. Doc McCoy shouldered his .270 and got off a single shot. Then the buck disappeared over the terrace top in a blur of gray and white. Even though they dutifully went over to check the ground for blood, both hunters knew that they had missed cleanly.

When they returned to the log fifteen minutes later, they were still in a state of great excitement.

"Did you see the white on his face, Roscoe?" Hutch asked. "And his double white throat patch? Did you see it while he was standing there looking at us? It was my buck, all right. . . . It was Old Whitey for sure!"

"I got a gander of that double throat patch," Doc McCoy answered. "I also got a good look at that split brow tine I was tellin' you about. I think we'd better start trying to pool our resources, ol' buddy, because Old Whitey and Old Slingshot seem to be one and the same animal!"

The two hunters continued talking about how they had missed and about how big the trophy animal actually had been.

"He'll be a lot more difficult to hunt in the future," Doc McCoy said. "Now he knows we're up here chasing after him."

"I suppose an incident like this should count as a real emergency, shouldn't it?" Hutch replied. "Maybe we oughta have a good slug of that heart attack medicine before we both succumb!"

"Sounds like a good prescription to me," Doc McCoy said.

Once again he took out the flask and unscrewed the top. As always, he offered the first drink to Hutch.

"Here's to the demise of one double-throat-patched, double-brow-tined mountain monarch!" Hutch said.

He held up the flask and took a long drink. Then he handed the flask back to Doc McCoy.

"Here's to Old Whitey and Old Slingshot!" Doc McCoy said. "I might've missed a shot today, but I haven't had this much fun since we used to steal watermelons out of old man Wilson's watermelon patch when I was a boy!"

After the drink, both men sat quietly reflecting for a few moments.

"I've got an idea," Doc McCoy said. "Let's make a pact. Let's have one more toast, then let's hide the flask right here in the hollow of this chestnut log. Sort of as a shrine to Old Slingshot. Next year, at 1:00 P.M. sharp on opening day, we'll bring it out and drink again."

"I hope we'll be celebrating a kill," Hutch added. "And since we haven't opened the can of peanuts, let's hide them, too. They'll keep for a year."

"Until next year, then," Doc McCoy said. "Same time, same place."

"I'll drink to that!" Hutch said.

"To a worthy adversary," Doc McCoy said. "To Old Slingshot!"

He took a drink and handed the flask to his friend.

"To Old Whitey!" Hutch said. "The best buck I've ever missed!"

* * * * *

Precisely one year later, Doc McCoy made the long trek up the mountain in the predawn darkness and walked over to the chestnut log on opening day. After hunting all morning without seeing a trace of Old Slingshot, he arrived at the log early. He sat and waited for more than two hours, but Hutch never showed up. It didn't occur to Doc McCoy to dig out the flask and drink by himself. Instead, he worked his way over to the north side of the mountain in the hope of finding some sign of his friend.

It was the same story the next year. Doc McCoy had the whole mountain to himself for the entire season, and he never saw a sign of another human being. He saw several yearling bucks, but Old Slingshot seemed to have disappeared. By now Doc McCoy's age was beginning to tell on him, and his knees were starting to give him a lot of trouble. He knew his climbing days were numbered.

For the next couple of years, Doc McCoy hunted the knob erratically. He even missed one or two years. When he did climb the knob, he seldom ventured over to the chestnut log. During all of that time he never saw another big buck, and he figured that Old Slingshot had died of old age.

It was ten years later to the day when Doc McCoy decided to make one last pilgrimage to the knob, against the heavy protests of his wife. He had long ago given up all hope of ever seeing his friend Hutch again, but for some strange reason he had started thinking about the hidden flask of Jim Dickle.

*It's probably not even there any more*, he told himself. *Some critter like a raccoon probably found it and destroyed it long ago, but I'd still like to go see if it's there.*

The climb up the mountain was grueling, but Doc McCoy was determined. He finally reached the terrace below the top of the knob around noontime. When he reached the huge chestnut log, he was glad to see that it was still there. For some strange reason, he had harbored a crazy notion that the tree might be gone.

*Nothing stays the same,* he reasoned. *Father Time could have chipped away at the log until nothing was left.*

But the huge log was there, just as always. It looked no different than it had ten years before.

Doc McCoy sat down on it. For a long time he sat thinking about all the great memories the mountain had given him. Then he decided to look for the flask. He went over to the hollow where he had carefully packed it away so long ago. After pulling out quite a quantity of mulch, debris, and rotting leaves, he found the heavy wool mitten he had packed the flask in. The flask was as unspoiled and untainted as the heavy log itself, but there was no trace of the peanuts. Doc McCoy concluded that some varmint surely must have found the can and carried off the peanuts years earlier.

"Well, I guess it's just you and me," Doc McCoy said, addressing the flask. The top was slightly rusted, but he finally got it off.

"I hate to drink by myself, but at least I can drink a toast to all the good times," he said solemnly. "Here's to you, Hutch, wherever you may be. Here's to Old Slingshot, one of the finest bucks I've ever known. And here's to Sheriff's Knob, one of the most beautiful places the Good Lord ever created."

He held the bottle up and started to take a drink. All at once, he paused. Something came over him. He had that feeling again. His senses might have been a little dulled with age, but there was no denying that feeling. Someone was watching him. He wheeled around.

"Hutch? Is that you?"

"It's me, all right!" the man said. "A little grayer, a few more wrinkles, a little worse for wear, but it's the same old me. I had to make one more trip up here to the knob. You weren't really gonna take a drink by yourself, Roscoe, were you?"

Doc McCoy was stunned. "My, God, Hutch, it is you! All these years . . . I didn't know how to get in touch with you."

Indeed, Hutch had aged. His hair was almost pure white, and he carried the wrinkles of an old man.

"What happened to you?" Doc McCoy asked. "Where have you been all this time?"

"It was two weeks before opening day the year after we saw Old Whitey," Hutch began. "I would have been here right on schedule, but a drunk driver hit me head-on and kind of messed up my plans. I got pinned in the car, and both legs got busted up pretty good below the knees. They said I'd never walk again, much less climb a mountain. It took me five full years of working at it just to be able to walk normally again. Finally, this year, I knew I had to give the knob a shot. Everybody said I was crazy, but here I am! I made it. I'm almost as good as new. I had to find out if you ever got Old Whitey. More important, I had to see you one more time. I knew you'd be here today. Don't ask me how, I just knew it."

Doc McCoy was speechless. Tears were streaming down his face.

"I never knew how to get in touch," he repeated. "I didn't even know where you lived or your last name. And, no, I never saw Old Slingshot or Old Whitey again."

"None of that really matters now," Hutch said. "All I know is I sure could use a good dose of heart attack medicine. After making the climb this morning, my old heart is about to thump right out of my chest!"

"You got it," Doc McCoy said, pushing the flask toward his old friend.

Hutch took the flask in his hand. "By the way, what is your full name?"

"Dr. Roscoe McCoy, retired, at your service," Doc McCoy said. "And you?"

"I go by the name of Stanley 'Hutch' Hatfield."

"Well, I'll be doggoned," his counterpart said. "Hatfield and McCoy. What a combination. You wouldn't have any roots up West Virginia way, would you?"

"As a matter of fact, I was born there," Hutch said. "And you?"

"That's where all my people are from," Doc McCoy answered.

"Well, I reckon both of us'll be doggoned, then," Hutch said. "Life sure does play some crazy tricks on a fella, doesn't it? I reckon it was one of life's great ironies that brought us together in the first place, and it's brought us back together now."

"The biggest irony of all is in our names," Doc McCoy said.

"The feud's been over for a long time," Hutch countered.

"True, but I never expected to be huntin' buddies with someone by the name of Hatfield."

"Nor did I ever expect to be huntin' with a McCoy," Hutch said. "What would our relatives say?"

"It could only have happened with two grizzled old deer hunters like us," Doc McCoy offered. "I reckon there's a lesson to be learned here somewhere, if we can just figure it out!"

Hutch smiled broadly. "I'll drink to that!" he said.

# An Old Hound Named Willard

## Chapter 17

The old hound wandered into our camp just as Buddy and I were getting started setting up the tents. He was a swaybacked and skinny old bluetick, long past his coon-hunting days. At first we didn't pay much attention. But as he stood watching us work, I noticed a certain look in his eye. It was a look that could have been gained only by living long years of life's bittersweet experiences. It was almost as if he were trying to tell us that, despite everything, he forgave the world for its many injustices. It didn't take him long to win my friendship and respect. Buddy and I figured that he was probably from the farm a few miles down the road. Since the arthritis in his joints told us that he wouldn't be running deer, we decided that he was a welcome guest in our camp for as long as he chose to stay.

We later named him Willard, after one of the former club members. As things turned out, he chose to stay with us all season. As always, it was a lively, cheerful camp. After the season got underway, some twenty hunters from all walks of life called it home for the entire eight days of hunting.

The long-established camp sprang forth each year amid a secluded stand of tall pines at the end of an abandoned logging road. There were two rows of neatly spaced tents facing each other and lined up in military fashion, except that these tents were far from uniform. Beyond the row of tents in a well-trodden clearing was the large fire circle, bordered with rocks and filled deep with the remains of countless campfires that had burned brightly through many a cold night in seasons past. This was the social gathering place of camp both before and after dark, and the clearing was dotted with stools and chairs claimed by the various hunters.

Directly across the clearing from the fire circle stood the cook tent. It was the largest tent in camp, a 10x10 square walk-in canvas structure of the sort you see in Western hunting camps high in the Rockies. It had originally been white, but years of smoke and weather had turned it a dingy gray. The well-stocked cook tent was the heart and soul of camp. Jess Ferguson, our self-proclaimed camp cook, who had never hunted a day in his life, made certain that an empty belly was as rare as an antlered doe.

Buddy and I were the youngest members in the camp. We were both sixteen then, and neither of us had yet killed a buck. Because we were the youngest, the camp elders burdened us with most of the chores—cutting wood, picking up litter, and doing all the greasy dishes. We grumbled a lot, but we loved every minute of it.

Of all the characters in camp, and there were a considerable number, Dexter Smith was our all-out favorite. He was by far the best hunter of the bunch, having brought down many a fine buck in his day. But the reason Buddy and I liked him so much was that he always took time to teach us something about deer hunting. He often took us out and showed us firsthand the ways of the woods. Above all, he made it plain that he cared about us, and he wanted us to shoot a first buck almost as badly as we wanted to ourselves.

The afternoon before opening day that year, Dexter piled us into his truck and took us down to the river to sight-in our rifles. He was forever expounding upon the subject of gun safety, and as we slowly drove down the dirt road, keeping a careful eye out on both sides for fresh deer tracks on the shoulder, he began one of his frequent lectures. I'll never forget his words: "A deer rifle can make an awfully big hole in a deer, but you won't believe what it can do to a man."

As always, the days of the short season flew by, and at last we were down to our final morning. Several good bucks had been hung on the meat pole during the course of the all-too-brief week, but Buddy and I had yet to see a set of antlers in the woods.

I suppose all deer clubs have a camp cutup, and ours was the son of one of the oldest club members, Cap Sullivan. Cap's son, Mickey, fresh out of college, seemed to jump from one frying pan into another. He seldom hunted, opting instead to party while in camp. When he was not in camp, he was always looking for trouble in the closest town. Mickey and his friend Roy Turner stayed mostly to themselves in a converted school bus camper that they kept parked out in the woods some distance from camp. They drank heavily, but as long as they were not hunting, their antics were tolerated by the others out of deference to Cap.

Whatever inspired Mickey to go hunting on that last day of the season will always remain a mystery. It was about 10:30 A.M., and most of the men had already returned from the morning's hunt. Judging from the whoops and hollers that had come from the school bus during the night, Mickey and Roy had partied into the early morning hours. However, by some quirk of fate, Mickey had decided it was time to go hunting. He proceeded to load his gun inside the bus. Roy was still asleep when Mickey grabbed his gear and prepared to go. As always, he was in a hurry.

As he unsteadily lurched from the bus, Mickey stumbled and fell forward. The .30-06 he was clutching discharged. Sixty yards away, through the trees, Cap Sullivan sat considering how to play his hand at a five-minute-old card game. Buddy and I were in the cook tent a few yards away doing the breakfast dishes when the horrible explosion rocked the woods. Glancing quickly into each other's eyes as we ran for the door, we knew it could mean only one thing. Everyone knew it could mean only one thing.

Cap never knew what hit him. The bullet ripped into his chest, killing him instantly. He was dead before he slumped to the ground. Buddy and I were standing only a few feet away as the lifeblood flowed from Cap's body.

That season ended right there for everyone. After all of the legal problems had been taken care of, the entire camp was quickly dismantled. In a few short hours, the once lively camp was as bare as it had been the day Buddy and I first started putting up the tents. But we knew that more than another deer season had ended.

Buddy and I were the last ones to leave. Just before we got into the car and drove off, we stood silently for a long time, trying to contemplate the horrible thing that had happened, and knowing full well that our happy, tranquil camp would never be the same.

As we started off down the narrow logging road, Willard, the old hound, emerged from the woods. During the week of hunting he had grown to be the camp mascot. He seemed to favor me in particular, and he never left my side when I was in camp. Now he stared at us as though we were deserting him. Buddy and I gave each other a long look. I slowed the car, and Buddy stepped out and opened the back door. Willard jumped in, and we drove off.

# A Revolutionary Breakthrough in Hunting Attire

## Chapter 18

*This is the second story in this collection taken from the author's popular column "The Misadventures of Arnold and Waldo," which ran in* North American Whitetail *magazine from 1997 to 2003. In the magazine, the stories were written under the author's pen name, D. A. Deerslayer.*

* * * * *

Buck Hurricane was the first to notice the shocking front-page headlines in the afternoon edition of the *Okefenokee Star*. He promptly called Arnold. Arnold phoned Waldo, who then called Jackknife Sandow. Late that afternoon, all four hunters were sitting in a corner booth at the Swamp Side Diner, chewing over their options.

"I always knew he was a little strange," Jackknife said.

"You never know about your closest friends," Arnold agreed. He eyed Waldo dubiously. "In this crazy ol' world, I reckon people are capable of anything—even the people you think you know best."

"The question is, What are we gonna do about it?" Buck Hurricane asked. "After all, he is president of our huntin' club this year. As such, I reckon he thinks he's the leader of the pack. You know what they say about the alpha male in a wolf pack—he likes to bare his teeth and growl once in a while."

"I didn't know the ol' goat had it in him," Arnold said, grinning.

"Wait just a dadgum minute!" Waldo yelled. "We're not talkin' about some two-bit ax murderer here. We're talkin' about Doc Bragg, for crying out loud. *Our* Doc Bragg. A fellow deer hunter! A God-fearing family man with a dog and a wife!

He's the salt of the earth, even if that salt does get a little lumpy from time to time in the south Georgia humidity."

"Oh, yeah? Then maybe you'd better start doing some serious explaining!" Three angry voices were directed at Waldo in unison.

A copy of the newspaper lay on the table, and Arnold pointed to the headlines. "Explain this!" he said.

Waldo glanced down at the ugly headlines for the umpteenth time that day. They seemed to jump off the page at him like the light of a flashing neon sign.

**Prominent South Georgia Dentist Arrested for Indecent Exposure**

Dr. C. L. Bragg, a well-known Ludowici dentist, was arrested this morning in a wooded area near his plush ten-acre residence after Mrs. Deloris Atwater, a neighbor, filed assault charges. In an exclusive interview with the *Okefenokee Star*, Mrs. Atwater alleged that while out jogging, she was accosted by Dr. Bragg. According to sworn testimony by Mrs. Atwater, the dentist, wearing nothing but a mask and a pair of combat boots, was hiding behind a tree in an isolated wooded section near her home. He was armed with a large-caliber weapon. Despite the attempt to disguise his identity, the frightened woman recognized her assailant immediately.

"I'd know him anywhere, with or without clothes on," the terrified woman stated. "We've been neighbors for years. I've been concerned about him ever since he performed a root canal on me in 1985. He's one of those people you always need to watch!"

Acting in self-defense, Mrs. Atwater, who holds a black belt in karate, attacked her assailant. After rendering him unconscious, she summoned the Sheriff's Department. The naked assailant was found crawling through the woods by deputies. He is currently being held in the Ludowici jail in lieu of $500,000 bond. A long list of charges has been filed against the Georgia dentist.

"There's got to be an explanation," Waldo insisted. "As sure as a turkey has sixteen tail feathers, there's a snake in the grass somewhere."

"Oh, there's an explanation, all right," Arnold said. "Your friend Doc Bragg is a pervert."

"He's *our* friend!" Waldo declared. "You know how the media is—Why, they can ruin a man's reputation quicker than a feist dog can tree a 'coon. We've got to get inside the jail and find out what really happened. Doc Bragg doesn't have the temperament to be in jail. That place'll chew him up and spit him out like a plug of bad tobacco."

"How do you plan to do that?" Jackknife asked. "This is the biggest story to hit this area since they tried to drain the swamp. They're probably guarding that jailhouse like Fort Knox. At the very least, we'd need a press pass."

Six eyes suddenly turned to Buck Hurricane.

"Me? You're kidding!" Buck Hurricane said. "I'm just a no-name sports writer who does a little radio show and the obit page when somebody dies. I don't work for the *National Enquirer*."

"You do now," Waldo said. "If we don't get in there and figure a way to spring him, you might be doing *his* column. I'll go with you."

Waldo and Buck Hurricane left for the jailhouse immediately. Just as they arrived, a hollow-eyed Doc Bragg was walking out the front door with his attorney. He had cuts and bruises all over his face, and his right arm was in a sling.

"You two are a sight for sore eyes," Doc Bragg said, smiling.

"So are you," Waldo replied. "How in tarnation did you post bond?"

"Didn't have to," Doc Bragg said. "I'm free to go, thanks to my attorney here. It's all been a terrible mistake."

"We figured that," Waldo said. "What in the Sam Hill happened?"

"It's a long story," Doc Bragg said. "I was having a right good day until that antihunting whacko-feminist neighbor of mine came along." Doc Bragg then proceeded to relate his unbelievable tale of woe.

"I got up this morning and started gettin' ready for work just like always," he began. "I was standing in the shower, whistling away and thinking about what a great weekend we have coming up for deer huntin', when my wife yelled in at me.

"'Honey, look out the window, quick!' Edna yelled. 'There's a big deer standing in the backyard. I think it's a buck.'

"The window was all fogged up, so I took a wash rag and wiped it off. Sure enough, I could see a big deer standing behind some tall azaleas. This particular deer looked like a right sizable animal, so I grabbed a towel and jumped out of the shower. Dripping wet, I ran into the kitchen for a better look. I couldn't believe my eyes when I looked out the kitchen window. It *was* a big buck!

"All my huntin' gear was right there by the door," Doc Bragg continued. "I ran over and grabbed my rifle so I could get a better look through the scope. I didn't have any intention of trying to shoot him, but I decided to sneak outside to get closer. My boots were right there on the floor, and I slipped 'em on so I wouldn't have cold feet. There was also a box of bullets sittin' on the shelf. For some reason, I took out one bullet and held it in my mouth like a cee-gar. Then I grabbed the camo face mask that was hanging by my coat. I put it on, thinking that if he looked back at me, he wouldn't be able to see my eyes. Then I sneaked outside.

"The buck started walking away, so I went after him," Doc Bragg explained. "It took me about one hundred yards to catch up. When I did, and when I finally got the scope on him again, I realized he was the biggest buck I'd ever seen. He had a beautiful basket rack, with long tines and thick beams. I got pretty excited. After all, gun season was open, and I was on my own property looking at a trophy buck through the scope of my rifle.

"The next thing I knew, I was propped against a tree with a loaded rifle. I got him in the cross hairs and fired. He took off like a freight train, but I knew it was a good shot. He wasn't going far!

"I must have gotten a little touch of buck fever after that, and I went running after him. Somehow the towel I had wrapped around my waist got snagged in a bush. It came off, but I didn't even notice. He ran right to the edge of my neighbor's property line before he dropped. I'm sure I looked pretty ridiculous flashing after a deer in my birthday suit. But it was still early in the morning, and I wasn't worried about seeing anyone on my property.

"I had almost reached him when I saw that busybody neighbor of mine comin' down the trail. An old woods road runs between our two property lines, and she was power-walking down the road with her arms just a-swinging. I didn't want her to see me or the deer, so I dodged behind a tree. About that same time, I realized my towel was gone. I knew I was in a heap of trouble!

"Before I could do anything, she was in front of me—yelling out all those karate words and kickin' and choppin'. She must have gotten in a good lick, because the next thing I knew I was down for the count. When I regained consciousness, I grabbed my rifle and started staggering back toward the house. That's when a car full of deputies drove up. They jumped out with their guns drawn. They handcuffed me and took me to jail. Fortunately, they also got my deer and took him to a cooler."

"After I called Harry, my attorney, he got to doing some checking around. It turns out that my 'innocent' next-door neighbor has filed sexual harassment charges against just about every adult male in our county. She's a real kook! I didn't attack her. She attacked me!"

"So they dropped all charges?" Waldo asked.

"Yep," Doc Bragg said. "I did have to pay a thirty-five-dollar fine for not wearing the mandatory five hundred square inches of hunter orange while deer hunting in the woods, but I'm gonna get my buck back. Thank goodness they dressed him out and hung him in a cooler. And he's a monster! It was almost worth everything I've been through just to shoot a buck like that. Also, since I wasn't wearing an orange vest. . . ."

". . . or anything else," Waldo said with a smile.

"True," Doc Bragg continued. "I was ordered to take the next hunter safety course when it comes up. But I'll do that, gladly!"

"I'm real embarrassed about what my newspaper did," Buck Hurricane said. "I'll personally see to it that they print a full retraction."

"Oh, it's OK," Doc said, grinning. "After all, most folks around here think of me as being a little on the dull side. Maybe this'll boost my image!"

"No doubt about that," Waldo agreed.

"Puttin' my reputation aside, I wouldn't recommend huntin' in the buff to any of my friends," Doc Bragg continued. "It can lead to all kinds of serious complications."

"Seems to me it could also lead to a whole new style of deer huntin'," Waldo offered. "After all, you did end up with a mighty good buck! Maybe we could even figure a way to cash in on it. I can see it now—grown men running through the woods wearing nothing but boots, orange vests, and camo masks. Swamp Ghost, look out! Huntin' *au naturel* may just be bigger than two double-piggy-back-trailer-truckloads of grunt tubes and rattlin' horns!"

8731 DOC

# Deer Hunting Fools

## Chapter 19

Sammy Sparks and his cousin Randall Black were deer hunting fools. As sure as the first killing frost of November would begin to cull back the vast oceans of kudzu so common in much of the countryside each fall, you could count on one thing: Sammy and Randall would be outdoors chasing woods-wise whitetails every available minute between Thanksgiving and Christmas. Nothing could keep them from hunting the gnarly old "he-bucks" that roamed the nine-hundred-acre farm belonging to Sammy's grandmother.

Years earlier the farm had been nicknamed "He-buck Heaven" by Sammy's grandfather, who had since passed away. In more recent times, it had lived up to its reputation of being a veritable trophy whitetail factory—thanks to the efforts of Sammy and Randall.

To these two dedicated hunters, a he-buck was no ordinary animal. A he-buck was a real brute of a whitetail—in both body size and headgear. Sammy and Randall rarely shot a he-buck that dressed out at less than 220 pounds, and the deer's rack would usually match its body. Much to the chagrin of the local deer hunting community, though, Sammy and Randall seldom invited any outsiders to hunt with them at He-buck Heaven.

Sammy and Randall were brickmasons by trade. They were good at what they did, and they worked hard for their money for nine months of the year. The moment deer season opened, however, they said good-bye to work and took a leave of absence. For the next three months, they lived in the woods.

Sammy and Randall had developed a reputation for being the best brickmasons in town. When Dr. G. Aubrey Riddle, one of the town's leading physicians, decided to build a new home on the outskirts of town, Sammy and Randall were hired to do the masonry work. They spent most of September working on the good doctor's dream house.

Although bricklayers may be a world apart in social status from men of medicine, Sammy quickly found that he and Dr. Riddle had a lot in common—at least in some areas. Both men were avid hunters. Sammy learned that Dr. Riddle was a dyed-in-the-wool bird hunter. Despite the fact that Dr. Riddle had never set foot in the deer woods, he had an insatiable curiosity about hunting that much regaled big-game animal. As the construction work progressed, he and Sammy spent hours talking about the various aspects of Sammy's favorite pastime. One day after quitting time, Sammy offered to drive the doctor over to his house to show him some of his trophy bucks.

Sammy's cluttered den was like a natural history museum. Numerous mounted animals, including turkeys, squirrels, wild boars, and coiled rattlesnakes, filled the room. At least a dozen mounted deer adorned the walls. In addition to hunting on their grandmother's farm, Sammy and Randall always took a trip together out West each fall to hunt mule deer in Colorado. Over the years the two men had brought home some superb Western trophies.

One look at Sammy's impressive antler collection was more than enough to convince the doctor that he needed to try his hand at deer hunting.

"Do you suppose you could take me and my partner, Dr. Bennett, deer hunting with you at He-buck Heaven some time?" Dr. Riddle asked Sammy one day.

"We'd love to take you with us!" Sammy said with a big smile. "The only thing we ask of you and your partner is not to shoot any small bucks. We try to let the little ones go so they can grow big racks. If that's OK with you, you tell your partner to be ready for the hunt of a lifetime on opening day!"

"That's fine with us," Dr. Riddle agreed.

Dr. Riddle promptly bought himself a Weatherby .300 Magnum. He also went to the local sporting goods store and outfitted himself with all types of deer-hunting gear. By the time opening day arrived, he had purchased enough new gear to go on an extended safari to the Dark Continent. With Sammy's help, Dr. Riddle got his new rifle properly sighted-in, and at Sammy's insistence he practiced enough to become quite proficient at ranges reaching out to two hundred yards.

Opening day in November that year turned out to be one of the coldest days in years. Being accustomed to hunting in all kinds of weather, Sammy and Randall were undaunted. They were a little concerned about their guests, though. Before they left for the woods early that morning, Sammy encouraged the two doctors to pile on everything warm they could find.

Well before the first hint of daylight, the two veteran hunters placed their guests in two prime stands located about three hundred yards apart on a wide power line easement. A large swamp was situated near the power line, and several exceptional bucks had been taken out of each stand in years past. Sammy told the doctors that he and Randall would be by to pick them up for lunch around 11:00 A.M. unless they heard shooting sooner.

"Now remember," Sammy reminded his guests. "Try to be selective. Please don't shoot any of our younger bucks."

"Oh, I'll to be selective, all right," Dr. Bennett replied coarsely to his good-natured host. "I intend to select the first buck I see! If he so much as has nubs on his head, he's dead meat!"

That comment didn't sit too well with Sammy, but he managed to hide his feelings. After all, Dr. Riddle was a respected friend. Sammy shouldn't expect the good doctor to be responsible for the actions of his disagreeable associate.

Being good hosts, Sammy and Randall came out of the woods much earlier than usual. Just after 10:00 A.M. they met at a designated spot and walked up to a high point on the power line, about three-quarters of a mile from where their guests were positioned. They began glassing the area below them to see if there was any activity in the vicinity of where the two doctors were hunting. Not a blade of grass was moving. The open power line right-of-way looked like a frozen expanse of arctic waste. With the help of their binoculars, Sammy and

Randall did happen to notice a strange glowing light way down at one end of the right-of-way next to the tree line.

Somewhat puzzled, they decided to investigate. Driving around through the woods for a closer look, they soon realized this glowing light was a blazing bonfire. As they neared the scene, they could see the two doctors huddled as close as they could get to the life-giving warmth of the fire. They got out of their truck and walked up to the two men of medicine.

"See anything?" Sammy asked cheerfully.

"Are you kidding?" Dr. Bennett answered. "All we've seen this morning is icicles, and all we succeeded in doing was wasting a lot of time and freezing our behonkers off! It's downright c-c-cold out here!"

"Yeah," Dr. Riddle agreed. "As soon as we thaw out, I'm afraid we're heading for the hacienda!"

"You can have your whitetail hunting!" Dr. Bennett added rudely. "This kind of hunting is for fools and idiots!"

"I'll say this for you," Dr. Riddle stated, addressing Sammy and Randall, and obviously embarrassed at his partner's behavior. "You two fellas are really dedicated to get out in this kind of cold."

"Heck, we're just doing what we're supposed to do," Randall replied with conviction. "Doesn't it say somewhere in the Good Book that a man's supposed to provide meat for his family? We're just trying to do what the man upstairs wants us to."

"Yeah," Sammy added. "And if that meat happens to be wearing a good set of antlers, well, that's just an extra bonus!"

"I think I'd rather sleep with the devil than have to undergo this kind of cold," Dr. Bennett replied rudely. "No antlers are worth this kind of suffering."

As soon as the two doctors had gotten some feeling back into their fingers and toes, they asked Sammy to take them to their car. They both said that this cold weather deer hunting business was the most miserable outdoor experience they had ever endured.

"It's just not our cup of tea," Dr. Riddle admitted.

Sammy breathed a big sigh of relief, overjoyed that the obnoxious friend of Dr. Riddle's had not tried to shoot one of their younger bucks. Sammy left Randall to mind the fire while he drove the doctors out to the edge of the property, where Dr. Riddle had parked his Cadillac. Sammy was eager to rejoin Randall for a fast lunch so that the two hunters could get back to their stands as quickly as possible. On a cold day like this, he felt that deer movement might to be best during the middle of the day.

The two doctors bid Sammy a hasty good-bye. Then, gathering all their gear together, they walked over to the Cadillac. They paused for a moment and started talking. Suddenly, as Sammy watched, a heated argument broke out. Sammy rolled down the window to see what all of the commotion was about.

"I thought you had the keys," Dr. Bennett said rudely to his partner.

"No, I told you to get them!" Dr. Riddle replied emphatically. "You were the last one to get something out of the car!"

The two men looked inside the locked car simultaneously and realized that the keys were still in the ignition. Since Sammy was an old hand at getting into locked cars, he opened the door of his truck and stepped outside.

"Can I help?" he offered.

Dr. Bennett looked over at him with a wild glare. "No you can't!" he roared. "Haven't you done enough already? The keys are locked inside, and we've both had our fill of this deer hunting!" Then, with an air of superiority, he said, "Civilized bird hunters should never have to go through this kind of ordeal." Before Sammy could respond, he added, "But at least this high-powered cannon is good for something."

With that, Dr. Bennett took the butt of his rifle and bashed in the rear window of the nearly new Cadillac. Dr. Riddle watched in horror.

"Sorry about that, Aubrey," Dr. Bennett told his partner. "But I'm ready to get the hell out of here. I'll pay for a new window! Hell, I'll buy you a new car if you'll just take me somewhere where they have a heater!"

While Sammy stood there with his mouth open, the two doctors unlocked the front doors and climbed into the well-ventilated automobile. Dr. Riddle cranked the engine and started to drive off. As he passed by Sammy, he opened the front window and slowed down.

"I don't think we were meant to be deer hunters," he said lamely.

"For crying out loud, Aubrey. Turn on the damn heater and let's get the hell out of here!" Dr. Bennett yelled. "It's like an igloo inside this car!"

With that, Dr. Riddle sped off toward the highway. Sammy stood there for a long time, looking down at the three or four pieces of shatterproof glass on the ground. Then he shook his head and started walking toward his truck.

"I'll never understand it," he said out loud. "Why in the world would somebody make such a big fuss over shootin' a little ol' bird about the size of my big toe when they could be huntin' for a he-buck the size of a young steer instead? I reckon some people just ain't cut out to be deer huntin' fools like me an' ol' Randall. Oh, well. This is the best opening day we've had in years, and this fool's going to the woods!"

# The Ghost Gobbler of Nacoochee Mound

## Chapter 20

### Part I

Clay Kenimer was seething. Three times in the last seven days he had tried to sneak up the trail leading to the Indian Mound, where the three longbeards frequently roosted. All three times he had spooked the crafty birds off their roost in the predawn darkness. The old logging road leading up to the mound from the paved highway wound directly underneath the three giant trees known as the "Three Sisters"—three huge white pines that a man couldn't reach around. The turkeys seemed to have a decided preference for those trees. But no matter how dark it had been or how carefully Clay had inched his way up the path, they had sensed his presence each time and exploded from the high limbs overhead into the inky darkness.

Clay knew all too well that once the birds were spooked off their roost, the hunting was over for the day. Because the Indian Mound was situated on the highest piece of ground in the area, the frightened birds could glide downhill in almost any direction for at least a quarter of a mile, sometimes much farther. If a spooked gobbler decided to pitch down into the wide valley below the steep southern slope of the mound, for example, it could actually glide for more than half a mile into any corner of the sprawling cow pasture that bordered the river. By the time it was light enough to see, the bird would be long gone.

Clay had experienced the same problem with spooking the gobblers off their roost during the two previous seasons. Now, in his third year of hunting, he had dubbed these crazy birds the Indian Mound flock, and he was beginning to think he was jinxed. Clay was not stupid, but he certainly didn't expect the birds to roost in the same trees every night. Furthermore, they appeared to be able to see as well in the pitch black of night as they could in broad daylight.

To compound the problem, only one trail led up to the top of the mound. It was hard enough to follow the winding trail in the dark of night without a light, and it would be almost impossible to approach the mound without using the trail. The surrounding woods were simply too thick and full of impenetrable downfalls. But Clay knew he had to do something different. So, hunting for the fourth morning on the eighth day of the fledgling spring season, he decided to go for broke.

*What the heck,* he thought. *There's nothing to lose. Instead of following the trail in the dark like I've been doing, I'll make a wide detour around the Three Sisters and try to fight my way through the woods just west of the mound. I'll take it slow and easy and allow myself plenty of time to reach the hole.*

The "hole" was a three-foot-deep pit located about one hundred yards from the very top of the Indian Mound. It was situated about two hundred yards from the Three Sisters on a contour of land some twenty feet below the elevation of the flat-topped mound, and it was a perfect place for a turkey blind. Fresh scratchings could always be found in the leaves around the hole, and turkeys were apt to feed through this area at any time of day.

The foxholelike pit had been made years earlier by treasure hunters who often sneaked up on the mound property without permission in search of Indian artifacts. Clay had stacked some logs and branches around the hole to camouflage it, and once inside he was well hidden. Jakes and hens frequently came to within a few feet of his makeshift blind without ever noticing him, but so far the much more vigilant gobblers had always given it a wide berth.

Just as he expected, fighting his way through the thick woods proved to be rough going in the predawn darkness. Surprisingly, though, he reached the hole in plenty of time to get settled in before first light. What's more, he did it without disturbing the woods or flushing any roosted turkeys.

*This is a first,* he thought as he sat down on a small cushioned stool in the hole and waited. Other than an occasional early morning truck out on the highway, the woods were quiet.

Clay tried to picture the three longbeards in his mind—roosting contentedly high up on a limb. It always fascinated him to watch a band of six or eight turkeys fly up to their roost in the fading light just before dark. One by one they would awkwardly and noisily start flapping their wings for all they were worth, rising almost straight up off the ground in a gravity-defying burst of strength and energy. Once they had settled down on their chosen limb and stopped flapping, they stood out like a whale out of water. But then something magical always happened. After a few minutes, they would shift around and begin to blend in with the limbs and branches. Suddenly they would become almost invisible, and Clay would have to stretch and strain just to see them.

*No need to roost the three Indian Mound gobblers,* he thought. *They go to the same spot almost every night.*

In the past, he had tried every trick in the book to make these birds gobble on the roost. Much to his annoyance, they proved to be the most uncharacteristically lockjawed birds he had ever encountered. Now he no longer even tried to make them gobble. He simply took his stand and waited for the new day to arrive.

A large number of crows were already raising Cain somewhere down in the valley below the mountain as the first hint of dawn began to open up the woods around him. Clay got out his slate and made several ultralight tree calls.

*Maybe I can entice at least one of those bad boys to fly down in my direction,* he thought.

They were there, all right. Every once in a while he could hear a faint cackle up in the trees over near the Three Sisters. The three birds were talking to themselves, but as usual, they were not about to gobble. Twenty minutes after first light, he heard them pitch down one by one on the opposite side of the mound and join up with a group of noisy hens that were already on the ground.

For the next hour and a half, Clay could hear the raspy calls of several hens as they fed through the woods on the far side of the mound. He got out his box call and tried to talk to them several times, but the flock continued to feed away from him. Finally, the only sounds he could hear were those of the infernal crows.

"There must be a million crows in this valley," he whispered. "One of these days, I'm gonna come up here after turkey season and wear them out."

Knowing the turkeys were long gone, Clay got up in disgust just after 10:00 A.M. and made his way over to the snaking trail that led from the top of the mountain down to the Three Sisters and on to the highway below.

"Damn these mountain birds," he said in total frustration.

When he reached the Three Sisters, he paused to study the fresh droppings and small feathers left by the roosting birds in the pine straw under the trees. The entire northern slope of the Indian Mound—encompassing some eight to ten acres—was covered with a beautiful stand of mature white pines. Clay's grandfather had been offered a lot of money for that timber, but he had refused to sell.

Facing the Indian Mound, the Three Sisters stood just to the left of the trail. They were clustered together in a roughly fifty-foot circle. Each of the huge white pines had a diameter of nearly thirty inches, and they were the largest trees on the property. They stood more than eighty feet tall.

To the right of the trail, a fourth giant white pine tree—even larger than the Three Sisters—had once dominated the mountain ridge. Well over a century old, this great tree had been struck by lightning and killed three or four years earlier. The rotten skeleton had finally collapsed into a huge pile of rubble and debris during a windstorm. Clay had cleared some of the debris off the trail, but several sections of the tree and several large limbs still blocked a portion of the passage.

Clay stood pondering the three trees and the three elusive birds that roosted in them.

*Talk about a pattern,* he thought. *These birds are here just about every morning. It's almost like they're three sentries, standing guard over the Indian Mound.*

The Indian Mound was located on a fifty-acre tract of wooded land just across the highway from a large two-story country farmhouse that had been in Clay's family for over a hundred years. His grandfather, Guy Kenimer, had been born and raised in the historic old house. Now in his early eighties, "Kenimo" was still going strong. By most turkey hunting standards, the Indian Mound property might be considered too small to fool with. But that didn't matter to Clay. The property was home to a sizable flock of birds, and no one else set foot on it during turkey season without permission.

Despite the fact that there was no shortage of turkeys on the Indian Mound, Clay never could seem to get the upper hand. These wary mountain gobblers didn't act anything like the flatland birds he was used to hunting. Not only were they nonvocal, they also had an uncanny ability to detect his presence. No matter where he set up in the woods around the mound, they always seemed to make a wide detour around him and parade by at a safe distance just out of range—as if they knew he was there.

Nacoochee Mound was not a typical Indian mound in the normal sense of the word. Nor was it a burial mound like some of the other ancient mounds found near the river in the valley below. It was a temple mound, used in prehistoric times for ceremonial and religious purposes. Although Nacoochee Mound had been altered by early man, it was not a man-made structure. Instead, the mound bearing the same name as the winding river valley below was nothing more than a mountaintop roughly the size of a football field that had been painstakingly flattened off some eight hundred to a thousand years earlier by the early inhabitants of the valley. They had achieved this engineering feat with primitive tools, by digging out and carrying off one bucketful of earth at a time.

The Indian Mound had been constructed centuries before those early inhabitants evolved into the well-organized and powerful tribe that would later be known as the Cherokee. After the early Mound Builders evolved into an organized tribe, they thrived for several centuries in a large village that stood adjacent to the Chattahoochee River in the sprawling valley just below the mound. In 1540, Hernando De Soto came through the area, leaving a legacy of death and persecution across the southern Appalachians wherever he went. That marked the beginning of the end for the Red Man.

Although it was still as flat as a pancake on top, the Indian Mound had gone back to nature over the past one hundred and fifty years. Where it had once been open, it was now covered with tall pines and hardwoods. The local turkeys never roosted on the very top of the mound. Instead, they always roosted in trees fifty to sixty feet below the pancake-flat summit, where they could be sheltered from the wind and weather.

Because of the Indian Mound's historical significance, Clay always got an eerie feeling whenever he hunted on the property. Perhaps his feeling stemmed from the fact that the mound had been a holy place to his Indian forefathers. Clay had a small bit of Indian blood running through his own veins. Along with it came a deep and abiding respect for Mother Earth and the natural world that had always been so much a part of his life.

* * * * *

It was midmorning when Clay returned to his grandfather's house across the highway. He normally stayed in the woods until early afternoon, but on this particular day he decided to eat an early lunch and return to the mound around 3:30.

*Maybe I can catch those three longbeards off guard later this afternoon as they go to roost,* he thought as he walked down the winding gravel driveway toward the house.

Kenimo was out in the backyard hitting a few golf balls toward a white stake in the ground one hundred yards away that served as an imaginary hole. Clay leaned his shotgun against a tree and picked up a club.

"Mind if I hit a few with you?" he asked.

"Not at all," Kenimo said. "You're back early. No turkeys this morning?"

"They went the wrong way—again." Clay sighed.

Clay lined up a ball with his club and sliced it toward the stake. It rolled to a stop less than six inches from the target.

"Nice shot," Kenimo said with approval. "Golf is a frustrating game for most people, but you've got a good swing. You're a natural."

"Thanks," Clay said. "I wish it was that easy with the turkeys. There's nothing more frustrating than turkey hunting."

"They get the best of you this morning?" Kenimo asked.

"This morning and every morning," Clay answered. "No matter what I do, it's wrong. These mountain gobblers beat anything I've ever seen. They're totally different from the flatland birds I've been used to hunting."

Kenimo was silent for a moment as he lined up a ball on the ground and gracefully hit it toward the stake. Despite his advanced age, he could still hit a golf ball with the best of them. "I'm a golfer, not a hunter, but you oughta go talk to old Perk Barker," he said. "You remember Barker, don't you?"

"That old poacher who lives across the river?" Clay asked.

Kenimo nodded. "He's not really a poacher."

"That's not what I hear," Clay said. "I heard Perk Barker used to be the biggest poacher in White County."

"He grew up hunting and trapping around these parts when a man didn't have to ask permission," Kenimo said. "It was a different way of life back then. I don't think he's ever been a poacher. It's just that when people started posting their land up and down the river where he had hunted, trapped, and fished for more than fifty years, he felt like he still had a right to use it. Back in his day he was the best turkey and deer hunter in White County, and that's a fact! It wasn't all that long ago, either. No, he's not a poacher. He's more of a hermit now, since his wife died. It's been pretty hard on him."

"I never knew he had that kind of reputation," Clay replied.

"It's a fact," Kenimo said with a smile. "You probably also didn't know that the two of us used to be the best of friends when we were in grade school. Barker knows the property in and around the Indian Mound like the back of his hand. He's hunted it a thousand times. He lives only three-quarters of a mile from the top of mound, as the crow flies."

"How old is he getting to be now?" Clay asked.

"Seventy-seven and sharp as a tack," Kenimo said with a grin. "Almost as old as me, but nobody's quite that old. He'd still be huntin' turkeys if his knees weren't so bad. He can't climb mountains anymore. Hell, he can't hardly even walk to the mailbox without a cane. So he just sits on the front porch most of the time pining about Lucy. They were married for fifty-seven years.

"Go pay him a visit, and tell him I sent you," Kenimo added. "He won't steer you wrong. In fact, he'll be glad to talk to someone who likes to hunt. He's never been one to give away any of his closest huntin' secrets, mind you, but if he likes you—and I'm sure he will, bein' you're my grandson—he might be willing to give you a tip or two. It couldn't hurt."

"Nothing could hurt at this stage of the game," Clay said. "I can't get within a hundred yards of those blame birds."

"If anybody on this earth can help you kill a gobbler off that mound, Barker's the man!"

* * * * *

An hour later, Clay was in his Jeep crossing the narrow one-lane bridge that spanned the Chattahoochee River in the valley. He slowly made his way down the rutted dirt trail that served as Barker's driveway. Barker's house stood on an elevated knoll about a hundred yards from the river's edge. Just as Kenimo had said, Barker was sitting on the front porch in a rocking chair. An old bluetick hound lay at his feet.

Clay pulled up in front of the house and cut the engine. Several mongrel dogs came out of nowhere to greet him. They appeared to be friendly, so he got out.

"Morning," he yelled.

"Howdy," Barker said.

"I'm Guy Kenimer's grandson, Mr. Barker—from across the river," Clay yelled. "Mind if I talk to you for a minute?"

"Whatcha wanna talk to me about?" Barker asked.

"Turkeys."

"Why would Guy Kenimer's grandson wanna talk to an ol' codger like me about turkeys?" Barker said, spitting black tobacco juice into a cup he was holding.

"Because Kenimo says you're the best turkey hunter in White County," Clay yelled. "And I need some advice."

"Is that a fact?" Barker said. "Well I ain't hunted no turkeys in goin' on four years, now, so I'd be a poor'n to be givin' out advice. But come on up on the porch and set a spell. I ain't goin' nowhere."

Clay walked up on the porch and extended his hand. "I'm Clay Kenimer," he said.

Barker shook his hand and nodded. "Pleased to meet you," he said. "Me an' yer granddaddy go back a long ways."

"I know," Clay said.

Clay sat down on a bench and started rubbing the bluetick's head. The dog stank to high heaven. "Ever hunted 'coons with him?" Clay asked.

"Used to," Barker said. "'Fore my knees give out. Now what was it you was wantin' to know about turkey huntin'? You ain't aimin' to try to shoot the Ghost, are ya'?"

"The Ghost?"

"Yeah, the Ghost Gobbler," Barker said. "On yer granddaddy's land. Leastways, that's what I call him. You may have a different name for him. You are huntin' on the Indian Mound, ain'tcha?"

"Yeah, how'd you know?" Clay asked.

"A feller'd have to be an idiot not to know," Barker said. "Somebody's been spookin' them birds off the roost over there. Ever' time it happens, they light right down here across the river in the bottoms, and I see 'im out there at first light. Why, three of 'im come down yesterdee mornin'."

Clay's face turned red with embarrassment. "Were they longbeards?" he asked. "Three big longbeards?"

"They was gobblers, but they wasn't no sho'nough limbhangers," Barker said. "They were prob'ly two-year-olds."

"That was me," Clay admitted. "They roost on the other side of the mound. I tried to slip by them in the dark, but they must've seen me. I never knew turkeys could see in the dark, but I swear, that bunch can!"

"I know exactly where they roost," Barker said. "Always right aroun' them four big sisters. Only, I reckon they's only Three Sisters left now, 'cause one of 'im got hit by lightnin' a while back."

"How do you know about the sisters?" Clay asked.

"I named 'im," Barker said. "Ast yer' granddaddy if ya' don't believe me. Hell, that stand of white pines is one of the finest in all of north Georgia."

"I believe you," Clay said. "I know you used to hunt on the Indian Mound. That's why I wanted to ask your advice. I've hunted birds all over the southern part of the state, but never up here in White County. That is, until three years ago. This is my third season. But everything I do is wrong. This year I got on those three longbeards right away, but I can't get them to come to me—no matter what I do."

"Mind if I ast ya' a question?" Barker said.

"No, go ahead."

"Why ya' wastin' yer' time with them little minners when they's a genuine whopper out there to be caught?" Barker asked. "Why don't ya' go after the Ghost? Now there's a real limbhanger!"

"I don't know anything about any Ghost," Clay said. "All I've seen are those three longbeards. They stay together a lot."

"That's why I call him a ghost," Barker said. "I first seen him up there about ten year ago, standin' on top of the mound in all his glory. It was in the fall, when the bucks was whistlin'. I was huntin' a big eight-pointer that was usin' the top of the mound up there right regular. Had a rub line goin' from one side of the mound to the other. Them ol' rubs're still there, I reckon. I got up there expectin' to see a big buck, but instead, I run slap-dab into the Ghost.

"I swear he looked like he'd just been struttin'," Barker continued, "even though it was way past struttin' season. He stood there with all them feathers bristled out like he owned the place, aglowin' in the morning sun like one a' them bronze statues—regal and stately an' glintin' with all them colored feathers. His head was so blue it was might nigh purple, and he just turned around and walked away like I wasn't even there. When he started walkin', I swear he looked like he was draggin' a rope 'tween his legs, and his spurs was so long that he had to walk pigeon-toed just to keep 'im from rubbin' on his legs." Barker grinned mischievously.

"He was only about thirty yards away when I first seen him, and he knew he had been had. Since he was on top of the mound, I run up there lickety-split figurin' he couldn't get acrost to the other side 'fore I could get up there to get another good look—bein' that it's so flat and open up there and all."

"What happened?" Clay asked.

"I'll tell ya' what happened," Barker said. "He disappeared into thin air, that's what! One minute he was up there walkin' across the middle of the mound, and the next thing I knew he just melted away into nothin'—just like that." Barker snapped his fingers. The bluetick lifted his head and looked up.

"What'd you do after that?" Clay asked, patting the dog.

"Well, bein' that we ain't got no fall turkey season, I waited till spring 'fore I went back after him," Barker said. "I never did get that buck, neither. I seen the Ghost a few more times up on the mound that year, and I seen him struttin' a bunch of times across the river yonder on the far edge of the pasture. But I never could get nowheres close to him. Kinda like you and them three bodyguards you been aseein'."

"Bodyguards?" Clay said.

"Yeah, I reckon they have to be bodyguards if they're a'roostin' up there with the Ghost."

"Funny you'd put it that way," Clay said. "I kind of think of them as being sentries myself. They're always up on the mound like they're guarding something."

"I'll say they are, by jiminy!" Barker said with conviction. "They're guardin' the Ghost!"

"Let me ask you something, Mr. Barker," Clay said. "If you saw this ghost gobbler ten years ago, how could he still be alive?"

"That's just it," Barker answered. "He ain't no normal bird, and the Indian Mound ain't no normal piece a' ground. He's the Ghost!"

Clay had always been quite superstitious himself, but he wasn't about to buy into this ridiculous tale.

*Perhaps old Barker is a lot more senile than Kenimo realizes,* he thought.

"These three bodyguards beat anything I've ever seen, Mr. Barker," Clay said. "How do you hunt 'im?"

"For starters, mountain birds don't act like no flatland birds," Barker said. "Nosiree. Mountain birds always roost up high, on the side of a high ridge just below the top. That's why they like it up there on the mound so much. It's the highest ground aroun'. Up there, they can watch the whole world and be the first in line to bring in the new day when the first light a' mornin' replaces the darkness and the stars. Why, when they roost up there on the mound, they can see clean across the valley—all the way over to Mount Yonah, where they's another big flock aroostin'. I swear, sometimes I think them two flocks talk to each other when they've a mind to." Barker grinned broadly, displaying a mouthful of tobacco-stained teeth.

"After it turns light," he continued, "and after they get themselves a bellyful of watchin' and listenin', they'll usually fly down in the valley somewheres 'cause they're thirsty after sittin' on that limb all night. They'll be alookin' for a drink—usually out in one of them little coves along the edge of the pasture.

"Then the gobblers start hookin' up with the hens, and slowly they all trickle back into a big flock. Within the hour—five days outa seven—them rascals'll feed right back up to the top of the mound. Then they'll begin workin' their way crost them rollin' hardwood ridges just west a' the mound. By early afternoon, they might be plumb down the other end of the valley somewheres. By late afternoon, when all the hens has broke away, them gobblers'll start headin' right back over toward the top of the mound where they plan to roost. They's safety in numbers.

"And whenever ya' see that flock workin' its way thu' them woods around the mound, ya' know the Ghost is close by, even though ya' can't see him. He's there all right, ghostin' thu' the woods, lettin' them three young gobblers feed out ahead of him like a buck deer so he don't get in no trouble. That's why he's so hard to kill. He can flat make himself invisible when he wants to."

Clay smirked.

"Ya' don't believe me, do ya'?" Barker said.

"I know a big gobbler like you're talking about can pull a disappearin' act whenever he wants to," Clay said. "But I don't think he can make himself invisible."

"You gotta believe, boy," Barker said. "This bird ain't no normal bird."

There was a long silence. Barker seemed to be poring over something important in his mind. At last he spoke.

"They's two more things I wanna tell ya', and after that I ain't gonna say another word," Barker began. "First off, if ya' aim to try to kill the Ghost, yer' gonna have to be faster and trickier than he is. Second off, and this is pretty doggone serious. . . ." Barker cleared his throat and spit into his can.

"Look, I'm just a simple ol' country boy," he said. "I ain't educated like yer grandpa. We grew up together an' all, but I never did go to college like he did. But it don't take no wizard to figure some things out in this world. That Indian Mound is a sacred piece a' ground, son. Once you understand it and treat it thataway, it'll be OK to go up there and try to defeather the Ghost." He paused and smiled benevolently. "It might even be OK to bushwhack one of his friends as well—bein' that we got a three bird limit here in Georgia—but ya' don't ever wanna overdo it on a piece a' ground like that. You understand what I'm tryin' to say?"

"I think so," Clay answered.

"Good, 'cause if ya' don't, you're wastin' yer' time."

## Part II

Clay Kenimer didn't know what to think about his conversation with Perk Barker as he left Barker's house. When he got to the narrow one-lane bridge that spanned the river, he parked his Jeep and got out. He stood on the bridge for a long time, poring over what Barker had told him. He looked down at the crystal-clear water as it rushed over some rocky shoals just below the bridge.

"Maybe I ought to be trout fishing instead of turkey hunting," he said out loud.

Twenty minutes later, he pulled around to the back of his grandfather's house and parked his Jeep. Kenimo was sitting on the back porch, drinking a glass of iced tea.

"Well, what'd you think of my old buddy Barker?" Kenimo asked as Clay ascended the steps leading up to the long wooden porch.

"He's a real character, like you said," Clay said.

"And . . .?" Kenimo asked.

"We got into some pretty deep stuff," Clay said.

"Like what?" Kenimo asked. "Have a seat and tell me about it."

Clay sat down on the top step and looked out across the backyard. "Barker claims there's a big gobbler on the mound that I've never seen," he said. "He calls him the Ghost Gobbler. He says he saw him for the first time about ten years ago, and he swears he's still up there."

"He usually tells it like it is," Kenimo said. "He's not one to mince words."

"It would be mighty unusual for a gobbler to live that long up here," Clay said.

"Unless he's got a guardian angel looking over his shoulder," Kenimo said. "Barker really believes in that spiritual stuff in a big way, especially when it pertains to the Indian Mound."

"I think Barker is getting a lot older than you realize," Clay said.

"You think he might be getting a little addled in his old age?"

"Yes, I do."

"What else did he tell you?"

"He said the Indian Mound is a sacred place."

"You believe that, don't you?" Kenimo asked.

"Yes, but I don't see what that has to do with hunting turkeys, or deer, or anything else for that matter," Clay replied.

"I guess it depends on how you look at it," Kenimo said. "A thousand years ago, a group of people living in the valley thought enough of that piece of ground to flatten off the entire mountain top and use it for a sacred meeting place, like a great prehistoric church. Two hundred years ago, it was still hallowed ground to the Cherokee. They believed the Great Spirit dwelt there. Their medicine men went there often to pray and to drive away evil spirits. Some of the medicine men or high priests probably even lived up there on top of the mound in little houses all by themselves.

"The sick were even brought there to be healed," Kenimo continued. "That's why very few artifacts have ever been found up there. It was a meeting place, full of spiritual significance. Young braves might go up there to greet the rising sun in the east and pray for good luck when they were about to embark on an important hunt or other adventure. From the top of the mound you can see Mount Yonah, or 'Bear Mountain' to the Indians, and it, too, was a sacred place."

Clay smiled.

"What're you grinning at?" Kenimo asked.

"Barker says there's a flock of turkeys over on Mount Yonah that can sit there on the roost and talk back and forth to the Indian Mound flock," Clay said. "It's only what, three or four miles away?"

"Barker might get a little carried away sometimes," Kenimo admitted. "But who knows what a turkey can hear on a clear morning? Sound travels pretty far on a clear day. You can sure hear a rifle shot from over there."

"Do you believe the Indian Mound is still a sacred place today?" Clay asked. "The Indians have been gone for a long time."

Kenimo smiled contentedly. "Is a five-hundred-year-old cathedral in France or a monastery in the Himalayas built a thousand years ago still sacred today? You bet they are!"

"I still don't see what that has to do with me and hunting turkeys," Clay said. "I have as much respect for nature and the animals I hunt as anybody."

"Maybe you need to try to tune in to the spiritual side of it a little more," Kenimo said. "The Indian Mound is a very spiritual place. Maybe that's what's missing in the equation."

"How?" Clay asked.

"I can't answer that," Kenimo said. "That's something you'll have to figure out for yourself. Go up without a gun. Go with the intention of greeting the rising sun some morning like the Cherokee did. You'll find it. I'm sure you will, but I can't tell you how to do it."

"This is crazy, really crazy," Clay said. "But maybe I'll do just that. Maybe I'll go to bed early tonight and get up and go over there first thing without a gun."

* * * * *

Clay seldom dreamed while he was sleeping, and when he did, he could never remember what he had been dreaming about the next day. Early that morning, however, just before it was time for the alarm to go off, he had a strange dream. He was sitting against a tree with his shotgun across his lap in some open woods one hundred fifty yards from the top of the mound. The sun was already up, but the woods were unusually quiet. Not even the crows were making any noise. The only sound that could be heard was a faint rustling from the light breeze blowing across the mountain.

Three hens had been roosting on the steepest side of the mountain, just below the top of the mound. Clay watched them pitch off the limb they were on and one by one, in slow motion, fly down into the open pasture below. Then five gobblers flew down into the open woods in front of Clay. They had been roosting near the Three Sisters. They gathered together in a small group without making a sound and started working their way around the mountain to the other side of the mound. Their bright red heads and big black bodies contrasted greatly with the dull gray of the winter woods.

They paraded past Clay in single file and within easy range, but for some reason he could not lift his shotgun. Then, just as the three real longbeards had done, they joined up with a group of hens that were calling faintly from the other side of the mound.

Using his box call, Clay made a series of perfect calls in his dream, but there was no response. Suddenly he saw a flash of red over to his right, where the contour of the land dropped off abruptly toward the cow pasture below. Thinking it had to be the head of a gobbler, he raised his shotgun and fired. The red head disappeared. He quickly ran over to the edge of the dropoff and looked down. To his horror, he saw he had killed a large pileated woodpecker instead of a turkey. The big woodpecker had apparently landed on the ground to capture an insect.

The alarm clock went off, and Clay sat straight up in bed. It was 5:00 A.M. Clay realized he had been dreaming and that he remembered almost the entire dream—especially the end. He went downstairs to fix a pot of coffee, then sat at the kitchen table drinking coffee and thinking about his crazy dream.

Thirty minutes later he was inching through the black darkness around the western slope of the mound, toting all of his usual turkey-hunting gear except for one key item—

his shotgun. He decided not to sit in the hole. Instead, he went around to the edge of the hardwoods near the south side of the mound and sat down against two large pine trees that grew there only a few inches apart. It was a good stand, and he had watched numerous turkeys from that same spot.

The woods began to brighten. Unlike the uncanny silence in his dream, the crows started up with their usual racket. It seemed as though there were always dozens of crows making a ruckus around the Indian Mound. Clay listened intently for the next forty-five minutes, but he never heard a single turkey fly down. Nor did he hear anything that sounded even remotely like a turkey. Sometimes it was easy to mistake the sound of a distant crow for that of a feeding hen, but not on this morning.

Clay watched the sun come up over the distant trees to the east. It was a beautiful spring day. The trees around him were just beginning to bud out with their new growth. In a few more weeks, everything would be green.

Around 10:00 A.M. Clay detected movement down the hill to his right, about eighty yards away. Two deer were walking up the hill directly toward him. The first deer was a buck. As it got closer, Clay could see that it was still in the process of shedding its winter coat. Large blotches of gray winter hair were being replaced with the red hair of summer. The buck had two big bulbs atop its head, about an inch and a half in diameter. The two bulbs were just beginning to branch into a *Y*.

The second deer, also a buck, was much smaller in body and had much smaller antlers. Three-inch, pencil-thin velvety knobs stood straight up on top of his head like a TV antenna. Both bucks walked behind Clay without scenting him and headed toward a far ridge that Clay knew was a favorite bedding area. Clay made a mental note that the lead buck would be worth watching in the future.

*He might be a good eight-pointer when he reaches full growth,* Clay thought.

Clay sat there until high noon without seeing or hearing a single turkey.

*It certainly didn't happen like this in my dream,* he thought. *So much for a spiritual encounter.*

He stood up and made his way over to the main trail that led down toward the Three Sisters. When he had reached the three big white pines, he looked around in the pine straw for fresh sign. None of the droppings he saw looked fresh. A lot of debris still covered the trail from the huge white pine that had been hit by lightning, including a portion of the tree's huge rotten midsection. Whenever Clay came down the trail, he always made a habit of picking up several broken limbs or other pieces of debris and throwing them over in the woods.

*It'll take a chainsaw to move that section of trunk,* he thought.

Clay grabbed a jagged limb that was partially embedded in the ground and pushed it off the trail. As he did so, something shiny and black on the bare ground caught his eye. He reached down and dug the object out of the red clay. It was a large black arrowhead.

"Man, this is really a nice one," he said out loud as he held it in his hand.

The triangle-shape obsidian arrowhead was an inch wide and nearly two inches long. It was extremely flat, and one side had a slight groove going down the center like a Clovis point. It was in perfect shape, being almost as sharp on the finely serrated edges as the day it was made. Clay stood holding this treasure in his hand and studying its every detail. He wondered how long it had been in the ground and how it had gotten there. He thought about the skilled craftsman who had made it so long ago. It was truly a work of art.

As soon as he got back to the house, Clay showed Kenimo his find.

"You need to show this to Barker," Kenimo said. "I've found good arrowheads all up and down the valley, but I've never seen one this beautiful. Barker will want to see it for sure."

Clay ate a quick lunch and drove over to Barker's house. Barker was sitting on the porch with all his dogs, as usual.

"Well, did ya' kill 'im this mornin'?" Barker asked. "I ain't heard no shootin', but ya' must have some reason for comin' over to my side a' the river."

"I do," Clay said. "I want to show you what I found this morning."

Clay walked onto the porch and reached into his pocket. He pulled out the piece of rock and held it in his palm.

"I found it in the trail right under the Three Sisters," he said.

Barker took it out of Clay's hand and studied it carefully.

"It's a nice'n," he said. "Reckon where the rock come from that it's made out of. Ain't no rock aroun' here like this. Most arrie heads I've found in the valley are either quartz or flint."

"It's obsidian," Clay said. "Probably from up in Ohio or somewhere like that. Kenimo says the Cherokee often traveled long distances and traded for things they couldn't find locally."

"It's big enough to be a huntin' point, but it's almost too purty, ain't it?" Barker said.

"What do you mean?" Clay asked.

"Lots a' times the Indians made points and knives like this jes' for ceremonies and nothin' else. Say ya' found it near the Three Sisters?"

"Yes," Clay answered. "It was right on the trail under some limbs from the dead tree."

"Is that a fact?" Barker said. "I'll be dogged."

Barker sat there for a long time without saying anything. Then he stood up and hobbled toward the front door. "Come on inside," he said. "They's sump'n I wanna show ya'."

Clay followed him through the front door and stepped into a large, pine-paneled living room filled with rustic furniture, much of which had probably been handmade. Several deer and turkey prints and other folk art covered the walls. To the right, a large stone fireplace with a long mantel of heart pine took up nearly the entire wall. An antique percussion mountain rifle hung just under the mantel. The top of the mantel was littered with all sorts of dusty objects, but the thing that stood out most was a framed 8x10 photo of Barker's wife.

Barker hobbled over to the mantel and grabbed several turkey feathers out of a cobalt-blue Mason jar. He turned around and held the feathers out to Clay. "Notice anything strange about these-here wing feathers?" he said.

Clay took the feathers and studied them. "Yes, they look like they've been burned somehow," he said.

"Set down on the couch there," Barker said, pointing. "They's a little story I wanna tell ya'."

Clay sat down as ordered. Barker settled into a comfortable-looking, green easy chair and lifted his legs up onto a matching footrest.

"Now I don't wantcha to take this as braggin', but I've killed 319 wild gobblers in my lifetime," Barker began. "Mostly in Georgia and Tennessee. I've got a log book settin' right over there on the chest to prove it. After I set my sights on a certain bird, they ain't been too many of 'im that got away. But that Ghost bird, why, he's a horse of a different color.

"After I seen him that first time up on the mound, I got a few more glimpses of 'im here and there, an' I saw 'im struttin' a bunch a' times 'cross the river in the valley, like I told you yesterdee. But danged if he didn't have me plumb buffaloed.

"It was right at four seasons ago when it happened. I'd been ahuntin' that ol' Ghost bird right regular, at least five or six years by then, I reckon, and they was one thing I knew about 'im for certain. He was roostin' in the same tree near-abouts ever' night. It was a big white pine. May've even been the biggest white pine in all of White County, but for sure it was the biggest on yer granddaddy's property."

"You mean the tree that got hit by lightning?" Clay asked.

"The very same one," Barker said. "He'd go to that same tree almost ever' evenin' like he owned it, jus' like them three bodyguards you been seein' that roost in them Three Sisters. It was on a Friday night in late March. I remember it well, 'cause it was the night before openin' day of turkey season. I'd been over there just before dark and heard the Ghost fly up in that big tree.

"I come home all excited that night. I told Lucy I had 'im dead to rights, and I was plannin' on gettin' 'im for sure the next mornin'. Well, we went to bed like always, and long about two o'clock in the mornin', a gollywasher of a lightnin' storm come barrelin' up the valley. No one coulda slept thu' a storm like that, and we were layin' there listenin' to the rain and the wind outside when the biggest bolt a' lightin' I ever heard in my life struck over there somewheres near the Indian Mound. I'm here to tell ya', it shook the earth. I kept expectin' to see a fire break out over there, but the rain never slacked off, an' I reckon it put out any fire that mighta' started.

"Bein' that the next mornin' was openin' day, I headed on over there 'way before daylight and took a stand in them hardwoods, jus' west a' the mound. I figured he was gonna fly down in that direction for sure. Well, nothin' ever happens like you figure on. An hour after daylight, I still ain't seen hide nor hair of that ornery bird. So I decided to look around some. When I got over on the other side of the mound, I looked down toward the roostin' tree, and I seen a jagged white gash comin' all the way down that tree from top to bottom like a fish that'd been gutted with a big knife. Long splinters of wood was alayin' all over them woods, some as far as a hunerd feet away.

"I knew that ol' tree was doomed the minute I seen it, an' it made me right sad jus' thinkin' about it. Then I realized the worst thing of all—the Ghost had been aroostin' up there when it got hit! I went on down the trail, expectin' to find 'im lyin' dead on the ground somewheres. But when I got underneath the tree and started lookin' around, the only thing I could find was a handful of these-here wing feathers that was all scorched around the edges."

"What do you think happened to him?" Clay asked.

"They ain't a bird alive anywhere that could've survived that kind of electric shock, but like I told you yesterdee, the Ghost ain't no normal bird."

"You mean, you think he actually lived?" Clay asked.

"I know he did," Barker said. "Hell, I seen him two weeks later up on the mound in all his glory, gobblin' like a fool! He was a little frazzled lookin', an' I'm not sure he could a' flew all that good till he grew out some new wing feathers, but he was alive, all right. After that, I give up tryin' to kill 'im."

"Why?" Clay asked.

"I reckon he'd done earned the right to live," Barker said. "Anyhow, I took it as a sign. Like I told you yesterdee, that Indian Mound is a sacred piece a' ground."

"Do you think I should be hunting up there?" Clay asked.

"Yes, now more'n ever," Barker replied. He was still holding the black arrowhead in his hand. Grasping it between his thumb and forefinger, he held it up to the light of a nearby lamp. "This here's a sign, too, young man. First, lightnin' hits the tree the Ghost is roostin' in. Then, you find this right under the very same tree. It was meant to be, boy. If anybody was meant to defeather the Ghost, I reckon it's gotta be you."

Barker leaned forward and handed the black arrowhead back to Clay. "You ever hunted with a bow and arrie?" he asked.

"Yes, I've been bowhunting for deer for about ten years," Clay answered.

"You any good?"

"I've killed thirteen with my bow—mostly does, but I have taken three bucks."

"You ever tried to stick an arrie in a turkey?"

"No, but I've thought about it a lot," Clay said. "I even have a turkey target at home that I practice on. Killing one of these mountain gobblers with a bow would be a real feat."

"It's a lot more'n that," Barker told Clay. "That-there arrie-head is a sure sign you're meant to kill the Ghost with a bow. I know it as sure as I'm settin' here."

"How would you go about doing it?" Clay asked. "How do you come to full draw on a big gobbler when he's less than twenty-five yards away—especially when he's coming in looking for you?"

"They's only two ways, I reckon," Barker said. "Ya' either gotta be huntin' over a decoy, or ya' git somebody else to call for ya'."

"If you teamed up with a caller, how would you set up?" Clay asked. "He'd still see you."

"Not if ya' done it right," Barker said. "The man callin' sets up about fifty'r sixty yards behind the man huntin'. The bird's gonna be lookin' for the caller, so he'll walk right past the hunter if he's hid good."

"Yeah, but the hunter still has to draw his bow back," Clay said. "You can't do that in front of a big gobbler."

"Ya' either let 'im walk past you, or, ya' wait till he walks behind a tree," Barker said. "Like I told you to start with, if you aim to kill the Ghost, you're gonna have to be faster an' trickier than he is."

"How would you do it with a decoy?" Clay asked.

"With a little luck, ya' hope he'll come in and start struttin' aroun' the decoy," Barker said. "As soon as he turns his back to ya', you draw down on 'im."

"Would you be willing to call for me?" Clay asked. "If I could get somebody like you who knows what he's doing to call, I think I might be able to get a shot with my bow."

"No way," Barker said. "I ain't been out in the woods in three years, like I told ya'. I passed the torch to young whippersnappers like you the year that big roostin' tree got kilt by lightnin'. I been officially retired ever since."

"Have you ever heard of Charlie Elliott?" Clay asked. "He was a big turkey hunter. He wrote several books on turkeys."

"Why, yeah," Barker said. "We hunted together one time jus' up the road in the Soque Valley. Must've been twenty, twenty-five years ago. He wrote sump'n up about it in one a' them outdoor magazines."

"He hunted turkeys until he was ninety-two," Clay said. "The last season he hunted, he was almost blind and he had a bad back. You're just a kid compared to him."

"Is he still alive?" Barker asked.

"No," Clay said. "I believe he was ninety-five when he passed away."

"He was a dang good turkey hunter," Barker said. "Knew his stuff."

"So are you," Clay said. "We might have a chance at the Ghost if we worked together as a team. You've still got a lot of hunts left in you."

"They ain't no way I could get myself up on the Indian Mound," Barker said. "I wouldn't make it fifty feet off the paved highway 'fore my knees give out."

"I could carry you," Clay insisted. "I could carry you piggyback. You're not all that heavy."

"Talk about spookin' birds off the roost! We'd spook every bird in the county," Barker said. "It ain't all that far, but it's a right healthy climb up to where we'd need to set up. We could never do it in the dark."

"Yes, we could," Clay insisted. "We could both hunt. I'll hunt with my bow and you can hunt with a shotgun."

"Me an' the Ghost Gobbler come to an understandin' after lightnin' hit that tree," Barker repeated. "I done had my day in the sun. Anyway, if I was to ever do such a fool thing as that, it wouldn't be for me, and I dang sure wouldn't be carryin' no gun."

"Then do it for me," Clay said. "I could sure use your help."

"I'm sorry, boy, but I can't."

"I've never even seen the bird you call the Ghost," Clay said. "I don't have much of a chance without your help."

"Ya' still don't believe he's real, do ya'?"

"It's not that," Clay said. "It's just that I've hunted on the mound a lot, and I've never seen him. It's hard to believe in something you've never seen. Anyway, he could be dead by now."

"He ain't dead."

"But he's got to be at least ten years old."

"Lots a' wild birds live longer than that."

"It would do you good to get out in the woods again, Mr. Barker."

"I ain't gonna be carried into the woods on someone's back like a cripple, an' that's final!"

Clay stood up. "I've enjoyed talking to you, Mr. Barker. Thanks for your help. If you change your mind, you know where to find me."

## Part III

Clay drove back to the house and told Kenimo about his disappointing conversation with Barker.

"What should I do?" he asked his grandfather.

"That ol' Perk Barker's as stubborn as a mule sometimes," Kenimo said. "He's got a lot of pride. Once he makes up his mind about something, he's not apt to change it."

"Do you think I should follow his advice and hunt with a bow?"

"Yes, I do," Kenimo said. "Barker's always had good instincts about things like that. If he says you should hunt with a bow, by all means, I'd do what he says."

"OK," Clay said. "I guess I'll drive down to Cleveland and pick up a decoy. If I'm gonna bow hunt, Barker says I need to put out a decoy."

"Do you plan to hunt this afternoon?" Kenimo asked.

"No," Clay said. "I think I'll shoot my bow some this afternoon and hunt in the morning. Since I'll be using a decoy, my chances will be better in the morning."

When Clay got back to the house, it was late in the afternoon. Kenimo was sitting on the back porch, as usual. Clay showed him the collapsible hen decoy.

"Looks real to me," Kenimo said with a smile. "Oh, by the way, Barker called while you were gone."

"He did? What'd he say?"

"He asked me to give you a message. He said, 'Tell the boy he can sleep in tomorrow morning. Tell him I'll be waitin' for him at 6:30 sharp. Tell him to pull right up to my front porch so that I can step in his Jeep. Tell him I'll have a fresh pot of coffee on. Tell him to be prepared to stay in the woods all day.' I think that's about all," Kenimo smiled broadly.

"All right!" Clay yelled. "He must've reconsidered. But I don't understand. . . . Are you sure he said 6:30?"

"As sure as I'm sitting here," Kenimo answered.

"It's already daylight by 6:30."

"That's what he told me to tell you. I'm certain of it." Kenimo said.

Clay set up a broadhead target and practiced shooting until dark. That night, after dinner, he attached the black arrowhead to a leather thong and tied it around his neck. Before he went to bed, he said a little prayer to the hunting gods. "Please, let tomorrow be the day!"

* * * * *

Clay pulled up in front of Barker's house and parked next to the porch at 6:30 A.M., as instructed. It was just beginning to get light. There was a misting rain, and it was threatening to rain much harder. Barker opened the door and greeted him excitedly. He was dressed in dark brown coveralls, old leather boots, and a faded camouflage jacket and hat.

"Come into the house and getcha some coffee and donuts," he said. "We got plenty a' time yet."

Clay went in and sat down at the table with a puzzled look on his face. Barker poured a steaming cup of coffee into a large mug and placed it in front of him.

"I reckon you think it's a mite late to be headin' for the woods," Barker said.

"It's almost fly-down time," Clay said, with a serious look on his face.

"Yep, it shore is."

"They might already be on the ground by now. I don't understand."

"I figured ya' wouldn't, but I got a little scheme up my sleeve," Barker said. "After you left outa' here yesterdee, I got to thinkin'. Since they's birds roostin' all over the top a' that mound—hens an' gobblers alike—it's awful hard to get in there 'fore daylight without gettin' busted. So I says to myself, *What can a feller do to be smarter and trickier than them longbeards?* I set on the porch an' studied 'bout it a right good spell, and then it come to me outa' the clear blue. *What if a feller waits till after they fly down 'fore he goes asneakin' into the woods?* I says to myself. Say aroun' 7:30 or 8:00 o'clock? Thataway, he wouldn't be spookin' 'em off the roost.

"Here's the thing," Barker added. "Them birds roost near the top of the mound in the same trees nearly ever' night like we've talked about. That's the good thing about mountain birds. They're easy to figure out. After they fly down, what do them rascals usually do?"

"Like you said, they go down in the valley for water, and they start looking for hens," Clay answered.

"And then what?" Barker asked.

"After they gather back into a flock, they usually start workin' their way up the steep side of the mound, feeding as they go," Clay answered. "By around 9:00 o'clock, they're usually near the top again."

"Right back where they started from," Barker quipped. "And then whata they do?"

"They feed down off the mound into the hardwoods."

"Exactly!" Barker said. "They been follerin' this same pattern, now, since creation—almost ever' day, unless sump'n happens. So today, we're gonna have a little surprise for 'em. We're gonna slip in there while they're gone, and we're gonna be waitin' on 'em when they get back. Drink up that coffee, boy. We got us an important appointment with an old man that wears a beard, and today, we're not gonna be late!"

Clay sat deep in thought. It took several minutes for Barker's words to sink in. Suddenly, a deep smile crossed his face.

"I get it," Clay said. "If they do what they're supposed to do, we have around forty-five minutes to an hour to slip in there and set up before they come back." He paused. "But it's drizzling outside. What if they stay on the roost late?"

"We'll give 'em plenty a' time," Barker said. "Let's get one thing straight, though—'fore we leave outa' here. Today, it's all or nothin'. Today we're huntin' the Ghost bird. Don't be tryin' to kill nothin' else. And if ya' do get lucky and get a crack at the Ghost, you'll probably only get one chance, so make it count. If you mess up, it's doubtful you'll ever get another."

"If I see a big gobbler coming in, how do I know if it's the Ghost Gobbler?" Clay asked.

"You'll know," Barker said, smiling. "Ain't nobody gonna need to tell ya'. You ever seen a big buck walkin' thu' the woods with a rocking chair on his head?"

Clay nodded.

"Same difference," Barker said. "When you first set eyes on the Ghost, there won't be no question 'bout who he is!"

They finished their coffee and piled into the Jeep. Clay drove over to the highway and pulled off on the shoulder just down from the entrance to the logging road. Several trees had fallen across the old road not far from its intersection with the highway, and Clay had left them there intentionally to keep trespassers out.

By then it was 7:30 A.M. Because of the misting rain, they decided to wait in the Jeep until eight o'clock before starting up the old road. While they waited, Barker told several of his favorite turkey hunting stories. Then he began a long discourse about why turkey hunters are better woodsmen than deer hunters.

"Fact is, most good turkey-holics are fair-to-midlin' deer hunters, but not all deer hunters are good turkey-slayers," Barker said. "But they's one thing for sure. True turkey-holics are gobbler-chasin' fools. They're kindred spirits, and they like to go where they please. That's why they often go where they ain't s'posed to go." He grinned broadly.

Clay smiled, too. He thought about some of the rumors he had heard about Barker being such a notorious poacher in his day. Of course, Kenimo had vouched for him, and Kenimo was seldom wrong about such important things.

"Deer hunters tend to stay put more in one place," Barker continued. "It takes a lot of skill to be a good deer hunter, and I ain't takin' nothin' away from that. But deer huntin' in most cases is real predictable. Ya' go scout an area, put up a stand, and then ya' sit there mornin' after mornin' hopin' yer buck'll come along. It's a waitin' game. But turkey hunters know they have to go where the birds are gobblin'. They're always breakin' in new ground, an' always lookin' for what's over the next ridge."

"You sure don't have that problem around here," Clay said. "The birds on the mound hardly ever gobble."

"I've heard 'im shake the mountain up there when they've a mind to," Barker said. "Ya' never know what them scoundrels is liable to do. That's why ya' gotta be flexible. I've spent many a day in the woods without hearing a single call, and without makin' a single call my own self, but I knew jus' the same they was birds in the woods all aroun' me. If they ain't in a mood to gobble, it's easy to run 'im off if ya' try to force the issue.

"That's why huntin' longbeards takes things to another dimension," Barker said. "To me, turkey huntin' offers the truest form of outdoor freedom they is. Ya' go where you gotta go to find the bird you're after. Ya' get out early in the mornin' way 'fore daylight and try to locate 'im. Or, ya' try to 'put him to bed the night before as he goes to roost. But the next morning, they ain't no guarantee he'll fly down in yer direction. I reckon it's time to go do battle. Ya' ready?"

Clay looked at his watch and nodded. They got out of the Jeep and sorted through their gear.

"I sure hope I ain't too much of a burden on ya'," Barker whispered. "I only weigh about 145, drippin' wet!"

"We'll manage," Clay replied.

Barker held the bow while Clay stooped down and picked him up. Carrying Barker piggyback, Clay started walking carefully up the trail.

When they reached the Three Sisters and the huge white pine that had been hit by lightning, Clay stopped to rest. Barker got down and scoured the woods for turkey sign.

"I wondered how long it would take for this ol' timer to come acrashin' down," Barker whispered. "What a tree. She was like an ol' friend. I can't tell ya' how many times the Ghost bird roosted in 'er."

"It's a shame," Clay whispered. "I plan to get a chain saw and get these big sections of the trunk moved off the trail after turkey season."

They still had the steepest part of the trail to climb. They took it slow and easy, listening intently for the sounds of feeding turkeys in the woods ahead. They went around the mound and down into the woods where Clay's hole-in-the-ground blind was located. He set Barker down next to the hole.

"I've never tried it, but I think this'll make a pretty good bow blind," Clay whispered. "I thought I could hunt from here and let you get back in the woods behind me."

"That sounds good to me," Barker said. "I've hunted outa' this very hole my own self a time'r two. If them turkeys come feedin' across the mound like I figure they will, they should come right down thu' these woods and give us a run fer our money."

Clay nodded. "I've had hens and jakes all around me in this blind," he whispered. "Within four or five feet."

Clay left his gear in the hole. Then he picked Barker up, and they walked back about sixty yards and started looking for a good spot for Barker to call from.

"This'll be good right over here," Barker whispered. "I'll lean against this-here tree and put some a' these limbs in front of me. I'll be well hid."

Clay helped Barker put some downed limbs in front of his tree. Then he quietly tiptoed back to the hole and ducked down inside. He sat down on the small stool and got all his gear ready. The inflatable decoy was still in a bag at his feet. He knocked a broadhead and practiced drawing back several times from inside the hole.

*Perfect,* he thought. *I've got plenty of room to shoot.*

Clay tied his face mask tightly against his face so that it wouldn't interfere with his bowstring. Then he settled down on the stool with the bow across his lap and waited. It was still misting rain, and the woods were silent.

Thirty minutes went by before Barker began calling. Clay couldn't figure out whether Barker had actually heard something in the woods, or whether he was simply calling at random. Barker made several light calls with his homemade glass slate. A hen answered immediately from up on the mound.

*That settles it!* Clay thought. *Barker must've heard them, and here they come!*

Clay couldn't believe his eyes as he looked up toward the top of the mound. Eight or ten hens and at least five or six jakes were working their way down through the hardwoods like a miniature army, walking toward him in one great rolling motion. They were about eighty yards away, but they were walking rapidly, making little cackling sounds as they moved forward.

*They'll be on top of me in just a second,* Clay thought.

Clay tried to hunker down in his hole as much as possible. He took a deep breath and waited, straining to try to locate a mature gobbler in the bunch. He reached up and rubbed the arrowhead that hung around his neck inside his shirt for good luck.

The hens paraded by him on both sides, paying little attention to the blind. Barker hadn't made another sound, but the hens were making a beeline for his position.

"Please, Lord," Clay whispered. "Don't let them spot him."

As the last hen walked by Clay, he glanced up toward the mound. Three large gobblers—the three bodyguards—were walking down the ridge from the top of the mound as if they owned the place. Clay's heart started beating uncontrollably. They came within ten yards of the blind and filed past him within easy bow range. They were much larger and blacker than the hens, and each bird sported about an eight-inch beard. Barker had told him they were probably two-year-olds.

Clay could hear Barker's words over and over again in his mind, and he knew better than to take a shot at one of the bodyguards. "Today, it's all or nothing. Today, we're huntin' the Ghost bird."

*Just my luck,* he thought. *The one time I'm offered a perfect chance, and I have to hold back.*

Clay held his breath, waiting for one of the hens to give the telltale alarm *putt* as soon as she spotted Barker, but no sound ever came. Somehow, Barker managed to stay concealed.

Fifteen minutes went by. Clay could hear the hens feeding on down the ridge well behind Barker's position. The light drizzle had stopped, and the woods got deathly quiet. Clay took a deep breath. All at once, a strange transformation seemed to sweep through the woods. It was almost like a sudden atmospheric change that a person could feel physically. Clay didn't understand it, but he sensed it immediately; it was very real.

Then, strangely, the soft-spoken voice of his grandfather suddenly popped into his mind.

"Everything was sacred to them," Kenimo had told Clay the day before, when they had been discussing the Cherokee. "The Indians believed that the murmuring creeks and rivers reflected the voices of their fathers and forefathers, and the breeze that blew through the valley reflected the breath of their ancestors. They lived a lot closer to nature than we do today, and through their senses, they could feel the heartbeat of the earth."

Clay had thought about these haunting words several times. Now, it was almost as if he could feel the heartbeat of the earth himself.

*This is really strange,* he thought.

He looked up, as if he knew something was about to happen. From his position in the hole, he could barely see the top edge of the Indian Mound some eighty or ninety yards away. He scanned the horizon back and forth, but nothing moved. The woods were still deathly quiet. The birds had stopped singing, and even those infernal crows had completely stopped their racket.

Then, during this almost mystical moment of silence, Clay looked up toward the edge of the mound again, and there he was. One moment there had been nothing. The next, the Ghost Gobbler was standing there in all his glory. Clay's heart skipped a beat. He almost dropped his bow. His legs started trembling. Just as old Barker had said, there was no question in Clay's mind about which gobbler this was.

The lord of the mound stood there in all his magnificence, looking out over his kingdom like a prince. He was large-bodied and erect, with a long red neck, a deep blue head, and a long sweeping beard. His wing feathers were slightly outstretched and almost touching the ground, and his tail feathers fanned almost in a strut.

He held up his head and emitted thunder. It was a heart-stopping sound that could wake the dead, and it seemed to shake the ground. It echoed down into the valley below, and Clay was sure it carried all the way over to Mount Yonah several miles away. The Ghost bird gobbled three times in succession, and then he came snaking down the ridge in a slow, deliberate walk directly toward Clay's blind, totally alert. His huge beard was at least twelve or thirteen inches long.

Clay was trembling, but he had control. He fumbled with his release and got ready to draw back. It seemed like hours, but the Ghost was there in a matter of seconds. Clay wondered if Barker could see him coming through the woods. The Ghost walked behind a large oak tree, and, at twenty yards, Clay instinctively drew back.

*Not yet, not yet . . . now!* The Ghost stopped, and Clay released the arrow.

It looked like a perfect shot. It was headed right for the vitals, but in the split second it took to reach its destination, the arrow hit a tiny sapling and deflected. It veered an inch in front of the Ghost Gobbler's huge, translucent breast and stuck into a tree with a hard *thud* ten feet beyond the startled bird.

Before Clay could knock another arrow, the Ghost jumped back, looked around, *putted*, and quickly trotted over toward the steep side of the mountain. He disappeared over the edge.

Clay stood there in shock, with his second arrow partially knocked on the bowstring. He waited several minutes. Then he climbed up out of the hole and walked over to retrieve his arrow. He could see Barker standing up now, and he walked down to Barker's tree.

"I missed," he said. "I missed the Ghost."

"Ya' tried, and that's what counts," Barker said. "You give it yer all. What's done is done."

"If I'd been hunting with a gun, I'd. . . ."

"If you'd been huntin' with a gun, you never woulda' seen him," Barker snapped.

"What do you mean?"

"You couldn't feel it when he first come?" Barker asked.

"Yes, I felt it," Clay said. "It was almost spiritual, the way it happened. No I take that back. It *was* spiritual."

"I felt it, too," Barker said. "It was so strong you coulda' cut it with a knife. I couldn't see 'im up on the mound, but I knew he was there. You didn't do nothin' wrong, son. Ya' jus' had some bad luck."

It had started raining, and Clay realized for the first time that it was raining fairly hard.

"What do we do now?" Clay asked, looking up into the rain.

"I reckon we head for the house," Barker said.

* * * * *

It was the last week of the season, in mid-May, and Clay hadn't been back to visit his grandfather or hunt on the mound since the ill-fated day of his missed shot.

The telephone rang on Thursday night.

"Hello."

Barker's voice blared out on the other end of the line. "Where ya' been hidin' all this time?"

"I've been working," Clay said.

"Ya' been doin' any huntin'?"

"No."

"Why not? Ya' ain't gonna kill no limbhanger settin' at home."

"I couldn't kill one if I was sitting on the same limb with him," Clay said.

"How ya' know?"

"You said so yourself, Mr. Barker," Clay answered. "A man only gets one chance at the Ghost."

"I been wrong before," Barker said. "Look, that arrie spooked him a little, but it didn't scare 'im all that bad. Leastways, not like a shotgun woulda' done. He never knew either one of us was there, an' he never knew nothin' was wrong. For all he knew, it coulda been a limb fallin' off a tree."

There was a long pause.

"I been thinkin'," Barker said.

"Yeah?"

"They's sump'n I want ya' to do."

"What's that?" Clay asked.

"Ya' still got that black arrie head?"

"Yes, it's right here," Clay answered.

"I wantcha to put it on the end of an arrie."

"What for?"

"So's you can hunt with it."

"Hunt with it?" Clay asked. "How can I put a rock arrowhead on the end of an aluminum shaft? Anyway, what's the point?"

"The point is, that's what ya' need to do if ya' wanna shoot the Ghost. I know it sounds crazy, but it's sump'n we shoulda' done the first time aroun'."

"Maybe so, but it's too late now," Clay said. "I've given up on tryin' to kill the Ghost."

"What're you talkin' about, son?" Barker piped. "You ain't even got started good yet. I'm the one who's give up on 'im."

"There's no way that arrowhead will go on the end of an aluminum shaft," Clay said again.

"Listen up," Barker said. "All ya' have to do is cut a notch in the end of a shaft and set it in there like the Indians done. I used to do it all the time when I hunted with a bow."

"You used to bow hunt?"

"Yes, sir. I hunted with a recurve bow for years. I used to make my own huntin' points outa' nails."

"You never told me that."

"You never ast," Barker said. "As I was sayin', all ya' have to do is cut a notch in the end of a shaft and tie that arrie head on good with real thin wire or cord."

"Even if I did get it on there, I couldn't practice with it," Clay argued. "I wouldn't know how it shoots."

"You don't need no practice," Barker said. "All ya' need is one more chance at the Ghost. I wancha' up here on Saturday morning."

"I appreciate your help, Barker, but. . . ."

"Don't *but* me, son," Barker said. "When you ast me to go up on the mound with you, I let ya' carry me up there like an ol' cripple. I done what you ast. Now I'm astin' you to do the same for me. Think it over, and call me back. I wancha' up there early, early."

* * * * *

Clay was sitting on the small stool in the hole, going over his last-minute mental checklist for the third time. It was just getting light enough for him to see the faint outline of the hen decoy standing in an open hardwood flat twenty yards away. In another twenty or thirty minutes, the birds would be flying down.

The woods were dramatically different than they had been six weeks earlier, when he had missed the shot at the Ghost. The leaves had emerged on all the trees and shrubs, the wild azaleas and dogwoods were blooming, and everything was green in spring renewal.

It was Saturday morning. The season would be over in two days. In compliance with Barker's request, Clay had driven up to his grandfather's house the afternoon before. He had called Barker upon his arrival to ask what time he wanted to be picked up in the morning, and it was then that Barker had dropped the bombshell on him.

"Ya' don't need me to tag along," he had told Clay. "I'd jus' be in the way. This time, ya' need to do it on yer own."

So Clay had come to do battle on the mound alone. The night before, he had taken a hacksaw and cut a half-inch-long notch in the end of one of his truest-shooting aluminum arrow shafts. Then he had carefully bent the notched ends of the shaft slightly outward and placed the obsidian arrowhead into the slot. Finally, he had secured the arrowhead tightly to the shaft with thin cord and glued the cord for extra strength. He had no idea how this primitive stone point would shoot. For all he knew, it might pull six inches to the right or left at twenty yards, but it was on straight, and it looked lethal. He would have to leave the rest to chance.

He had left his grandfather's house an hour and a half before daylight. Instead of using the trail, he had worked his way up and around the mountain, through the woods in the darkness, the way he had done once before. He had debated whether he should hunt from his hole-in-the-ground blind or find another spot. But Barker had been adamant about his using the hole.

"It's been several weeks, an' the Ghost has had plenty a' time to cool off," Barker had told Clay. "Anyhow, like we talked about, ya' really didn't scare 'im all that bad. If it ain't broke, don't fix it! They's one more reason ya' need to hunt there, too."

"What's that?" Clay had asked.

"Ever notice how yer hole blind is sittin' right slap-dab in the center of a raised piece a' ground?" Barker had asked.

"Yes, that's why it's such a good spot," Clay had answered. "You can see all around you in every direction."

"Ya' ever wondered how that piece a' ground got raised like that, when ever'thing aroun' you's a lot lower?"

"No," Clay answered.

"It's the site where the high priest's house used to sit," Barker said. "You know, the Cherokee medicine man. I jus' thought you oughta know."

So Clay was back in his familiar "hole" blind, wondering what the morning would bring and thinking about the Cherokee medicine man or shaman who used to live on this same piece of raised earth so long ago. Of course, this time, he was on his own.

Twenty minutes after good light, three hens flew down in the hardwoods just above him. They immediately went over to investigate the decoy. Then, two longbeards came walking through the woods from the direction of the trail, just below the top of the mound. They slowly made their way down toward the decoy, strutting and putting on a good show for the plastic hen while the three real hens milled around.

*It's two of the bodyguards,* Clay thought. *I wonder where the third one is. Maybe somebody killed him.*

Clay was totally preoccupied with watching the show these two gobblers were putting on. All at once, they starting walking directly away from the decoy toward the edge of the mountain, as if something had alarmed them. The hens followed.

*What's going on,* Clay wondered. *There's no way they could have seen me.*

Then he sensed something directly behind him. He froze, not daring to turn his head and look back.

P-f-f-f-t! P-f-f-t-u-u-u!

Clay's heart almost stopped beating. A gobbler was strutting behind him, only a few feet away. He knew he couldn't move.

*Could it be the third bodyguard?* he wondered.

Then he knew.

*No,* he thought. *It's not the third bodyguard. It's HIM!*

The big bird circled slowly around on Clay's right side. He continued over toward the decoy with his back to Clay. Clay's bow was pointing to the left, and there was no way he could move or try to shoot. The Ghost was simply too close.

The Ghost Gobbler walked all the way around the decoy, strutting and puffing as he went. When he had almost completed his circle, he again turned his back to Clay. Clay quickly shifted his body and came to full draw in one sweeping motion. The Ghost Gobbler was fifteen yards away, and you could hear a pin drop.

The big bird slowly pivoted around, facing Clay at a slight angle, looking regal with his great tail feathers opened in a perfect fan. Then he stopped and raised his blue head straight up in the air. For a split second, he appeared to zero in on the man with the bow, but it was too late. The arrow was on its way.

It was a good shot. Clay's arrow flew true—this time, with nothing in its path to deflect it. To Clay, it traveled through the air as if it were moving in slow motion. The Ghost was facing slightly to the left, and the arrow struck just below his neck with a loud *thunk*. The force of the arrow spun him around. Clay couldn't tell where the arrow went after that, but the Ghost never missed a step.

Instead of going down, as Clay expected, the great bird started flapping wildly, trying to get airborne. But his wings would not work for him, so he started running. He ran to the edge of the terrace dropoff, and he half jumped and half flew over the edge.

Clay was up and out of the blind in an instant. He ran for the edge of the terrace after the bird, knocking another arrow as he ran. Just before he got to the edge, he slowed down and took a deep breath. His heart felt as if it were in his feet. He got his bow ready and started tiptoeing ahead.

He could hear the wings of the turkey flapping before he peered over the edge. When he did look over, he couldn't believe his eyes.

Barker was standing about thirty yards below him with one boot on the Ghost Gobbler's head, pinning him to the ground. The great bird was in his final death throes, and Barker had a boyish grin on his face.

"Barker?" Clay asked. "What're you doing here?"

"I figured it might take the both of us to get this ol' boy outa the woods, so I hobbled acrost the pasture way 'fore daylight and waited down below. Seen a bunch a' jakes and hens makin' a big fuss down there. Then I started workin' my way up the mountain."

"What about your knees?" Clay asked.

"Knees, heck," Barker said. "They's only one Ghost in the world, an' if ol' Charlie Elliott could still get out there at ninety-two when he was half-blind and plagued with back trouble, why, I figured I could force these ol' knees to climb one more hill. So I took a couple a' aspirin, and here I am. Looks like my timing was jest about right."

Clay stood there with his mouth open.

"Congratulations, boy!" Barker continued. "This's got to be the most beautiful bird I ever laid eyes on. He must weigh thirty pounds if he weighs a ounce. And look at them spurs—an inch and a half at least, and a beard to beat the band! I reckon this is one a' the biggest birds to ever come out of White County. Yes, sir. Congratulations, boy! You finally done it!"

"No, Barker," Clay said with a big smile. "We did it together!"